The Elf-Queen's Bounty

Joshua Calkins-Treworgy

A Novel of Tamalaria

BooksForABuck.com
2010

Joshua Calkins-Treworgy
The Elf-Queen's Bounty

BooksForABuck.com
January 2011
ISBN: 978-1-60215-136-9

Dedication

For my brothers, Colin and Newton. They doubted me never, and inspired me ever. May you both always be with me, in heart if not in body.

A Note From the Author

Greetings, reader, and welcome once again to the mythical land of Tamalaria! We will once again be following the enigmatic man known as Portenda the Quiet, a Simpa Bounty Hunter (see also *A Hunter and his Prey* and *Lizard at Arms*) whose primary goal in life is to eventually retire from the Bounty Hunting business and settle into a quiet life as a landlord. For now, however, our werelion/tiger man half-breed friend is devoted to the life of a hunter of men. And herein lies another tale of his exploits.

We'll also be running into an older hero of the lands of Tamalaria in the form of one Shoryu Tearfang, the Cuyotai Hunter (read: archer) who defended the land with Byron of Sidius in the *Freedom or the Fire* books. Many years have passed since we last heard from the Cuyotai, but rest assured, life has been moving along quite smoothly for him since the one-eyed warlock perished at the Dread Knight's hands.

The events of this story unfold about a month after the events in the short story entry in *Lizard at Arms* that showed Portenda taking on the only man who ever gave him a real run for his money, Ignatious Stockholm. The Bounty Hunter has since recovered nicely, and it's back to business as usual for him. However, what possible connection could he have with Shoryu Tearfang, Councilor of the Elven Kingdom? Read on, friend, and we shall see.

Prologue

The city of Whitewood, capital of the Elven Kingdom, sat peacefully and quietly under a blanket of darkened sky, the moon providing only a vague glimmer of lunar light on the city below. With most of its residents able to see quite well in the dark, a natural ability for the Elven people, torches and street lamps were left doused on most nights where the moon provided light to the city. For this night, several would regret this custom, in the long run.

Atop one of the city's Historical Society buildings, a pair of crouched figures crept toward the squat block atop the building that opened on the stairwell leading inside. Wrapped in dark green tunics and with their weapons tucked in soft, black leather sheathes, the shorter of the figures reached into a compartment on his deep, cerulean-shaded belt, and withdrew several blackened steel instruments. The taller, more slender man remained crouched a few feet away, scanning the surrounding rooftops for anyone who might be looking at their activities from the distance.

"All clear," he whispered to the shorter figure, who had already started manipulating his tools on the lock of the door to the stairwell. The tall man in the green tunics took a deep breath, enjoying the odors of the forest that surrounded the city. *I almost miss this scent*, he thought.

After a few minutes, the shorter man finished his work and eased the door open on its hinges.

No sound issued from the iron fittings, and moving in a half-crouch, the two men entered the Historical Society building. Silence filled the stairwell as they entered in plush cotton shoes, specially fitted for such work as theirs.

Down two flights of stairs they slunk, neither man making a sound. Deep, regulated breaths inflated and deflated their lungs, their nerves undeterred by the work at hand. On the second lower landing from the roof, the taller man once more deferred to the little fellow, who cracked the door on the landing open a few inches, and removed another tool from his belt. The tool appeared to be a thin, jointed pole of steel with a tiny mirror attached at an angle.

"What the devil's that for," the tall man whispered.

"Checking for guards around the bend," answered the short fellow. His voice was high and nasal, but kept low so that it only carried between the two burglars. The shorter man angled the pole into the barely opened doorway and peered at the mirror. After a moment, he pulled it away, and tucked it away. He looked up at the tall man, and made a series of hand signals. He put two fingers to his eyes, then made a hooking sign. Then, he held up two fingers again, this time in front of his chest, and made a flat hand with his palm up toward the ceiling.

Having spent plenty of time in the military, the taller fellow, an Elf who was very familiar with the city of Whitewood, nodded. He mentally translated the signals in his mind: *I see two men, facing away from us.*

Finally, the smaller fellow, a Human, made a little walking motion with his fingers, and then held up eight fingers.

Eight feet from the door, the Elf thought. *Facing away, good.* He nodded to the shorter fellow, and the two of them pulled the door open silently, and moved out into the corridor beyond.

The mixed scents of dust and aged parchment filled their nostrils as they crept into the hallway. No torches were lit here, and to the right of the door, down near the bend in the hall, stood two young Elven men in military uniforms. They faced away from the intruders, and could be vaguely heard whispering with one another.

Hmm, the Elven intruder thought, *the uniforms haven't changed much from my time.* His heart began drumming just a little harder in his chest as he drew a long knife from his leather sheath, moving on bent legs toward the building's guards. They wouldn't be the only ones on duty, but the Elf and Human breaking into the building only had business here, on the fifth floor.

The Elven intruder, decked out in his dark green garb, blended almost seamlessly with the darkness of the corridor. Across the hall now from him, moving in the same crouch, the Human intruder drew his weapon as well. Both weapons were made of tempered black steel, the only reflective surface being the honed edges of the knives. With only an occasional window letting in lunar light, the two burglars were all but invisible as they crept up on the two young Elven guards.

"Don't worry about it too much, Sam," one of the guards said to the other, neither man aware in the slightest of their near fate. "You have to give these things time to develop on their own."

"Yeah, easy for you to say," the other guard replied. "You've already gone through the whole mess. I'm just afraid my parents are going to do something to completely embarrass me."

The conversation might have gone on like this all night, but the intruders chose that moment to make their move. The Elven intruder swung one hand around the older guard's mouth and rammed his long knife home into the guard's kidney, pain exploding in a firestorm through the guard's lower body as waste product and blood flooded his body and the floor of the hallway.

The Elf-Queen's Bounty

The Human intruder made his own strike much quicker and deadlier, pushing the younger guard's head forward as he ripped his long knife along the man's throat. From years of practice, the Human intruder had learned that pulling a man's head back before slashing the throat actually striates the muscles in the throat. That, in turn, requires a deeper, stronger slash of the throat, and the Human intruder knew he wasn't very strong, physically speaking.

Blood spewed from the younger guard's throat, and his hands flew to his lacerated neck, clawing and grappling with his wet flesh as he dropped to his knees, his field of vision blurring swiftly. He'd planned a wedding for this upcoming weekend, his own in fact. Until a few moments ago, his biggest concern had been what his parents might do to embarrass him at the rehearsal dinner. Now, his biggest concern was trying to get fresh oxygen to his lungs and brain through the ragged tear in his throat.

The other guard, older by three years, had lost all of the strength in his arms and legs, and was going limp as the Elven intruder's long knife struck home a fifth time. The first two stabs had gone to one kidney, the third and fourth into the other kidney, and the fifth and final stab hit him in the right lung.

Losing blood onto the hardwood floor at a pace that rivaled running tap water, the older guard fell forward onto his face, his life flashing before his eyes. His childhood, his adolescence, and finally, his young manhood, all blurring past as Death hovered near, waiting for the very last moment. His dying thoughts were of his wife and the child she carried for the last four months. Who would guide their son now, he wondered?

Both intruders had used their free hands to grab the collar of each guards' upper tunic, guiding them slowly, soundlessly to the floor to die. The deed done, they sheathed their weapons, and darted around the corner the guards had posted themselves at, moving silently and stealthily.

In the northern corridor, guided by the blueprints of the building that the Human had stolen from the Tax and Excise office, both intruders halted before a sealed door. Using the keys lifted off of one of the dead guards, the Human cycled through the keys until he got the one that opened the sealed door, and popped the lock.

The chamber on the other side of the door held various weapons, armors, shields and other artifacts that had long since been named national treasures of the Elven Kingdom.

"You know what to do," the Elven intruder said.

The Human smiled broadly, his rat-like face wrinkling at the corners of his eyes. "Yeah, yeah, I've got the picture. How many should I take?"

"Pick a number between three and ten," the Elven intruder said, his eyes sweeping over the walls and the pegs that held the various collected items. There, on the left wall, the Elf spotted a bow with a plaque beneath it. The name on the plaque, and the bow itself, sent sparks lighting through his mind. He knew that name, he knew that weapon. A hatred that had been forgotten for years rose from its mental grave, filling his mind entirely. He crossed the short distance to the wall, and his eyes widened at the description beneath the name of the bow's owner. "Councilor? He's a Councilor now? Since when does the Elven Kingdom allow Cuyotai to be Councilors? No, this won't do," the Elven intruder growled mostly to himself, taking the bow down from the wall and feeling the magic of the weapon flow through his fingers.

"What you got there, boss," the Human asked.

"Something I should have taken from a dead man a long time ago," the Elven intruder said, looping the bow over his shoulders. "Come on, our work here is done, Sean." The Elf headed out of the room and back into the corridor.

The Human followed after stuffing a few more artifacts into his rucksack, and they moved back toward the stairwell. As the two men passed by the dead guards, the Elven intruder looked down at his racial kinsmen. "Sorry, kid," he whispered. "Sometimes, shit happens."

Atop the building, the Human prepared the rappelling equipment on the edge of the building, and looked up at his employer. The Elven man had insisted upon coming along himself, instead of sending any of the Human's three younger brothers. Sean Browler, the Human intruder, wondered how his brothers were holding up at the moment, serving as distractions for the other guards throughout the city of Whitewood. He checked his wrist timepiece, and estimated that they had about another ten minutes before his brothers retreated to the rendezvous point, where the five of them, four Browler brothers and their employer, would then further retreat on horseback to their hideout.

"Tell me something," Sean Browler asked of his employer as the Elven man secured his rappel line. "Why are you doing this?"

"Even though it's none of your business, Mr. Browler, I'll indulge your curiosity," the Elven man said with a glib grin. "I am doing this in order to secure the interests of a former compatriot, a man who knows how things are supposed to be in the Elven Kingdom," the Elven man said.

"So you've been hired by someone else too?"

8

"Yes, in a manner of speaking," the Elf said. "You see, I used to be a major in the Elven Kingdom's military. By helping my, er, friend, accomplish his task, I will be securing my return to the kingdom. He shall grant me a pardon for my previous offense."

"The one that got you booted from the area, you mean," the Human asked as they began their descent.

"Yes," the Elven man said. "With my help, this friend of mine shall be able to move into a position of high authority. At that time, I shall be reinstated into the military forces. Yes, Mr. Browler, I shall once again be James Svelk, major of the Elven armies."

"So the weapons and artifacts, they really were just a cover for that other building we hit up," the Human asked.

"Indeed, Mr. Browler," Svelk said as his feet touched the floor of the alley between the Historical Society building and the neighboring apartment building. "Now let's get the hells out of here before we're spotted."

Without another word or noise, the two intruders made their way through the alleys and streets, and out into the woods. There they met up with the other Browler brothers and their horses, and they rode slowly off toward the kingdom's borders, away from the scene of their crimes.

The bodies of the two guards wouldn't be discovered until the next day.

Chapter One
A Queen Calls Out

The Grand Meeting Hall in the palace of the Elven Queen stood some fifty feet from floor to ceiling, with wondrous paintings and tapestries hung everywhere to add to the overall richness of the chamber. The odors of lavender and wildflowers could be smelled upon entry, and in the center of the chamber, dominating most of the room, stood a long oak wood table, polished to a high shine and laden with candles and fine, expensive ornaments. Glass and pewter soldiers were set in formations along the table's length, and figurines depicting the various heroes of the Elven Kingdom's history stood out prominently, made larger than the foot soldiers and marching army figures.

Seated around the thirty-foot table were the kingdom's High Councilors and several of the Elven army's highest-ranked officers. Some general murmured conversation was made as they all awaited the arrival of the last man called to this meeting, a Councilor who resided in the city of Whitewood itself, as did most of the other Councilors. Unlike the men and women seated in the Grand Meeting Hall already, however, the man they all waited on was not an Elf: he was a Cuyotai.

At the head of the table, far opposite the twin steel doors that opened on the room, the Queen of the Elves rested her chin on her balled fist. Dressed elegantly in the most beautiful, flowing petticoats and dress the maids had made available to her, the Queen felt like more of a centerpiece than a diplomat or leader of her people. She had called this meeting together, and looking around at the simply clad Councilors and the armored militiamen, she felt vaguely envious of them. They didn't have to contend with all of the burdens that came with being the ruler of the kingdom. They didn't have to hold meetings with foreign heads of state, meetings arranged months before the actual meeting was held.

General Bergen might be able to help out a bit with that soon enough, the Queen thought, looking to the seat to her right. The gentleman there was a handsome, middle-aged Elven Knight, and for perhaps half a year's time, he had been formally courting the Queen of the Elves.

The General looked away from his present conversation with General Mortenson and graced the Queen with his almost boyish smile, sending her heart aflutter. Oh yes, she would gladly forfeit her command of the kingdom to him as king if only he would propose marriage openly.

No historical precedent was set for such a thing to happen, but then again, she mused happily, there was no precedent set against it, either.

Bergen wore the formal uniform of all officers of the kingdom, a half-plate armor suit over thin cotton tunics and covered by a bright green over-cloth that was open on the sides. The emblem of the Queen, a green field with a yellow falcon crest in its center, sat in the dead center of the over-cloth, and his medals of commendation and prestige sat pinned to the upper-right side, just over the breastplate of his armor. On the shoulder of the over-cloth and beneath it, affixed directly the shoulder plate of his armor, sat three solid golden circles, denoting his rank of major general. Only one man in the whole of the Elven army had higher rank than he, and that was four-peg General Mortenson, who sat to his right. The two generals returned to their conversation, leaving the Queen of the Elves longing for another of General Bergen's boyish smiles.

The Queen was the only person at the long conference table who noticed one of the steel doors opening opposite her. This was followed by the discreet, silent entrance of a tan-furred Cuyotai, who smiled charmingly at one of the guards inside of the chamber. He carried several books under his left arm, his plain, grass-green tunics flapping loosely about his wiry frame. His bushy tail flipped this way and that as Councilor Shoryu Tearfang tiptoed toward his usual seat on bare feet, his face filled with silent worry at his lateness.

"Shoryu Tearfang, good friend of mine," the Elven Queen said aloud, bringing an immediate end to all of the other side conversations in the room.

The Cuyotai's hair stood on end, and his right hand clamped down hard on the back of the chair he had been just about ready to slide down into. His eyes wide, Shoryu turned his head to face the Queen with a broad, 'please-don't-kill-me' smile plastered to his furry lips.

"Today, I ask that you be seated to my left," she continued, indicating the empty chair on her left that she usually reserved for General Mortenson.

Shoryu shrugged, and began greeting the others around the table amiably, all of whom rather liked the Cuyotai Hunter. None of the Councilors or military men were quick to forget why exactly Shoryu had stayed in the Elven Kingdom's capital, or how he had fought alongside Byron of Sidius to defend the city, the kingdom, and overall, the realm of Tamalaria as a whole. If anyone at the table held a grudge with Shoryu, they kept it bottled away in some deep, dark space in their very soul.

11

The Queen looked at the Councilors and militiamen and marveled silently at the warm, open smiles they had for Shoryu. The Cuyotai seemed to have that effect on everyone he came in touch with, bringing warmth and friendliness with him wherever he went, and spreading it like a benign virus.

As he passed each councilor and shook hands, however, Shoryu sensed the tension that hung about them all. Something big had happened for a meeting like this to be called, something he was still out of the loop on. After he reached across the table and shook hands with Generals Mortenson and Berger, Shoryu bowed to the Queen and took his seat.

"I thank you greatly for this high honor, your grace," he said to the Queen in his lilting voice.

All of these years have passed since those dark times, the Elven Queen thought, *and yet none in this chamber have changed one bit. Some new scars, some new mannerisms, but physically, almost no visible time has passed.*

Shoryu looked briefly around the table, his eyes lingering for a moment or two on major general Bergen, whom he knew to have a courting relationship with the Queen. It was good, he thought, that the Elven Queen should finally decide to settle down with a man to sit beside her as king. Of course, the Cuyotai didn't expect that the actual balance of power would shift at all: he had become too accustomed to the Queen's way of ruling her subjects to think the Elven Kingdom could be run any other way.

"Councilor Tearfang, do you know why I have called this meeting?" The Queen of the Elves addressed the Cuyotai but looked out over all of the assembled faces. Other than the queen herself, only five people present: the two generals, Councilor Vanessa Tandril, and Chief of Constables Karaman Sutton and his High Deputy, Deacon Llanos, knew the issue at hand.

"I must confess that I do not." Shoryu looked around at his fellow Councilors. He noticed the worried countenance of Councilor Tandril, however, and thought that perhaps she had an idea. "However, I assume that at least a few other than yourself and Chief Sutton know the situation." The Elven Kingdom hadn't been engaged in military operations in a long time, so Shoryu assumed that whatever the situation was, it dealt with law enforcement. And since ambassador Runefleet was not present in the Grand Meeting Hall, he felt he could safely rule out political reasons for a meeting.

Seated next to Chief Sutton, Deacon Llanos cleared his throat. "That much is true," said the high deputy. Llanos was a highly respected magic user, dedicated to mastering the studies of both Aquamancy and Gaiamancy: water and earth magic. His skills as a combat mage had helped him rise through the ranks of the constabulary to the position of high deputy. His diplomatic skills, however, had earned him a seat in the Queen's cabinet.

"Councilor Tearfang, I have known you well since your move into the capital many years ago. I know you to be capable, perceptive, sly, and a man of family traditions," he said solemnly.

The hairs on the back of Shoryu's neck started to stand on end, and for a moment, he felt certain he was about to be sacked from his position as a Councilor. After all, he was the only person in the room at the time who wasn't an Elf.

"I also know that you have a, um, strange temper at times," Llanos added tactfully.

Shoryu thought back to his journey with Byron, to the time they'd spent up in the Northwestern Mountain territories. He thought about the pack of Khan troopers he'd slain with a single well-aimed shot from his mystic bow, crushing them under tons of mountain rock and snow. He remembered smiling to himself as he sat atop the pile of rubble that covered their corpses, the odd glee that ran through his blood with each confirmed kill in combat. He looked at Deacon Llanos, who had seen him in combat a handful of times, and raised an eyebrow at the Elven mage. "Yes, sometimes I have a bit of a temper," Shoryu admitted. "So what?"

"Well, the incident we are about to discuss is sure to disturb all here gathered," said Chief Sutton. "I've written out copies of the report taken down by one of my captains, and Deacon will now pass out a copy to each of you," Sutton said as his high deputy did just that. "One of the fine details is certain to make you a little angry, Councilor. That, I believe, is Deacon's concern in addressing you, sir."

Shoryu picked up the report and started reading. The previous night, according to the report, someone had broken into the Historical Society building on Armor Way. From the northern display chamber on the fifth floor, several artifacts and weapons of value had been stolen. When Shoryu looked down the list of items taken, his eyes stopped on the final item noted, his heart leaping up into his throat.

The Tearfang Ancestral Bow.

Sanguinary fog rolled in on the edges of Shoryu's vision, and for a moment, he thought he might scream aloud or launch into a lycanthrope rage. His bow, the very weapon with which he had fought alongside Byron of Sidius in defense of the lands, had been stolen! Shoryu read on through the report, and felt the fury mix with sorrow to see that two of the building's guards had been slain rather mercilessly. The author of the report suggested that at least two individuals had to be involved.

"I have something else to add as well," said Deacon Llanos.

All heads turned to look at him at that moment, hoping for some good news.

"But only after you note something very important about Captain Serge Tolwen's report. He states in the report that at the time of the robbery, there were only minimal numbers of guards present in the building, due to the other ruckus that was being raised throughout the city."

"Indeed, I had noticed rather a lot of commotion last night," said Councilor Ralph Martin. "What was that all about?"

"I'll answer that," said General Bergen. He rose to his feet, his hands clasped formally behind his back, and turned to face each Councilor and the constables in turn. "There was a large-scale disturbance in the northern district of the city last night. A group of three armed thugs started a bit of a riot in one of our taverns, fleeing on foot thereafter to start random street brawls throughout the area. Constables arriving on the scene of each incident were brutally beaten by these three men, many receiving grievous injuries, and in two cases, officers were killed."

This bit of information sent cringes through the assembled Councilors; the city of Whitewood had known great peace ever since the end of the War of Vandross and hearing of such violence in their kingdom's capital was too much for them to stomach easily. Only Shoryu and the generals didn't seem fazed by this information.

"We believe those three men started trouble as a distraction for whoever broke into the Historical Society building to use as cover for their activities," said Deacon Llanos. "However, I have maintained a Mage's Eye spell in the display chambers of that building for several weeks, renewing them when I've had the chance," the Elven mage said. "It's a relatively simple spell that any magic user can cast, and I have the intruders recorded on the Mage's Eye's record. Allow me to show it to you." Deacon summoned his mana and formed a square in the air before him, displaying a still image of the interior of the display chamber.

The image shifted in front of Chief Sutton, who watched it, and then waved it on to General Mortenson. In this fashion the Mage's Eye record was passed around, but Shoryu took extra time to watch the playback. He thought, for a moment, that he recognized the Elf in the recording. He asked Deacon to replay the display for him several times, and finally, he remembered the man in the image, his claws extracting themselves from the tips of his fingers as the name clicked into place and spilled from his mouth. "Major Svelk," he growled.

"You know one of those men?" Chief Sutton asked, eyebrow raised.

The Queen didn't remember any such man, but she would have to ask about him, she decided. An Elven man, possibly having committed murder in his own homeland? The very idea almost seemed impossible. Illeck, the dark Elves, she could see doing something like that. But a pureblood Elf? *Remember,* she reminded herself quickly, *even our people don't have the purest history in the world. Nobody's perfect.*

"Yes, I remember him," Shoryu said in reply to Sutton's question. "That son of a bitch caused me some troubles when Byron led the company here to help defend against Richard Vandross. And I've long suspected that he turned traitor."

"Actually, now that you mention it, that was confirmed some time ago," General Mortenson said suddenly. "A scout reported to his command that he'd seen Major Svelk speaking with some strange spider-demon out near a pond not far from the city. He gave the demon the location of the Orb of Eden's Serpent within Whitewood's city walls, selling out his own people. Disgraceful man," the general said to the murmured agreement of the Councilors.

"I see he's the very one who took your family's bow," said Councilor George Louiselle, seated on Shoryu's left. "Councilor Tearfang, I'm sure I speak for the Council as a whole when I say that I pray you aren't planning to do anything brash."

The Queen, Shoryu now noticed, had gone deep pink in the face, flustered with swelling rage.

"That man is the one who betrayed us to the warlock?" she asked, rasping the words harshly. "He is the reason that my father and brother are dead and buried?"

"I'd stake my honor on it," said Shoryu.

The Queen seemed to calm visibly, and rubbed her chin, mulling the situation over.

"Your majesty, we should take some time to consider our options," Shoryu said. "The Council will discuss matters among ourselves, and confer with the good General Mortenson. We will have a solution hopefully by tomorrow afternoon. Is everyone agreed?"

Shoryu saw the nods of heads around the table, and stood, collecting his books from the table. "Very good then. Your majesty, may we take your leave?"

"You may, good Councilors." She stood herself and gave the members of the High Council a graceful curtsy. "I must think this situation over myself as well. You are all dismissed, with the exception of you, General Bergen."

The Councilors, constables and the other general, the actual head of the Elven army, shuffled out of the Grand Meeting Hall one by one, until only the guards were left, and these men were swiftly dismissed as well. The Queen of the Elves glided over to one of the picture windows in the massive chamber, peering out into the city of Whitewood, her thoughts adrift. "Andrew, do we have any reserve forces available to hunt this Svelk down?"

"I am afraid not, my lady." The middle-aged Elven man stalked toward her, his heavy metal boots and leggings tromping and clinking as he made his way. He draped one arm around the Queen's waist, and pulled her close to his side as he too peered out into the city. "Most of our reservists are on assignment to explore the large island off the southwestern tip of our continent, your majesty."

"Ah, yes," she said, sighing. "I had forgotten about Steel Island. Do you have the most recent reports on that place?"

"The next one is due in a few days," the general said. "Your majesty, I shall go and see what I can do about getting some men reassigned, but it may take a few days. I take my leave of you, my lady," he said, raising her hand and kissing the back of it.

The Queen of the Elves waited until her courting gentleman had left her alone in the Grand Meeting Hall, and then immediately pulled a rope in the corner of the room. One of her scribes showed up through a side door into the chamber, his messenger bird on his shoulder.

"Your majesty." The young Elf gave her a low bow.

"No time for pleasantries, Heinrich," she blurted. "I need you to write down this letter as I dictate it to you."

"And to whom is this letter being addressed, majesty," the scribe asked innocently enough. He had been the first person to have any idea that the Queen and the general were courting one another, since he'd been receiving letters from the general and sending them to him from the Queen for months now. He assumed she wanted to write him again, but she surprised him this time.

"It is to be addressed to a man in Desanadron." She pulled a small black book from one of her petticoats. She thumbed through it and found the contact information she required, giving the scribe the address. "On the envelope, it is to be simply addressed as 'to the landlord'. Do you understand?"

"Yes, your majesty," the scribe said, and then he began taking down the dictated letter, his eyes widening as he went.

The Elf-Queen's Bounty

* * * *

As the sun started to poke its shy top over the horizon, spilling its golden light into the city of Desanadron, Portenda the Quiet poured himself his morning coffee and sat down to his daily paper, which he'd just brought in from the lobby downstairs. The Simpa was taller and broader than most men of his Race, a proud werelion whose lineage was also half Khan. Wide gray stripes of fur covered his bare forearms, which were as muscled as his hands were skilled. *Of course,* he thought rather bitterly, *not as skilled as they could be.*

Perhaps only a month and a half to two months before that morning (he quickly lost track of time between bounty assignments), Portenda had engaged in a melee with another of the city's inhabitants, the fearsome Ignatious Stockholm. The combat had gone well enough, he supposed, to not be a total embarrassment, but overall he'd gotten his ass severely kicked. As a result, he spent most of his time these days working as a handyman at his apartment buildings, and training endlessly. He hadn't taken a bounty assignment in a rather long time and, as he sat down to read the paper, he wondered if Jonah Staples really would ever pay him back monetarily for his efforts on his sister's behalf.

The Simpa sniffed deeply, and felt the warm aroma of the coffee fill his nostrils and lungs, a symphony of caffeine just waiting for him to imbibe. As the rim of the cup came up to his lips, a knock issued at his living room door, and he groaned, looking at the steaming liquid. He set the cup down, flopped the paper onto the table, and got up—with a heave and a grunt, lifting himself out from his specially designed kitchen chair. Grumbling all the way to the door in his native Simpa tongue, Portenda rubbed his eyes and wondered just who the hells would want to bother him at such an early hour, especially on a Sunday.

Portenda turned the knob on his door and pulled the door, letting a half-formed "Grana su magrashaken," out of his mouth before he found himself looking out into an empty hallway.

"Down here," a high-pitched voice said, and Portenda blinked and looked down, his eyes narrowing to look down at Mrs. Flecks, one of his residents, who lived three stories above his. "And you should be watchin' yer mouth, young man," the Gnome woman said, tugging on her short gray beard. Portenda's head dropped forward a little in defeat, and he scrunched his eyes shut for a moment, pinching the bridge of his wide, leonine nose.

"My apologies, Mrs. Flecks. I didn't know you spoke my people's tongue," he muttered. "Now, what can I do for you this morning?"

The Gnome woman crossed her arms over her chest, and cracked her neck, looking once again up into the face of the most feared Bounty Hunter in the lands of Tamalaria.

"Oi, I needs ya ta come down and patch up a hole in me livin' room. Me 'usband, Thomas, is a good man, but 'e spends all 'is toim out in the fields and farms, workin' on those useless old machines he sold to the farmers a few years back. I've been on 'im ta fix the hole in the wall, which he put there in the first place, an' he 'asn't gotten around to it." Her familiar sort of tirade was just what Portenda didn't want to deal with so early in the morning.

He put his hands up to stay her from speaking further, and when she prattled on for a minute more, he simply turned and walked back into his kitchen, the Gnome woman following and talking the whole while.

Hmm, Portenda thought, turning to the sports section as Mrs. Flecks launched into the second part of her full-blown sermon this fine Sunday morning. *The Destroyers beat out the Rock Warriors yesterday, interesting.* He sipped on his coffee. He mentally timed Mrs. Flecks, his ears tuned in to the beating of her heart, which was rather rapid, and trying to get a feel in the air for her level of anger. It rose still, meaning she had yet to get to the apex of her rant, and he patiently nodded his head where necessary, and grunted the occasional "You don't say?" when needed.

The Simpa Bounty Hunter read the reviews and recaps of the previous day's sporting events, then moved on to the classified section, looking for furniture sales and whatever other items he might need for the building.

Ah, heart rate declining, he thought, *her outward temperature is decreasing as well. About time to get to business.* He cracked his knuckles. He turned in his chair, looked down at the woman, who even as he was seated still came about half a foot shorter than he did, and cleared his throat meaningfully.

"So you need me to patch up the wall in your living room," he said bluntly, without inflection to his voice. "All right, let me get another cup of coffee, and I'll be right down."

Mrs. Flecks thanked him for his time and for listening, and made her way out of his apartment.

Portenda drained the last of his first cup of coffee, and got up to get himself a second cup, pulling open a drawer near the sink and drawing out a magazine he hadn't read since buying it four days before.

International Bounty, one of his favorite publications for obvious reasons, listed all of the high risk, public bounties that were presently available. As he sat down to his second cup of coffee, he looked through the recent wanted ads—and blew most of them off.

The Elf-Queen's Bounty

Finished with his second cup, Portenda got up and headed into the spare bedroom of his apartment, where he kept his tools and supplies for working on the building. He grabbed a bucket of wood-patching material, as well as a couple of metal scrapers that he would use to fill in the hole. The needed items in hand, Portenda headed upstairs to the Flecks' apartment, and opened the door without knocking.

"It's roit there," Mrs. Flecks said from her seat in the living room, where she crocheting a green and white blanket for her husband.

Portenda followed the line of sight from her finger up to the hole, where a strange metal object stuck from the wall. Must've tossed it up there, Portenda said, identifying the object stuck in the wall up near the ceiling as a Gnome invention called a 'radio'.

"I'll be right back. I've got to get a ladder." Portenda set down his patch and scrapers. He went back to his apartment, got the ladder, and returned to the Flecks' place, setting it up as he pried open the bucket of patch.

"You know, 'e doesn't have any patience, that's 'is problem," Mrs. Flecks began, and Portenda hung his head as he got halfway up the ladder with the patch and a scraper.

Gee, he thought rather venomously, *I can't imagine why he would want to spend his time out in the fields instead of enjoying your lovely conversation.* Portenda looked at the radio embedded in the wall, and thought to himself that he would have to break the radio in half in order to extract it from the wall. As Mrs. Flecks droned on, he pulled out a hammer from his tool belt, and swung it down hard on the radio, breaking it clean in half.

Crap, he thought, *I'll have to smash apart what's left in there to get it to fall out.*

He placed his left hand squarely on the wall next to the hole, and drew the hammer back in his right. As he was about ready to swing, Mrs. Flecks asked him a direct question.

"You expecting a letter, Mr. Portenda," she asked.

Distracted, Portenda managed to turn his head and see the one of the other residents, Bing Marvel, holding an envelope addressed to him. As soon as his eyes fell on his name, written in graceful common cursive on the envelope, the hammer came down directly on his left hand. Pressure built up in his hand from the smashed bones instantly, and he clenched his teeth together against the scream of pain that threatened to break loose from his lungs.

"No, I wasn't," he growled, putting the hammer back in its loop and staying on the ladder for a minute so he could regenerate the bones in his left hand. Finally, he descended the ladder, and sauntered over to Bing, a half-Jaft fellow who took greatly after his mother, large and muscular in the way of Jafts. "Thank you, Bing."

"Sure thing, sir," the half-Jaft boy said. "I was heading out when a bird showed up with that. Um, listen sir, I was wondering if maybe you could sign this as well."

"What is it." Portenda took a red clipboard from the boy.

Mrs. Flecks stood on tiptoe, trying to see whatever it was that Portenda was holding.

Friggin' nosy parker, he thought disdainfully.

"Oh, I need five references to apply for the police academy," Bing said.

Hearing this and seeing the header on the sheet of paper, reading the statement beneath it to confirm this statement, Portenda took the offered pen and immediately signed the paper before handing the clipboard down to Mrs. Flecks.

"Always good to have young policemen on the force, Bing," Portenda said, opening the letter addressed to him. He briefly scanned the letter, also written in the fine cursive that graced the envelope, and smiled broadly from ear to ear. He flicked the corner of the paper with one thick finger, and chuckled a little to himself before folding it and stuffing it in a pants pocket. "Mrs. Flecks?"

"Oi, what is it then," she said, handing Bing his clipboard back without her signature.

"You'll have to get Mr. Joiner to finish this up for you." Portenda shuffled out of the apartment right behind young master Marvel.

Mrs. Flecks followed hurriedly, her mouth agape.

"What, that part-timer you have on for handyman work? I'd just as soon deal wif lookin' at the hole in the wall! That 'orrible little man is a sneak thief, I knows it!"

Portenda shook his head sadly, thinking about his part-timer. Seth Joiner was a Wererat, and most of his Race consisted of thieves and brigands, that much was true. Joiner, however, was a likable, simple-minded fellow who enjoyed rough physical labor and an honest day's work. Portenda had hired him on part-time to do handyman work and collect the rent when he was in Ja-Wen or elsewhere on bounty business. The man was finally going to earn his pay.

"Mrs. Flecks, I assure you, Mr. Joiner is not a thief." Portenda stopped in the hallway and looked down at the Gnome woman. "I trust the man greatly. He's a hard worker, and he earns his keep around here for certain. He'll be by to work on this, if you ask him."

"Oi, I'd rather do it meself," she said, harrumphing loudly and planting her hands on her hips.

Portenda shrugged as if to say 'whatever'.

"Suit yourself. Joiner will be by to collect the rent next week in any event, or evict you. Your choice." He waved good-bye over his shoulder.

He headed directly down for his armor, weapons, and traveling equipment. As soon as he had them on, he decided, he'd head on over to Jonah's Alchemy shop and get himself some teleportation to Whitewood.

He had a date, apparently, with a Queen.

Chapter Two
Partners

Shoryu Tearfang awoke to another of the wonderful autumn days in the Elven Kingdom's capital city, Whitewood, and was immediately ambushed by his wife, Ellen. He sat up from his pillow in their large bed, and she burst into the room, entering his hazy, sleep-riddled view for a moment before she flung herself through the air and onto his limp form.

"Hooof," he managed as she clung around his neck, the two of them embracing for a moment before she moved herself to the edge of the bed, and handed Shoryu a sealed envelope.

"What's this," he asked, his voice still partially muddled.

"A summons, I believe," his wife, the Elven Gaiamancer Ellen Daires-Tearfang, said. "It has the Queen's seal on the back."

Shoryu turned the envelope over as he swung his legs over the side of the bed, noting the symbol of the Elven Queen embossed on the blob of cooled red wax on the envelope's flap.

"So it does." He stood and stretched his long tan furred arms. Dressed in his yellow pajama pants and open button shirt, he walked around the side of the bed and sauntered out into the kitchen, where Ellen had a cup of coffee waiting for him. He tore the seal open as he sat down at the table, and pulled out a brief, to-the-point letter from the Queen. 'Come to the Grand Meeting Hall at approximately noon today. This meeting is mandatory.'

"What is it, dear," Ellen asked her husband, sitting across from him, looking around and wondering where their children were. Amber, their daughter and older of the two Tearfang kids, would have to hurry and get off to school soon. Toshiya, son and younger sibling of the pair, didn't have to get going for another hour or so, as he took fewer classes in school.

"It's a summons, like you thought." Shoryu passed the letter to his wife and picked up his mug of coffee. He blew on it and took a sip, enjoying its warmth in his throat and stomach. "It's only been a couple of days since the last meeting, but as you can see, she must have a solution in mind. She usually does when she's curt like that." He tipped his cup toward the letter in Ellen's hands.

She scrutinized the brief note, and noted the wording of the second sentence.

"I thought all of her meetings were mandatory." Ellen raised an eyebrow at Shoryu as he finished off his first cup of coffee and set his mug down.

He tapped the side of the mug, indicating that he wanted a second cup, and Ellen moved to refill it.

"Not all of them. We all show up anyway, most times. I think I've missed one meeting in eighteen years," he said with a smile.

"Well, you didn't have much choice then, now did you," Ellen asked with a grin. Eighteen years ago, an hour before Shoryu's third meeting with the Queen and the High Council as a group, Ellen had gone into labor with their daughter, Amber. Shoryu had sent a runner to the Queen, begging her forgiveness, at which the Elven Queen had laughed rather delightedly. There's no need to apologize for such a beautiful thing, she had replied via messenger.

Fifteen hours later, Shoryu Tearfang became the proud father of an Elven-born Cuyotai daughter. As expected, she had been born in her humanoid form, but the involuntary shape-shifts had begun days later, when they took their first born home.

As with all children born of such heritage, Amber had developed very quickly, physically speaking. She'd been born at nine pounds, and twenty-one inches in length. However, on her fifth day home from the hospital, Ellen had prepared herself for another breast-feeding session and found not a smiling, gurgling little Elven girl in the crib, but a small coyote up on all fours, prowling around the crib's interior. Mystified by the unseen transformation, she turned to Shoryu for advice, and as he would prove in the years to come, he was more prepared for the upbringing of the hybrid child than she.

He had reached down into the crib with his jaws and picked up the infant by the scruff, setting Amber Tearfang gently down on the bed in his and Ellen's room. There, he placed his hand on the nape of Amber's neck, as she stared up at him with her intelligent, animal eyes. He gave her a brief pinch on the neck, and before her parents' eyes, Amber made her second transformation, back into an Elven child.

Ellen had nearly shrieked at the sound of breaking bones and shifting muscles and other tissue, but Shoryu held her still by the shoulders, and the two of them watched as baby Amber drooled on herself and giggled her infant's laughter.

Two weeks later, baby Amber, in her Elven form, stood up and started toddling around the cottage. Ellen was completely startled; Shoryu not so much so. "It's typical, actually," he'd remarked as he opened his arms toward their daughter, who ran right up to him and literally jumped up into his lap. He sat her on his knee and bounced her a little, and Ellen decided to head to the city's library to look up any books they might have on the subject of rearing a lycanthrope child.

Now, at the age of eighteen, Amber Tearfang had developed into a beautiful young Elven-Cuyotai woman. She seemed to age much faster than a pureblood Elf, reaching puberty at the age of sixteen, but Shoryu explained to Ellen that this, too, was common among Cuyotai. "She isn't going to mature any further until she's about fifty, physically," he had explained. "She's more Cuyotai than Elf, physiologically speaking."

Their younger child, Toshiya Tearfang, had developed much the same way, though his physical maturation seemed to move along even more quickly.

"The males always grow faster than the females," Shoryu had said.

Ellen knew this, however, from having read about lycanthrope child rearing. She also knew, however, that the boys didn't get out of puberty for a great deal longer than the girls of Shoryu's kind.

Her thoughts returning to the present, Ellen brought Shoryu's second cup of coffee over to the table, and was nearly knocked flat as Amber ran past her, just shy of a full-on collision. "Sorry mom, hi dad, gotta run," she exclaimed as she ran out the front door, leaving neither of her parents any time to get a look at her. Shoryu and Ellen exchanged a worried glance, and then both grinned and pointed their fingers at one another.

"She gets it from you," they said in unison. They shared a good laugh, and Ellen sat down, passing Shoryu the sugar bowl. "Any idea why she sprinted out of here like that," Shoryu asked before sipping his coffee.

"I suspect it's what she's wearing. Again."

"Something I should know about," Shoryu asked.

"Well, I don't exactly approve of the clothes she's been wearing to school lately. I don't remember buying her anything like she's been wearing, and it's a tad bit, erm, revealing," Ellen said.

Shoryu set his mug down after taking another sip of his coffee.

"Care to clarify," he asked, planting his right foot on the floor, tensing up a little bit.

"Well," Ellen said, rubbing her hands together, hopeful that her husband wouldn't explode into one of his occasional fits of anger. "Last Thursday she wore a sky blue dress that cut off a few inches above the knee, and the neckline was, well, plunged, let us say," Ellen said.

Shoryu raised an eyebrow at his wife, and felt his blood begin to boil slightly.

"Define plunged," he groused.

Ellen hooked a finger into the top of her own sundress, and pulled it down enough to give her husband a good gander of her full cleavage.

"I see. Well, we'll have to put a stop to that." He took a large swig of his coffee.

From behind him, coming down from his room, Toshiya cleared his throat.

Ellen let go of her dress, letting it return to its normal shape.

"Thanks, mom, I really needed to see that," the boy said rather sarcastically. Toshiya Tearfang stood at a full six feet in height at the young age of sixteen. With finely chiseled features, he appeared to be the definition of Elven athleticism. Well-toned musculature, high cheekbones, and a faintly effeminate countenance, he was handsome enough to attract the attention of most of his female peers, though he showed little interest in them. He walked around his father and sat down at the table next to him. "Can I get a cup of that too, mom?"

"After that little remark, you can get it yourself young man," she replied with a smile, getting up anyway to fetch her son his morning coffee.

"You know, you really should watch what you say to your mother," Shoryu said to his son, ruffling his hair. Shoryu craned his head back, and looked down to the back of Toshiya's chair. Once again, the Cuyotai tail was waggling up out of the back of the boy's trousers. "Still having a little trouble with the transformation, Toshiya?"

"Yeah," the boy said with a sigh. "It's no fair, dad. Amber can do it whenever she wants, any part of her body she wants to. I can't seem to control it, though, and it's been pretty awkward in gym class," the boy said. "Yesterday, we were playing football out on the field, and in the middle of a play, I shifted into my bestial form. Tore my clothes apart, and when I jumped up for the ball, I reached a good foot higher than I needed to. Dropped the damned ball," he growled.

"Now honey, you know you'll get a hang of it soon enough." Ellen handed her son his coffee. "You could always do what your father does and just stay in your bestial form. It's the most common thing for lycanthropes, you know."

"Most other lycanthropes are purebloods," Toshiya spat, immediately apologizing for being rude. "Sorry mom, I just get so frustrated." He picked up his mug of coffee and stared at the hairy, clawed hand holding it. "There, you see what I mean?" he asked quietly, hanging his head.

Shoryu put his hand around his son's shoulder and gave him a brief squeeze.

"Like your mother said, you'll get the hang of it," he said.

Toshiya remained silent the rest of the time, and headed off for school about forty-five minutes later. Ellen started for their reading room, then asked Shoryu when he'd be heading out for the meeting.

"As late as I can," he said. "What're you doing today dear?"

"I'm going to the library to do my usual checking up." One of Ellen's projects since becoming a mother had been to check the relevant reported facts in historical references regarding the War of Vandross. Whenever she found something she knew to be inaccurate, she wrote a letter to the author of the reference book, chastising them for not getting their facts straight, and then would continue on by correcting their error for them. Making these small, seemingly useless contributions had actually earned her a decent living over the last eighteen years. With Shoryu's added income, they did very well for themselves.

Shoryu sauntered into their bedroom, and decided that for today, he would change into the traveling gear he hadn't worn since returning to Whitewood with his bride, shortly after burying Byron Aixler. The tan Hunter pants, the sleeveless vest, and the black leather belt, all went on as he prepared for the meeting. *Hmm,* he thought, cinching the belt tight around his waist. *I'm smaller than I was back then.*

Shoryu turned to the closet, and drew out his enchanted quiver, the one his father had left him along with the bow. It never ran out of arrows; whenever he reached back for a projectile, there would be one ready for him. Without the bow, however, the arrows launched from his new ash bow would only be standard arrows, with no magical properties of their own.

Shoryu also took out his short sword, a weapon that he routinely practiced with, but hardly seemed to have gotten any better at using. Melee combat was certainly never going to be his forte, that much he knew. "Not that I'll ever see much combat again," he whispered to himself.

Dressed, armed and ready for the day ahead, Shoryu Tearfang left his humble two-story cottage home and headed for the Palace.

He didn't know how wrong he would turn out to be about his fighting days.

* * * *

Shoryu stepped into the Grand Meeting Hall, and wasn't the least bit surprised to find that he was one of the last members of the Council to arrive. He *was* surprised, however, to find that the Queen herself was not present at her high backed seat at the head of the table. General Mortenson was present, as always, checking his timepiece with a practiced, irritated look. General Bergen also seemed to be in a bit of a rush, however, and Shoryu wondered if perhaps he had drills to run that day.

A side wall panel slid aside amid the chatter of the Council members, and every set of eyes turned to see the Queen of the Elves walk gracefully into the Grand Meeting Hall in a billowing white day dress, her hair up in locks. She graced them all with a resplendent smile, and glided to her seat at the head of the table. "Gentlemen, ladies, today we have a guest. I have called him in via messenger to help take care of this problem facing us, regarding James Svelk and the burglary of our Historical Society center."

Almost as if on cue, the Councilors and heads of the military forces turned their eyes toward the opening double doors at the back of the room, where a thickly muscled, grizzled Simpa, armed to the teeth, stood with his arms folded over his tree trunk of a chest. Gray stripes stood out on his exposed forearms, and the plain, blank stare he gave each of the individuals in the room left each thinking one common thought: *he's cold and he's professional.*

The Queen cleared her throat and spoke up again. "May I introduce you, ladies and gentlemen, to," she managed before General Bergen interrupted her, standing to his feet in a rush and knocking his chair over.

"Portenda the Quiet," General Bergen said flatly, a trace of disdain in his voice. "A Bounty Hunter. Your majesty, may I speak freely?" he asked without taking his eyes off of the Simpa.

Tension filled the air as the Councilors looked back and forth from the Queen to her suitor, and then on to Portenda, and back to the Queen.

He turned his head, and saw that the Queen had given him the go-ahead with a nod. He glared up at the Simpa, standing at the top of the steps leading up to the double doors, unmoving and silent as a monolith. "I do not believe this is a matter for an outsider," he said, emphasizing the word 'outsider'. "I believe you should dismiss this interloper post-haste, and allow me to find someone among our military ranks to take on the task of finding and arresting Svelk."

Though there were a few murmurs and nods of agreement from the Council members and General Mortenson, the Queen and the Simpa just smiled evenly at one another.

This, Shoryu thought, *is going to get interesting rather quickly.*

If they continue courting one another, he also thought, looking back and forth with just his eyes from Bergen to the Queen, he will become King of the Elves. If that happens, will he take control of the kingdom, and rule in the traditional manner of the Elves? Or will he simply take the title, and continue to allow her to pretty much run things in the country?

Before he could muse further on the matter, the Queen spoke, taking everyone rather off guard.

"I respect and appreciate your cautious opinion, dear," she said, making the General blush as she openly admitted to their relationship indirectly. "But our resources of manpower are stretched thinly enough as it is. I have made it my business over the years to check up on potential outside help, you know, and always this man's name pops up. He's got a rather lengthy report sheet of successful bounty operations in other regions, General." She smiled at her suitor, who appeared to Shoryu to be fizzling out a little.

The Cuyotai also realized, a full minute after the fact had been revealed, that the good General already knew who Portenda was on sight.

Shoryu would have known him as well, but only after a few minutes' time. As the Councilor in charge of foreign diplomacy and intelligence, Shoryu often read and heard about those things going on outside of the capital and the kingdom itself. The most recent thing he had heard or read about the Simpa Bounty Hunter had involved an apparent brawl between Portenda the Quiet and a rather brutal Red Tribe Werewolf up north, in the city of Desanadron. It had been the first public record of the Simpa losing a fight to anyone, though most witnesses said it was more of a draw.

Looking at the lumbering Simpa, Shoryu wondered how fast such a fellow could possibly be. Holstered on his right hip, Shoryu saw that Portenda the Quiet had a mecha firearm weapon of some sort, most likely what was known as a pistol or a revolver. *Likely a last resort*, the Cuyotai thought.

The Queen once again spoke, and brought Shoryu back to attention. "By the way, Mr. Portenda, how did you reach us so quickly?"

"Your Majesty, I am friendly with a highly skilled Alchemist in the city of Desanadron, a young man by the name of Jonah Staples. As soon as I received your message, I went to him and requested that he prepare for me a Focus Site to teleport me somewhat north of the city. Science and magic make life easy, if used properly," he said with a small grin. *Also, I wanted to get the hells away from Mrs. Flecks*, he didn't add.

"The offer," the Queen continued as a matter of course. "Is it agreeable?"

Portenda nodded without comment or explanation to the Council or the Generals.

"Very good. A picture of the man you are hunting down will be provided. Do you have any questions for the Council or Generals Mortenson and Bergen," she asked.

"Just a few." He pulled a small notebook from one of his vest pockets. He'd been through scores of these little notebooks, using a new one at the start of most assignments. He took a pen from another pocket, and looked around the table at the Councilors and Generals. "Target's name?"

"James Svelk," said General Mortenson, taking a look around, finding Sheriff Deacon and asking him quietly to provide a Mage's Eye playback for the Simpa. "We believe he has aid in his doings and goings-on."

Portenda looked around the room at length, letting his eyes settle on the eyes of each Councilor and General in turn, not surprised as most of them broke contact right away. Only the Cuyotai and the General known as Bergen didn't look away from his gaze. The Bounty Hunter made a mental note of that.

"Dead or alive," Portenda asked, looking directly at the Queen and nobody else. After all, he reasoned, this woman had contacted him personally, so her subordinates had little or no say in the actual business negotiation of this contract.

"Preferably alive, that we may properly try and punish him for his many crimes. However," the Queen said, lowering her voice and tone, so that all ears were highly tuned in to her. "I understand that sometimes your line of business can get very risky, particularly when dealing with people who will kill in cold blood, as this man has. If it comes down to that, you have the go-ahead to kill him."

"His cohorts," Portenda asked, still jotting down the Queen's reply word for word.

"Deal with them as you see fit," said General Mortenson.

"Recovery," Portenda asked. When silence ensued for a few minutes, Portenda clarified. "Property to be recovered?"

Chief Sutton stood up, and approached the Simpa Bounty Hunter with a tightly rolled scroll.

Portenda unfurled it, noting the length of the list and the items on it. "Great Shioden," he grumbled. "I'll need a pack mule for all this stuff," he continued in a whisper. He rolled the scroll up once more and stuffed it away in his rucksack for later reference. "Timeline?"

"As soon as possible," replied the Elven Queen. "The lives of those guards who were slain are more priceless than the artifacts stolen. Councilor Tearfang's family heirloom, a bow, was also among the items stolen. I assure you that I know how much the return of it would mean to him."

As the Council and the Generals and Chief Sutton looked at him, Portenda mulled the situation over, tucking the notepad away in one of his outer vest pockets.

"I'll be off then," he said, turning on his heel and preparing to leave the Grand Meeting Hall of the Elven Queen's Palace.

As soon as he was out, Shoryu shot the Queen a questing glance. Much to his surprise and delight, she was already looking to him with a smile and a nod.

"Go, Councilor Shoryu Tearfang," she said. "You have the best wishes of the Kingdom and its peoples."

Shoryu thanked the Queen with a deep bow, nearly smacking his snout on the long, polished table, and darted out of the chamber after the Bounty Hunter. The doors of the chamber closed behind him as he chased after Portenda the Quiet, who he saw hadn't quite made it halfway down the long corridor.

Shoryu sprinted after Portenda, his long, loping strides helping him clear the distance with relative ease.

Shoryu reached up and half-turned Portenda toward him, panting slightly at the sudden exertion.

Portenda had heard him approaching from the rear, practically stampeding down the hardwood corridor, his lungs inflating and deflating audibly to Portenda's heightened sense of hearing. In a way, he had fully expected that this one particular man might come after him for an extra word or so, either him or General Bergen. Of all of the Council members, Shoryu Tearfang had met his gaze and held it the longest. In Portenda's experience, that either made Mr. Tearfang very brave, or very stupid.

"Wait," Shoryu said between breaths, staying at his full height, which almost matched Portenda's at nearly seven feet. "The bow was a family heirloom, mine by right of birth. I lost two fathers in order to attain it, and I mean to have it back in my hands as soon as possible. Also," Shoryu said, remembering how major James Svelk had met the Byron of Sidius's company all those years ago, with open hostility and violence. "I have a score to settle with Svelk. I'll inform my wife that I'll be coming with you on this errand."

"Wait a minute." Portenda held up one golden-furred paw, the fingers gnarled and scarred, the arm attached to it thicker around than Shoryu's throat. "You're married?"

Shoryu's face took on an inquisitive expression, and Portenda decided there and then that if the man really wanted to come along, he was going to give him a hard time, just as he had with Jonah Staples.

"Yes, yes I am," Shoryu replied after a minute. He gave the hulking Bounty Hunter a quick once-over, his eyes stopping once again on the enormous mecha weapon holstered on the man's hip. "Does that matter? I'm coming with you, Mr. Portenda," Shoryu's mind was decided on the matter. "I'll just go tell my wife, Ellen. She'll understand."

"Children," Portenda said, folding his arms over his considerable chest.

"Yes, two," Shoryu said, smiling.

Hmm, Portenda thought, he has children. Maybe I shouldn't bring him after all. A proud papa by the look of him.

"Amber, our daughter, and Toshiya, our son. They'll both still be in school at this hour, but I can wait to go with you until after they come home."

"You're not coming," Portenda said in his typically icy tone, turning and moving away without another word, his thickly muscled arms swinging easily at his sides as he strode off. He heard the sudden acceleration of the Councilor's heart. He heard the sharp, indignant intake of breath as the Cuyotai prepared to yell something at him. He also felt the air around the Cuyotai separate as he dashed around his side and stopped a few feet in front of him, spreading his arms out, blocking Portenda's progress.

"Why in the seven hells not?" Shoryu raged at the Bounty Hunter.

How dare he speak to me so plainly, Shoryu thought, his field of vision dimming, filling on the outside with the dangerous sanguine hue he recognized as his own mind coming apart in sudden fury. "Do you think me incapable of facing danger? I am not just some politician, you know! I am a renowned archer, with or without my family bow!"

Portenda closed his eyes and smiled to himself. *Well, at least he's persistent. That's a point in his favor.* The lumbering Simpa Bounty Hunter took one step forward, and the two lycanthropes stood almost nose-to-nose. On one side, the Simpa with his blunted leonine features, almost regal in stance and appearance; on the other, the Cuyotai with his long, slender, canine features, usually so full of mirth and laughter that there appeared to be permanent laugh lines carved just beneath the thin facial fur.

Portenda reached up and put his hands lightly on the Councilor's shoulders.

"Go home," Portenda said, still not raising or lowering his voice at all. However, he didn't put any of his icy professional aura into his words either. "Hug your wife, and play with your children. You will do them no good if you are harmed or slain in this errand."

Shoryu's arms twitched at the sudden gentleness in the huge warrior's tone, the seriousness he seemed to imply when speaking of Shoryu's children, who in truth hadn't played with him since they were little. Those days were over long ago, yet here, this giant of a man who had just slipped past him yet again, made Shoryu think back on those by-gone days.

Shoryu found himself standing stock still in the corridor, listening to the receding footfalls of the huge Simpa behind him. As he turned, he saw that Portenda chose that moment to stop and turn toward him once again. "I've got some things to research here in the city before taking up the pursuit, Councilor Tearfang. You seem to know the target somewhat, so I'll be by your residence later to speak further with you on the subject."

"Um, don't you need my address then," Shoryu asked in a voice just above a whisper, shaking his frozen muscles loose.

Portenda gave him a strange sort of lopsided grin, one that reminded the Cuyotai eerily of Byron's smile.

"Don't worry," Portenda said, turning away again and putting up one hand in a gesture of 'see you later'. "I'll find you." As Portenda turned at a hallway intersection, Shoryu couldn't help but think, *yes, I'm sure you will.*

* * * *

Far to the east of Whitewood, in the borderlands that separate the Fiefdom of Lemago from the free lands just outside of the Elven Kingdom, sat a small woodland about two miles in diameter. Several dozen yards north and west of its center stood a ramshackle one-story cottage made of darkened wood. The odors that poured through the small wooded area would remind anyone passing through of rotted fruit that had been left out in the sun and placed shortly upwind. Woodland animals roamed about freely in these woods, along with a handful of the more dangerous monstrosities that reside in the lands of Tamalaria. Rashums, froggrips, thresherbeasts and other assorted dangerous species sometimes roamed during the daylight hours, but they mostly came out at night.

Of course, none of these creatures could be said to be as dangerous as the four more sentient beings inside of the one-floor hovel in the woodland. Just inside the building's only exterior door, an ill-lit living room chamber held four young men, Humans all, each in the midst of some activity of their own. The oldest of the Human men, all of whom were brothers, sat at a small two-seater table near the only living room window, staring at an intricately engraved ring of some sort. At full height, the man stood at just an inch shy of five and a half feet, and weighed only a little over a hundred pounds. Sean Browler, eldest of the Browler Brothers Gang, was presently trying to estimate the amount he could pawn this ring off for.

His black long sleeve sweater was draped over the back of the chair he sat in, his bare upper body caked with sweat due to the horrible humidity of the day. He glanced for a moment at the long, arm-covering tattoos he had currently exposed, his eyes lingering for a long moment on the image closest to his right hand. It was a simple sketched headstone with the name of his mother, and the year she had passed away, engraved on it.

Six years, he thought. *It's been six years, Ma, and look at us now. Nothin' more 'n a bunch of hired goons. Sorry if we've disappointed ya, Ma.*

Sean hadn't seen or heard from the gang's employer, James Svelk, since they had parted ways the night before, but that bothered him very little. Looking around the living room of the rented cottage, he surveyed each of his younger brothers, and for just a moment, wondered if there was a way out of this lifestyle for any of them. His line of sight stopped first on the next brother in line, in accordance of age, Dean Browler. Dean had only joined Sean and the other two Browler boys about six months before while they had been passing through the region north of Desanadron. Dean stood at around five-foot-nine, and weighed around forty pounds more than Sean. He was rangy, with a mountaineer's muscles constrained beneath a charcoal gray Ninja uniform.

Dean Browler had spent the last couple of years away from Sean and his younger brothers, training under the instruction of Thaddeus Fly and Markus Trent in the arts of the Obura Clan Ninja. He had become a quiet, conserved assassin, and much to Sean's delight, he kept his private business private. Sean loved his little brothers all, but Dean often worried him. As an adolescent, Dean had been wild, uncontrollable, prone to fits of violence and petty acts of rebellion. Sean had been forced to reel him in on more than one occasion, and ultimately sent him to Fly for instruction and 'discipline'. The end results had been excellent. In fact, they had been almost, well, unbelievable. That was precisely what bothered Sean.

Onward his eyes roamed, to the next brother in line. Benjamin Browler, sitting on the floor with a pack of cards arranged in a game of solitaire, was the third Browler in line. At the tender age of twenty-two, he was hands-down the best Pickpocket Sean knew, aside perhaps for the Gnome Lee Toren. Scrawny and angular like his eldest brother Sean, Benjamin had a quick smile and a handsome countenance that helped him swindle many the young lady. Beyond picking pockets, however, Benjamin had one skill that Sean valued him for more than most; Benjamin had several contacts throughout the lands' diverse information networks. If the Browler Brothers Gang ever needed information, Sean needed only to turn to Ben and let him work his magic.

Finally, Sean turned toward the door of the cottage. Set against the wall, left of the door as one entered the building, was a long metal workbench. Bits and pieces of metal, and dozens of mecha tools and attachments lay scattered here and there along the long bench, which ran almost the entire length of the front of the room.

"Reggie," Sean whispered to himself, looking at his youngest, tallest brother.

Reginald Browler, age 19, was the only one of the Browler brothers who Sean thought might have a future outside of the goon racket, if someone could get the boy some mental help.

Bright sparks kicked up from the bench where Reggie sat, working away with his soldering and welding equipment.

Sean thought about approaching, and finally got himself up from the two-seater table, watching Ben move swiftly with the deck of cards to claim his abandoned seat.

Whatever, Sean thought.

He moved up right behind Reggie, and peered over his right shoulder.

For a brief moment, Sean's eyes snatched a look down at the partially exposed shoulder of his littlest brother, who was by all rights an Engineer of the genius caliber. A round, silvery plate of metal was just visible underneath his beige work apron, and the sight of it sent a shiver up and down Sean's spine.

"Whatcha working on, Reggie me boy?" Sean asked in his wispy tone.

The lanky Browler brother set down his soldering torch for a moment on its safety plate, killing the flame. He removed his safety glasses, and turned his head just far enough to the right to look up at his oldest brother. His left eye was a beautiful shade of blue, bright and intelligent. His right eye, however, gave Sean another of those racing, clammy chills in his back. A circlet of bulbous metal surrounded a deep violet orb that rotated around in his right eye socket. Sean could never tell if the eye was focused on him or not, and this only added to the oddity of being stared at with a mechanical eyeball.

The Elf-Queen's Bounty

"New equipment. Last touches, Sean," Reggie said in a plaintive voice. "I really think this one'll be better. I based it on the ancient combat models they unearthed in the northwestern mountains a while back."

Sean looked at the long, sleek object on the table, and noted the lethal aura that seemed to radiate from the lifeless piece of machinery.

"And Dean helped me find a rechargeable power source, too. See this?" Reggie Browler now sounded a little excited, an emotion he didn't often display, and for once Sean let himself be drawn into this one-sided conversation.

Reggie reached down and plucked a small blue crystal from the device, holding it up and turning on one of his work lamps, casting himself in a sort of bluish glow.

"What is it," Sean asked, looking at the priceless-looking object.

"Scale from a Cerulean Dragon. Dean got a bunch of scales when he was training in Desanadron. You see," Reggie said, swiveling the work chair around to fully face his brother.

Sean looked down toward the floor, and noticed the way the light glinted off of Reginald's metallic feet.

"This is wonderful, because they get their energy from sunlight. Through their scales." Reggie then slipped the scale back in its designed slot, and grabbed his left arm just above the elbow.

Oh Gods, Sean thought with a cringe, *I hate it when he does this.*

Reggie Browler gave his lower arm a twist, and there issued from the joint of connection a loud grinding noise as unscrewed the lower section of his left arm.

The section of arm he had just removed, he set on the workbench where it gleamed dully, just like the rest of the machinery and equipment laying about. He plucked up his new project, an artificial mecha arm, and slid it into place, screwing it in and letting the technology chips, plates and sensors connect and align themselves with his internal systems. Reggie's artificial eye glowed a brighter shade of violet for a moment, and his fleshy eye twitched back and forth in its socket. "Synchronization complete," Reggie said in an empty voice.

"Um, very nice, Reg," Sean said, moving away as his little brother turned back to the table to finish tinkering with his new artificial limb. Roughly fifty percent of Reginald Browler's body was cybernetic, all of his pieces based on the ancient robot designs of the lost ages, along with the theories and designs of the Age of Mecha. Aside from the Tinker Norman Adwar, nobody else in the lands of Tamalaria possessed the vast mechanical and technological knowledge that belonged to Reggie.

Sean headed out of the living room, down the one hallway to the kitchen, where he prepared himself a brief lunch of meat strips and a wedge of cheese. "Can't go wrong with the basics, eh, Ma," Sean asked the empty kitchen as he sat down to his meal. He was half finished with his lunch when a loud knock came at the front door, and he stood up as he heard it opened by one of his little brothers. He heard a familiar voice ask for him, and a minute later, James Svelk stood in the kitchen doorway.

"By your grace, it's warming to see you, Mr. Svelk," Sean said sarcastically, offering the Elven warrior a haphazard bow. "Pray come in, and allow us to give you succor."

Svelk, angular and dour-faced, grunted and stepped into the kitchen, the Tearfang family bow in his left hand. He toyed with the string for a moment, and then gave Sean a serious look. "Please, Sean Browler, let us dispense with your poorly rehearsed society-speak. Let us be plain, for my time is short. My own employer expects to meet with me in a couple of hours, and I've got a mage in the town nearby waiting to teleport me to his location."

"Sure thing, boss." Sean returned to his seat and resumed his meal. "What's on your mind?"

"The Cuyotai that this weapon belonged to," Svelk said, setting the enchanted bow down on the table across from Sean's plate. "He's a highly skilled Hunter, or archer if you will, and he's got a bit of a temper. He will most likely come looking for it himself."

"Anything we should worry about?" Sean asked, always mindful of getting information where and when he could.

"I doubt it," Svelk said confidently. "He's just a Cuyotai archer, after all. Besides, he's a Councilor in the Elven Kingdom, so I doubt he'll actually receive permission to come looking for it. But, in case he does come after me," he strung the weapon around his shoulders in the style of an archer, "I'll be in touch with you to take care of him for me. I've no desire to get my hands dirtier than they already are. That's what I'm paying you boys for, after all," the Elf said with a haughty grin.

Sean Browler could see the openly displayed disdain in that grin, and in the Elven man's eyes. *Thinks he's so much better than us,* Sean thought heatedly, minding his meal and keeping his temper in check. *Thinks we're just a bunch of hooligans. Well, we'll take care of his problem for him all right.* He looked down at his food. *And then maybe we'll take care of him.*

"What's this guy's name, this Cuyotai," Sean asked as Svelk abruptly turned to leave the cottage where the Browler brothers currently resided.

The Elf-Queen's Bounty

The former major in the Elven Kingdom's armies spun on his heel and smiled once again at his employee.

"Shoryu Tearfang. His name is Shoryu Tearfang."

* * * *

Portenda, meanwhile, sat in an uncomfortable and all too small oak chair with orange cushions on the seat and backing. To call them cushions, he thought dryly, they'd have to actually have some padding in them. The Office of Public Records didn't have much business with anyone with a frame as sizable as his. Even after adjusting his weapons, Portenda was forced to hunch forward on the chair so that his hips didn't push the sides out to splitting distance.

Overall, the atmosphere of this administration building was a lot more homey than most other government offices he'd visited. The Elven Kingdom for years stood as a shining example of what society could and should be like: polite and helpful citizenry, efficient and relaxed civil servants, and an orderly business populace. Whitewood's Office of Public Records seemed, to his perceptions, to meet those criteria perfectly. A smiling, handsome young Elven gentleman in blue trousers and a white button shirt had politely informed Portenda that he would have a twenty-minute wait while they located James Svelk's military records. The young man had offered him tea, which the Simpa Bounty Hunter had gruffly declined. When he asked about Svelk's criminal record, another of the office's administrative assistants, a shiny furred Cuyotai woman in tan trousers with a yellow blouse had told him she'd be 'more than happy to help with that.' The forced smiles and cheerfulness made him want to gag, and Portenda had excused himself to the records' viewing room.

Now, nearly an hour after entering the two-story house that had been turned over to the government for its own purposes, he had James Svelk's military record file open in front of him, and he had already leafed through roughly half of it. All of the reports and commendations had been written, frustratingly, in a decidedly atypical form for the Elven peoples: instead of being longwinded and descriptive, which would have been helpful for Portenda, they were stringently military in nature. Short, clipped statements lacking in personal opinion of any sort, relaying only the facts pertinent to his service. In other words, pretty much a dead end. Portenda let loose a low growl from his throat, glad to be in the viewing room alone so that nobody else could witness his aggravation.

The Elven Queen, however, and the Cuyotai, Shoryu Tearfang, had both made reference to the fact that Major Svelk had sold out the capital's defenses and the kingdom itself, to the warlock Richard

Vandross many years ago when the madman had assailed the city of Whitewood. His military file, however, only listed him as an abandoner, pegging him with a dishonorable, but not a criminal discharge.

Portenda grabbed the discharge papers and rose from his chair, wincing as it clung to him for a moment before falling off of his ass back onto the hardwood floor with a thud. "I wonder how bad it'd be for visiting Minotaurs," he muttered to himself.

Portenda headed back to the main desk with the discharge paper in his right hand, and set it down gently on the desk as he rang the bell for a clerk's attention.

The Cuyotai woman who had brought him Svelk's criminal record file, a much slimmer folder than his military record, came from a back room a moment later with a slightly dimmer smile than she'd had before. "Can I help you with something, sir," she asked, cocking her head to one side and looking down at the discharge paper.

"Yeah, right here," Portenda said. "It says here that he was listed as an abandoner and discharged dishonorably. But I don't see any attached notation to indicate that he was given a criminal discharge," he said.

"Oh, that's because abandonment isn't considered grounds for a criminal discharge in the Elven Kingdom," the woman explained.

Portenda, slightly flummoxed, only raised an eyebrow at her, keeping his cold, steel gaze on her eyes. "But it does earn them a dishonorable discharge, so an abandoner can't rejoin the military for a minimum of four hundred years. That's a long time," the Cuyotai woman said.

"Sure, for you or me," Portenda said, taking the paper up and turning to return to the viewing room. "Drop in the old bucket for a pureblood Elf though," he murmured under his breath as he took his seat once more.

Grousing and fuming internally that he didn't have a single lead to work with from the man's military record, Portenda wondered if perhaps there might have been incidents, as is common in military operations, that hadn't been accurately reported, if reported at all. Every army had its own dirty little secrets, after all, he reasoned. Why not the Elven Kingdom's military?

The Bounty Hunter was preparing to set the military file aside when he noted something on the very last paper in the folder. This last sheet was a copy of Svelk's payroll record at the time of his official discharge. A single box, with one letter in it, gave Portenda a jolt of hope that he might be able to find a lead on Svelk's background and profile. The box was labeled 'marital status', and underneath was the letter 'M', for married.

As he grinned to himself, a pretty young Elven girl, perhaps only a few years out of her adolescence, entered the room and brought him the fresh mug of cuppa that he'd asked for roughly an hour earlier. He took a hasty sip and cleared his throat.

"Is there anything else I can get you," the girl asked in a lilting, beautiful voice typical of her Race.

"A copy of James Svelk's marriage certificate, and the wife's current address," he said flatly without taking his eyes off of the application sheet.

The girl remained where she was for a moment, writing down his request on a pad of paper.

"And make it quick, woman. A copy should be readily available, so you won't have to write it up from scratch like you clearly did this cuppa," he said, his face now devoid of expression, his tone arctic wind. "Did you hand grind the beans yourself? I asked for this an hour ago," he continued, frankly surprised at his own sour attitude toward the girl.

As she smiled wanly and nodded at him, he realized that part of his aggravation was not at her or any of the other clerks in the office building. He knew that government offices took their sweet times with things like this, had experienced the 'administrative shuffle' more times than he could count. But he had a target now, and was actively pursuing his assignment. That was one factor of his irritable mood. The other factor, he knew, was that once again he was taking someone else along for the ride, against his better judgment. Unlike Jonah Staples, however, Shoryu Tearfang had a wife and children to go back to as well, which meant that Portenda would have to make doubly sure that no harm came to the Cuyotai archer.

The girl hadn't yet left the room, and with his heightened sense of hearing, he made out her mumbling to herself, "What an uptight asshole." She exited the room, and came back only six or seven minutes later with two yellow pieces of parchment outstretched to him. "Here you are, sir," she said amiably.

"Miss?"

The Elven girl turned back to face her enormous guest, and her smile faltered when her eyes locked on his. He could see her fear of him, but her fear did not outweigh the apparent sense of superiority she held over him.

Like all Elves, he thought, *this little woman thinks she is of the most superior and supreme Race in the lands of Tamalaria. Time to knock her down a peg.* "What's the most important thing for you to be in your line of work?" he asked, slanting his head to one side and folding his hands under his chin, elbows propped on his knees as he leaned slightly forward.

"Um, helpful and pleasant," she whispered, lost in the depthless gunmetal gray of his eyes. He gave her a small smile then, and the aura he exuded wrapped her up even tighter.

"Good," he said. "Personality traits you need to display in your job to do well and remain employed. Now, do you know what I need to be, in my line of work?"

In reply to this second question, the Elven girl could find no words to speak. She only shook her head slowly, her eyes still locked on his, her entire field of vision taken up by the Bounty Hunter's proud, leonine features.

He gave her a bit of a start then by dropping his smile completely and staring darkly at her. "Efficient and ruthless," he rasped, listening to the accelerating heartbeat of the Elven girl, smelling the salty sweat building up in her armpits. "In a word, what I must be is an asshole. Now," he growled, launching himself up onto his feet to loom over her. "Get out of my sight."

The Elven girl broke eye contact, turning and scurrying away, a rabbit that has seen the barrel of the rifle aimed at its head, but has been given a chance to dart for its burrow hole before the farmer opens fire.

As soon as the girl was out of sight and he was back in his too-small seat, the Simpa Bounty Hunter heaved a sigh and shook his head. A scuttling, venomous insect crawled around inside his heart, and he knew its name very well: guilt. But he wasn't about to apologize. He had sensed that the girl was haughty, arrogant and vapid, a two-dimensional young woman imposed on his multi-dimensional senses and thoughts. He shouldn't have been quite so harsh with her, but at the same time, he didn't like having to suffer such two-faced fools.

Before he heard the thundering, booming voice that only he would hear, regardless of its owner's volume, Portenda could feel the void-like presence filling the air next to him. WOULD IT KILL YOU TO BE NICE TO HER KIND?

"What kind is that," Portenda asked, looking of the corner of his eye at Death before returning his gaze down to Svelk's criminal record.

THE KIND I HAVE UPCOMING APPOINTMENTS WITH.

Portenda turned his head to fully look at the astral being, and quickly turned his head away, feeling even more of a heel than he already did.

"How," was his only question.

IT WON'T DO YOU ANY GOOD, KNOWING. YOU KNOW THAT, DON'T YOU?

The Elf-Queen's Bounty

When Portenda did not reply, Death simply shrugged his shoulders beneath his robes.

IF YOU MUST KNOW ANYWAY, SHE'S GOING TO TAKE A WALK OUTSIDE OF THE CITY THIS AFTERNOON. SHE'S GOING TO FAIL TO PAY ATTENTION TO THE PATH AHEAD OF HER, AND SHE'LL SLIP RIGHT DOWN A HILL AND BASH HER SKULL OPEN ON A ROCK. LIGHTS OUT, GAME OVER, the astral being said as he sat across from the Simpa Bounty Hunter, whose existence he was partially responsible for.

In silence Portenda scanned the few sheets of incident reports in which Svelk had arisen as a suspect to the kingdom's various law enforcement groups. He could think of nothing to say, no way to properly apologize for his behavior. *What should I say to him*, he thought. 'Sorry, I'm in a bit of a rush because I'm on an assignment?' That wouldn't exactly fly, not with this fellow. Before he could formulate a proper conversation with his guest, he looked up, and saw that the chair opposite him was empty. Before leaving the offices, he made a point to apologize to the girl for his brutish behavior, offering up the lame excuse that he was under a lot of stress, and made his way off.

* * * *

The scents of hearth and home always warmed Shoryu's heart, especially as he set the table for dinner. The clink and clank of the ceramic plates softly touching one another echoed gently in his ears, which stood on end. The sound of his son and daughter gently prodding each other and laying pranks for one another also gave him a Racially natural bit of pride.

In the kitchen, Ellen looked lovely and at peace in their family home, preparing a large meal as usual for a Friday. He had a view of her from behind and at some distance, but her radiant hair, the swan-like neck, and the shapeliness of her curves reminded him once more why she captivated him in the physical sense. She was as close to the Elven ideal of beauty as he was likely to ever be allowed near in his lifetime. As he watched her turn and bring over a large plastic bowl of stuffing, he gave her a brief kiss, which surprised her.

"What was that for," she asked, blushing slightly.

"It was for everything," he replied, being overly sweet. He leaned in close to her, his left hand reaching slowly to snag a bit of the incredible smelling stuffing she'd set on the table.

As he came to within an inch of his prize, his smile cool and calm, his lips pressed close to hers, he felt a sudden THWAK! on his hand and let out a coyote yelp, backing away and shaking his hand.

41

Ellen stood up straight, arms crossed and hips tilted, a gnarled board of wood reacting to her magic and flowing back into the woodwork of the table. He had forgotten for a moment that as a Gaiamancer—even dead wood reacted to her magical command.

"No snatchies before dinner," she scolded playfully, waggling her finger at him.

Shoryu rubbed his hand and moved behind her into the kitchen, grabbing up more plates and bowls for the meal ahead.

"So tell me again what this fellow is like, this Mr. Portenda. I want to know, so I can holler at him if he doesn't show up on time for dinner. I made a lot of extra food expecting him to come," she groused.

"Well, he's a Simpa," Shoryu said, trying to buy time for himself, think of a way to describe the Bounty Hunter without being too harsh.

"Right, lion-man, already knew that," Ellen said, returning to the stove. "Next?"

"Um, he's a very reserved fellow, very businesslike," Shoryu said a touch nervously, checking the clock. When Portenda had said that he would find the Councilor, Shoryu fully expected that he would be abducted in the middle of the night and whisked away by the burly brute. Somehow, that just seemed to fit in his mind with the stoic Bounty Hunter's attitude. However, he was hopeful that perhaps he would be interrupted during the evening meal, as often happened for his official post as Councilor.

As Toshiya and Amber ambled down the stairs from their respective bedrooms, grumbling at each other miserably, Shoryu heard the telltale knock at the door. As he whipped his head up and looked down the hall at the simple oak door, he wondered how much trouble the big man might have getting inside.

Ellen hadn't turned from the stove for a moment until the second knock came, much heavier and insistent than the first. "Good Gaia beneath us, is he trying to break the door in," she exclaimed, feeling tremors under her bare feet.

Before Shoryu's heartbeat could return to a normal pace, his lithe, slender wife brushed past him and headed for the front door, her simple green housedress swishing daintily on the wooden floor.

Shoryu, captivated by her femininity as always, momentarily forgot that she was about to open the door on one of the largest brutes she had ever seen in her long, long life. "Um, maybe I should get it," he stammered lamely and far too late.

The Elf-Queen's Bounty

Ellen Daires Tearfang, wife of Shoryu Tearfang and former ally and companion of Byron of Sidius, opened the front door of her humble, modified two-story cottage.

Standing before her on the other side of the doorway, a hulking Simpa with a black sleeveless vest loomed over her by about a foot and a half. His height, she reckoned, was not much more than Byron's had been. In terms of width, however, this Portenda fellow was muscular almost to the point of being vulgar.

"Mrs. Tearfang," Portenda asked, eyebrows twitching upward in inquiry. *My goodness,* he thought as he gave the Elven beauty before him a quick once-over, *the good Councilor is one lucky sonuvabitch.* This Elven woman was perhaps even lovelier than good Jonah's wife. To her credit, he noticed that despite his much larger and broader stature, as well as being armed like a one-man hit squad, she did not seem the least bit afraid of suspicious of him.

"Indeed I am," she replied warmly enough. "You must be Mr. Portenda. Please, come in. Dinner will be served shortly."

Hunching his shoulders slightly, the Simpa Bounty Hunter squeezed through the doorway and into the Tearfang home. Without meaning to do so, his mind immediately began recording vital scenario information. *Doorway is approximately three feet across and six and a half feet high,* he thought, his eyes darting this way and that, his ears pricking up. His nostrils flared several times as he sampled the air, and his nerves stood on end, trying to get a feel for the environment.

Front door opens on the den, he thought. *Three-seater couch, approximately five feet long from end to end, weight of probably between seventy and eighty pounds. Smells like rosewood. Might be wood polish for the coffee table. Two recliners, angled across from the couch. Family room. Games probably played on the coffee table. End table next to each recliner, oil lamp on each. Oil smells a little old, but he probably replaces it whenever he can; he is a Cuyotai after all. The smell must notify him sooner or later. Lamps themselves have glass bases, so they'd shatter pretty good, make for shivs. Den window looks to be about quarter of an inch thick, little insulation, four feet across and three high. Emergency exit.*

All of this he thought in the time it took to blink his eyes twice. When Portenda caught himself running through his usual mental prep, he grimaced slightly and chided himself for being so stringent. He tried to give Ellen a small smile, but he knew that what actually presented itself for viewing resembled a rictus more closely than it did a benign expression. Portenda the Quiet turned his eyes toward the kitchen then, which stood at the end of a short hallway past the den. A set of stairs was to the right of the hallway, almost opposite the actual family den area.

Ellen moved away from the front door, and Portenda started to follow, turned to close the door, and then returned his attention toward the kitchen.

The sweet aromas of homemade foods wafted through the air to him, and he instantly forgot about the oil lamps his nostrils had been so interested in before. His stomach spoke to him, reminding him that he hadn't had a decent respite in some time, and that it would like if he could kindly guide it and himself to where the grub could be found.

Upon entering the kitchen, Portenda's eyes did not follow the natural progression of his nose and stomach. Instead, they strayed to the long oak dining table, at which sat two Elven youths, both of them reading what appeared to be textbooks of some sort. The boy appeared to be a few years younger than the girl, but he didn't seem to have the natural slenderness of an Elf. *No*, Portenda thought, *he's a lot more like his papa in that regard.*

"Kids, go get washed up for dinner," Ellen said in her best 'we have company and must at least appear civilized' tone of voice.

The kids sighed to themselves, and rose from the table, heading toward the bathroom to take turns washing their hands and faces.

The girl, Portenda saw as she walked past, not daring to look up at the Bounty Hunter, seemed to have a bit of trouble with her lycanthrope nature. A tan-furred tail swished back and forth behind her, poking out of the top of her gray corduroy pants.

A slender hand patted Portenda on the back, and though he knew it was Shoryu Tearfang behind him by the man's scent, he couldn't help wondering if he should just react in a defensive manner, just to show the good Councilor that he was as good as advertised.

Better not, he thought, his eyes shifting for just a moment to Ellen Daires-Tearfang, the goodly Councilor's wife before he turned around to meet Shoryu's eyes. *She may not look it, but I know she's a force to be reckoned with.*

"Elven is their natural form," Shoryu informed Portenda, guiding him gently to a seat at the long dining table. "Amber has a good grasp on controlling her body-shifting, but sometimes she loses control of the tail."

"A mind of its own, eh?" Portenda quipped.

"Indeed," said Shoryu, upon whom the joke appeared to have been lost for a moment before he gave a soft chuckle. "Toshiya though, he's been having trouble with the shifting a lot in the last couple of years. He spends most days in his natural Elven form, and his bestial form at night. He cannot take on the form of animus at all," Shoryu reported in a low whisper as he looked at the chair he was about to offer to the burly Bounty Hunter. "Um, dear?"

"Yes hon." Ellen turned and wiped her brow with a handkerchief.

"Do we still have the redwood chair for our, erm, larger guests," Shoryu asked.

Ellen pointed down a small offshoot hallway off of the kitchen and Shoryu excused himself for a moment to go fetch it.

Portenda stood idly in the kitchen near the far end of the table, opposite Shoryu's designated seat, his nose working a mile a minute. He mentally ticked off the spices and herbs that Ellen had added to the meal she had prepared, a hearty dinner of stew, loafed meat and sticks of cheese boiled in pig fat with some sort of breading on them. The end result smelled good enough, Portenda supposed, and would probably taste great. He only wondered for a moment how bad the food was for someone trying to maintain a particular build to their body.

Before Shoryu returned with the chair, and as Ellen began the final preparations for the meal, Portenda looked down the hall where the bathroom was and spotted young Toshiya Tearfang returning with freshly scrubbed face and set of hands. He also appeared to be holding something small against his leg with one of those hands, as though to conceal it. Whatever it was, Portenda's sensitive ears could make out a low humming coming from it, so he figured it had to be a mecha device of some sort.

Approaching the table, Toshiya looked at his mother's back, then checked behind him, sweeping the room to see if the coast was clear. With an impish grin and a finger to his lips, indicating that Portenda should remain silent about what he was about to witness, Toshiya knelt and planted the device in his hand on the underside of one of the seats at the dining table.

Cuyotai, Portenda thought, are a playful species, tending to play pranks and practical jokes with one another as a means of social interaction and show of endearment. When Toshiya sat at the next seat down, he realized that whatever the device was, its target would be young Tearfang's sister, Amber.

At that moment Portenda's ears picked up the heavy respiration of Shoryu and the grinding of a redwood chair on the soft floor. The Simpa Bounty Hunter moved to the end of the offshoot hallway, finding the Cuyotai Councilor dragging the rather large seat along with a moderate amount of effort.

Portenda tapped him on the shoulder, and Shoryu turned his head to look back at the Simpa. "I can take it the rest of the way, Councilor," he offered.

Shoryu gave him a sheepish grin and stepped aside, letting Portenda pick the high backed redwood chair up in one arm and carry it to the table. It was indeed heavy, but for a man such as himself, it posed little problem.

Portenda moved the chair to the end of the table opposite where Shoryu would be seated, and just as he was about to settle himself in it, young Amber Tearfang flounced into the room, her hair tied back in a ponytail that bounced as she came to the table.

Ellen set the last of the serving bowls on the table and seated herself on Shoryu's right, and as she sat, so did Amber.

The moment Amber's bottom met with the seat, Portenda noticed the smallest twitch in Toshiya. The boy had his left hand in his pants pocket, leading the Bounty Hunter to conclude that whatever was about to happen, the boy was in total control of it.

Before anyone could properly adjust their seats or grab a plate, a loud buzzing sound erupted from under Amber's seat. The odor of charged ozone immediately filled the air, and the crackling sound of electrical current droned for a brief moment just before it was drowned out by Amber's shocked shrieks of rage and pain. The jolts from the mecha device had literally sent her about a foot and a half off of the seat and into the air, smoke curling from the charred bottom of her pants.

As she landed with a thud, Toshiya let out with snorting chuckles, guffawing and pointing at his sister excitedly.

"Oh man, you should have seen the look on your face," he managed to squeak between fits of laughter.

Amber groaned and tried to remain in her seat for fear of exposing the damage to the bottom of her trousers.

Shoryu stifled a laugh at his daughter's expense, mostly due to the look of pure, cold-blooded fury that welled up on his wife's face. There were, after all, several well-established rules in the Tearfang household, and most of them pertaining to meal times had been laid down by the wife and mother of the family unit.

Shoryu, knowing his paternal duties, stood from his seat and rounded the left side of the table until he was directly behind his son, who continued to giggle into his fist.

Shoryu balled his hand and clouted Toshiya just behind the ear, once, glowering at him as the boy looked up at his father while holding his head. "No fooling at the table! You know your mother's rules better than that," Shoryu chided, still muffling his own laughter.

Well, Portenda thought, *he may dish out the punishment, but it's pretty clear who sets the standards around here.*

Shoryu returned to his seat at the head of the table, and Ellen started passing out the bowls and plates. She handed one at a time to Shoryu, who passed them on until one of each dish and utensil reached Portenda and then on to Toshiya, Amber, Shoryu and finally Ellen herself. There was an empty seat at the table, Portenda realized, a sixth seat that would only be used if the Tearfang family had two guests over. Had they added the middle leaf to the table because they were expecting him, he wondered? Or perhaps they've always got the extra two seats out.

Ellen passed the food bowls around, and once everyone had a portion of everything on their plate, Portenda started to reach for his fork and knife.

A leg kicked him under the table, and with a barely contained snarl he directed his eyes at Toshiya, whose head was bowed low over the table.

The Simpa Bounty Hunter peered around at the other three members of the Tearfang family, and saw that every one of them had their heads in the same position, with their hands out at their sides, flat on the table.

Well, he thought, *when in Arcade, do as the Arcadians do.* He bowed his head and waited, his nostrils reporting all sorts of dangerously delicious and appetizing messages to his brain and, more importantly, his stomach.

After an agonizing minute in this posture, he heard a soft "Amen," from Ellen, and he risked a glance up. She had raised her head, and her husband and children had done the same.

Portenda raised his fork and knife, and started in on the simple but delicious homemade meal. *Ingest and observe,* he thought, mechanically shoving the food in but savoring the aromas and tastes of a decent meal. While he mostly ate for the taste and the fuel of the food, his senses of taste and smell consumed by the meal, his eyes, ears and nerves stood on end to observe and record everything he could about Shoryu Tearfang. If he was going to take the man with him on the hunt, he would need to know the measure of the man.

Throughout the meal, what he saw and heard was more than a little encouraging. The Councilor and his wife had both served with Byron of Sidius, it turned out. They had met while aiding the Dread Knight personally, a bit of information that Portenda had known about Shoryu, but which he hadn't confirmed about his wife. If they had been able to travel together through those sorts of hardships and come out on the other end all right, then perhaps he could take the Cuyotai with him after all.

When the meal came to its completion, with Amber and Toshiya chiding each other back and forth and their mother asking them about their plans for school the next day, Portenda hooked Shoryu under the arm near the archway leading from the kitchen into the hallway and pulled him aside.

Shoryu, a little surprised by the Simpa's brute strength, hadn't been caught off guard: he had a Cuyotai's nose, after all, and he'd scented Portenda in the hallway all along.

"Good," Portenda said, as if he had just confirmed something unbeknownst to the Councilor.

Shoryu raised an eyebrow at him, his canine snout twitching slightly.

"You were aware that I was here."

"Well yes," Shoryu said with a wry smile. "I did sort of watch you leave the kitchen after dinner."

"I could have gone anywhere else in the domicile, however," Portenda said. "You knew I was right here. Good nose."

"Thank you." Shoryu gave the Simpa Bounty Hunter a mocking half-bow. "I'm rather proud of it myself. Look, what's on your mind, Portenda?" He popped a mint into his mouth.

"I've changed my mind, Mr. Tearfang," Portenda said, keeping his voice low and devoid of inflection. "If you wish to accompany me on my search for James Svelk, you are more than welcome. However," he said, turning his eyes toward the end of the hallway and the kitchen, where Shoryu's family was still interred. "If you are coming, you should say your good-byes. We will begin the investigation tomorrow here in the city, but we will be busy much of the day. In order to maintain distance and keep focused, we will not return here to your home, even for rest or meals. Is that understood?"

While Shoryu wasn't particularly keen on being ordered around like some lackey, he understood the Simpa's reasoning. Were they to begin the work the next day and he returned to the comfort of hearth and home, he might be unwilling to proceed until he had eked out every bit of family time he could. Shaken by the steely, dead look in the Bounty Hunter's eyes, Shoryu turned away from him and headed down the dim hallway, toward the kitchen and the loves of his life. As he went to speak with his wife and children, Portenda the Quiet headed silently outside, to take a breather and be away from such a family gathering.

He hated being around happy families sometimes, considering his own family history.

The Elf-Queen's Bounty

* * * *

Portenda sat on the concrete stoop bordering one of Ellen Daires-Tearfang's flower gardens, enjoying the sweet odors of the various flowers she had growing there. A lilac bush, violet and vibrant even in the evening gloom, gave him a brief olfactory lift of mood which he enjoyed for the moment. His eyes darted up and down the street, across the cobblestones to the homes across from the Councilor's residence, and once more his mind fell into the observation mode he lived in most of the time.

Armored guards, he thought, *teams of three. They've passed by this way many's the time. They aren't really paying any attention at all to their footing, because they know this area by the feel of the street under their boots. Two Elves, one Half-Elf. The Elves are Hunters, the Half-Elf is a Soldier. Smells like one of them might benefit from more routine bathing. Sounds like one of them's a long-time smoker, the lungs are only filling to maybe half capacity.*

As Portenda made this observation, the Half-Elf drew a crumpled pack of cigarettes from one of his belt pouches, offered one to his companions, and shrugged as they waved his offer aside.

The grating sound of a sulfur match, Portenda thought. *Guy's thumb is major league callused from years of doing that little trick. Probably has about forty or fifty years before the Black Rot settles into his lungs. It'll work its way through him fairly slow. Hell of a way to bite it.*

Fifteen minutes after he'd exited the Councilor's home and seated himself on the waist-height wall surrounding the gardens, he heard the door open behind him. "Any problems, Shoryu," he asked, his nostrils still taking in the wonderful odor of the lilacs.

"Not for him," Ellen Daires-Tearfang replied, her voice soft and low.

Sort of loamy, Portenda thought, cursing himself internally for letting the plants overpower his nostrils and his keen powers of observation. He tensed, the muscles in his arms and torso bunching together rapidly, flexing and relaxing. He held no fear of the Elven Gaiamancer, but he knew what she'd be capable of if provoked. Here he was, a total stranger to her and her family, and he proposed to take her husband of thirty-plus years off on a mission that might endanger his life. He supposed he could understand the underlying current of fury pouring off of her in waves.

Vines from the garden at his back whipped up lightning-fast and lashed themselves around his wrists, holding him in place. "But there could be problems for you," Ellen growled as she approached.

The vines moved, and Portenda was stood up on the front walkway leading to the house, the plants secured to his arms as tightly as a pair of steel clamps. Oddly enough, he was reminded of the time Jonah Staples had accidentally made similar vines extend from his very body. "I understand why he feels compelled to go," Ellen continued, "and I know that he could retrieve his family bow on his own, through safer channels. You Bounty Hunters have a reputation for living, well, dangerously, Mr. Portenda."

Portenda took a quick sniff of the air as he flicked his wrists, using her attention on his eyes as a much-needed distraction. He took another sniff of the air, and realized he recognized the odor he had detected: razor thrush. A cord of the dangerous plant slowly crept and slithered up toward his groin from behind him, much like a snake from a charmer's basket. Though he did not flinch, he did worry for a moment about his future ventures in attempted urination if she were to really lose her temper too suddenly.

"If my husband comes home in any condition other than the one he leaves here in, remember this, Bounty Hunter," she said, spitting the last two words as though they were venom. "Wherever you go in Tamalaria, you tread upon Mother Gaia, and she answers my summons for her magic, my prayers for retribution against those who harm me and mine."

Portenda looked her hard in the eyes, and saw there all he had to see. She meant exactly what she had said, and her raw determination and instinct to protect her flock was, if nothing else, quite admirable.

"I believe I understand," Portenda said flatly, letting go of all of his emotions once again. The power of the Gaiamancy employed around him ebbed away, and the vines and razor thrush slithered back over the stone stoop and into Ellen's little garden of flowers. "Also, I must commend you on the concealment of your home defenses. You and your husband make quite a formidable fighting force, I should imagine."

Ellen smiled demurely, nodding a little as she folded her arms over her chest.

"However, you must realize that if you had attacked me just now, you would have died."

With an expression of stark amazement and confusion, Ellen turned her attention to her feet, where the Bounty Hunter was looking intently. Three strange, small objects sat there, and to her they appeared to be some strange sort of gray fruit.

Portenda snapped his fingers, gaining her attention, and with his right hand held up another small device with a red button atop it. "It's called a detonator," he said, grinning viciously at her.

"How," she sputtered. "My vines had you," she said rather lamely.

"No, they had my wrists, and not quite as securely as you would have thought, either." Portenda tucked the detonator away and stepped forward, bending down and retrieving his trigger grenades. He clipped each one to its appropriate spot around his equipment belt, and let out a long sigh. "Now, watch." He put his hands in the same position they had been in when Ellen's vines had been brought to life to restrain him. He extracted his claws and retracted them, bullet fast. "You see?" he asked, holding one of the grenades in his left hand and the detonator in his right hand. "I only had to turn my hands slightly to toss this one and get the others in the two or three seconds you were staring me down. When I tried to pull my hand back, your vine pulled on my hand, and I went with it, three times. The force was enough to get decent trajectory for the throw."

Ellen stared at the Bounty Hunter, mouth agape like a fool who has been duped by an Illusionist's trickery. When she finally recovered her senses, she planted her hands on her hips and gave him an appraising look and grin. "A Simpa with gray stripes who uses weapons of tradition and technology. A Simpa with a strange aura," she said, turning and shuffling back toward her front door. "A Simpa who is clearly both strong and cunning. Add to that what my husband tells me of your heightened senses and something becomes abundantly clear, Bounty Hunter," she said, opening the door.

"And what, pray tell, is that Mrs. Tearfang?"

She turned around with a graceful twirl of her dress, and gave him a curtsy.

"Yours is to be an interesting road in life, Portenda the Quiet."

* * * *

The Elven Gaiamancer's magical prowess had been impressive, but what surprised Portenda even more was her grace and willingness to forgive and forget. He had been invited to stay with the Tearfang family, and he had accepted their offer to stay overnight. However, the family couch had been rather smallish for a fellow of his size, a fact that he felt certain in the morning Ellen had been more than aware of when she had put the pillow and blankets on it for him. *Sometimes*, he thought as he awoke in the dead hours of dawn and cracked his neck, *subtle payback is the worst.*

As he stood and stretched, his bare upper body cramped from having to curl up into an improbable position to fit on the couch for sleeping purposes, he wondered quietly how close he was to retirement. Surely only another five or six years and he'd have the money, property and connections he needed to get moving on his career as a real estate dealer and manager. No more would he have to range across the continent, hunting down men and women and returning them to his client for whatever fate awaited them. No more would he be forced to slay the various beasts and monstrosities that made their homes in the wilds.

Portenda took a quick whiff of the air, and followed his nose to the one place he knew it eventually would, though he was surprised to find he was not the only person awake. Toshiya Tearfang sat at the kitchen table, a cup of coffee steaming in front of him.

Portenda rubbed his swollen, sleep-addled eyes and groaned, shifting uneasily around the table toward the youth. "Mugs?"

"Upper cabinet behind me," Toshiya said without looking away from the textbook in front of him.

Portenda maneuvered around behind Toshiya, reached up for the cabinet that the boy had indicated, and stopped with his hand halfway there. Something about the cabinet door appeared almost rigged, as though the boy had done something to it. Portenda scanned the countertop, grabbed a long handled wooden spoon, and holding the cup end, opened the cabinet.

With a rather loud SPRANG! the cabinet popped open, launching a bowl of whipped cream right across the room. The ceramic dish struck the opposing wall with such force that it exploded, sending shrapnel in all directions.

Toshiya let out a surprised yelp as bits and pieces of his mother's bowl flew about, one sticking into the textbook in front of him.

"What in all the mighty Heavens and Hells is going on out there," shouted Shoryu from his and Ellen's room in the back of the first floor.

Toshiya slowly rose from the floor, looking around at the whipped cream and bowl fragments. Before he could dart away in time to lay the blame at his sister's feet, the Simpa Bounty Hunter had him dangling in the air by his ankle. Various little gadgets, gizmos and old-fashioned tools of practical joking fell from his various pockets, and Portenda simply raised an eyebrow at the smiling, awkward boy who dangled from his grip.

"Um, I don't suppose you're going to let me get away with this one, are you," the boy asked sheepishly.

"Considering I was the target, no," Portenda replied gruffly, dropping Toshiya on his head as Shoryu stalked into the kitchen. "Your boy is growing up to be a fine example of the species," Portenda groused at the Cuyotai Councilor. He reached up into the booby-trapped cabinet and grabbed a mug, dwarfing it in his enormous hand.

"Yeah, he does me proud." Shoryu skirted past his son, who was trying to rub a new sore spot on his head. "Toshiya, quit clowning around and get to school. You're going to be late again," Shoryu admonished.

The Elf-Queen's Bounty

Toshiya grabbed his bag and headed out of the kitchen, down the hall, and out into the city of Whitewood. "What precisely did happen here, by the way?"

"I asked him where to get a mug," Portenda said, pouring coffee from the decanter.

Although he expected a more thorough explanation, Shoryu wasn't surprised in the least when the hulking Simpa turned and seated himself at the kitchen table without another word. For Cuyotai, such a statement explained pretty much everything. Shoryu poured himself a cup as well, and sat opposite the Bounty Hunter, silence developing between the two men.

After a few minutes of pleasant quiet, Portenda cleared his throat meaningfully. "Did you say your farewells?"

"Last night, before everyone turned in," Shoryu said quietly. He looked down the side hall branching off of the kitchen, toward the room he had shared with Ellen as husband and wife for the better part of thirty years. He had hired a contractor the year after the War of Vandross to add the hall and the bedroom, and then Morek Rockmight had brought some friends of his down from Traithrock to add the second floor to the cottage. For almost all of those years, he had lived comfortably within the confines of this house; now, he was once again setting out into the world. The key difference here, he thought, was that he wasn't being forced out of his home.

"Well, you'll get another chance," Portenda said. Shoryu nearly sprayed coffee out through his nose at this, but instead swallowed hard and looked at the seasoned Bounty Hunter. "We won't actually be leaving the city until tomorrow, you see. Today, we'll be investigating the most recent transgression, his background, and any leads we might get within the confines of Whitewood. But come, my friend," he said, taking the last of his coffee down in one enormous gulp. "The day is going to be long, and we have much work ahead of us."

Shoryu quickly finished his coffee and set his cup in the sink, sneaking off into his and Ellen's room to tell her that he wouldn't be leaving until the next day.

She gave him a brief and fierce embrace, and told him to get going.

Shoryu rushed out of the room and toward the front door in the living room, where he had his traveling gear set to go. "I suppose I can leave the travel gear here for today, then," he asked the Simpa, who was looming in the open doorway.

"Yours at any rate," Portenda replied, moving out of the portal and out into the early morning sunshine, soaking up the energizing rays of the sun. "I'll be at the Torten Hotel tonight."

"Why?" Shoryu stepped outside and buttoning up his green and gold upper tunic shirt.

"Because," said Portenda, cracking his neck with a sharp twist of the head to look Shoryu in the eyes. "Your couch sucks."

* * * *

Passing through the marketplace, Shoryu waved and smiled at passersby who recognized and greeted him, a few of them asking how his daughter or son were doing. He made idle small talk with a handful of ladies outside of a diner on a cigarette break, all the while trying to be mindful of the fact that he and the Simpa with him had work to get to. Saying his good days and good byes, Shoryu walked along with a slight spring in his step.

Portenda led the way, always ranging ahead of Shoryu by a few yards, which the Cuyotai didn't mind in the least. He was used to leading the way out in the wilds, leading the path as a scout.

At one of the royal guardhouses on Flame Way, Portenda stopped and turned toward the large oak door, stepping inside.

Shoryu entered right on his heels, and two of the Elven guards posted at the guard station's front desk smiled at the sight of the Councilor.

Both men stood and saluted the Cuyotai, beaming with civic pride. "Councilor Tearfang," the younger of the two guards said. "How may we be of service to you, sir?"

Instead of answering, Shoryu merely cocked his thumb to his left, indicating the Simpa Bounty Hunter.

Both guards gave Portenda the once-over with their eyes, each man's visual review stopping briefly at the revolver holstered to Portenda's right hip. *Foul mecha weaponry,* both men thought.

Portenda crossed his arms over his chest and waited until one of the guards addressed him.

"Sir?"

"I am certain you've been appraised of the situation involving James Svelk," Portenda said.

Shoryu watched as the meaning of this single statement sunk in with the guards. They turned from wary protectors of their city into willing and helpful civil servants at the Bounty Hunter and Councilor's discretion.

"Yes, the traitor," the elder guard fairly growled. "You are the Bounty Hunter, then?"

"I am," said Portenda. "We'll need a copy of Svelk's command files. Every commendation he's ever given or suggested. In addition, we need some idea of what sort of person would befriend him. A service psych report would be most telling as well, gentlemen." He rattled off what he required with a machine-like pace and tone. "Shorthand copies will do, as we have business elsewhere. Chop chop, people," he said, causing the two guards on the desk to spring into motion.

When they left the area immediately behind their front desk, a door opened on each side of the greeting area, and a different Elven guard stood in the doorway.

"Councilor, you may come in," said the guard on the left side of the room.

Portenda shot a quick look at the sign affixed above the door, which said Commons Office (Officers and Officials Only!). Portenda took a good look at the guard, trying to gauge if the young woman could be trusted. Often times on these sorts of government contracts, an opposing party almost always made themselves known fast and hard, he thought. But he didn't sense anything off about the young Elven guard, and so as Shoryu followed her into the Commons Office, he turned and looked at the male guard at the right side door.

"There is a waiting lounge where you can relax and await your requested materials, sir," the guard said, and Portenda let himself be led off that way.

Shoryu, meantime, had just closed the door to the Commons Office behind him and smiled at the young guard assigned to the chamber. He recognized her, he thought, but he just couldn't put his finger on her name or how he knew her.

"Councilor," the chain mail armored Elven woman said, prefacing her statement with an honorific out of respect. "Why are you with that man? Do you have any idea who that is? He's—," she managed to say before Shoryu cut her off.

"Portenda the Quiet, I know." He fixed himself a cup of coffee from the machine in the corner of the cozy official lounge. "I'll be traveling with him a while." Shoryu sipped his coffee and turned, looking the girl up and down. He smiled suddenly, remembering the young Elven woman. "Aren't you Jenny Marshall? Lynn and Edward's daughter?"

The girl blushed and smiled, her body loosening a little, less tense now that he recognized her. "That's right, Councilor. Shandra Massey and I now share an apartment in the seventeenth district."

"So no more watching the kids for Ellen and I, huh?" Shoryu asked. He began making a cup of coffee for the young guard, and thought back over the years of his children's lives. Jenny had babysat for Ellen and Shoryu on many occasions, giving the married couple the opportunity to go to the theater to watch plays, go to sporting events, and so forth. About two years ago, however, Jenny had ceased to be available, for reasons unknown to Shoryu and Ellen. However, they had agreed that Amber and Toshiya no longer needed sitters for just one evening, but only if they were both to be gone for several days. At those times, Ellen got in touch with Morek via messenger pigeon, and the stalwart Dwarven Boxer took a teleportation scroll to Whitewood to keep an eye on the children.

"No, sorry," she said, accepting the offered coffee. "This is what I've been training for the last couple of years. I finally passed the exam a couple of weeks ago, and this is my first post. It's a little frightening, though," she said, her eyes downcast.

"Why's that?"

"Well, the night before the break-in at the Historical Society building? That was going to be my first post, but my paperwork got mixed up in processing, so I wound up here," she said. An awkward silence filled the air as the two of them considered the weight of what she had said. "So," she finally said, breaking the silence. "How is Toshiya doing with the, uh, transformations?"

"Oh, still not so well," Shoryu replied as he took a seat in a soft green leather chair. "Anyhow, how do you know of our big friend out there?"

Jenny's eyes shifted toward the closed door of the Commons Office, and she shuffled her feet nervously.

"Well, Councilor, every law enforcement officer knows who he is. He's kind of a mixed bag, Councilor. He knows the laws of pretty much everyplace he goes, he uses both mecha and old world weapons, and he always gets his target. There's that, and what other people say who've been around him."

"And what's that," Shoryu asked as he drained his mug.

"They say he seems kind of, well, dead on the inside, sir. And he notices everything," she said in a low whisper. "For all we know, he's listening to me right now, sir! His senses are supposed to be supernaturally enhanced somehow, but mostly that's just a rumor I think." And a moment later, as though the Gods thought it might be amusing to respond to this statement, there came a hard rapping at the door.

"Tearfang, let's go," Portenda said through the thick oak door from the main chamber. "We've got an angry ex-wife to interview."

Chapter Three
The Hunt Begins

Shoryu almost couldn't contain his mirth as he looked over at his large companion. The Simpa Bounty Hunter pressed against the sides of the recliner in which he sat, his muscles bunched together from the effort of keeping himself as contracted as possible within the confines of the chair. As with the couch the night before, he was simply too large to fit comfortably.

Shoryu himself, on the other hand, being of the more slender variety of lycanthrope and individual, fit rather nicely in one of the dust-brown recliners. Both men sat across from a two-seat couch on which their hostess was going to seat herself, once she returned from the kitchen and set their tray down on the coffee table between the seats.

"Why don't you just shift down into your humanoid form," Shoryu whispered over to Portenda as the big man shifted himself forward in the chair, giving his thighs room to breath.

"Because I don't have one," the Bounty Hunter explained, growling. "I am as you see me. The only secondary lycanthrope form I can take is animus, thank you. I hardly think this woman wants to come back in here and find that in my stead a huge tiger-striped lion is curled up in a corner of the room."

"Why the corner?"

"I don't know," Portenda said, trying to maintain his emotional control. It was infuriating for him, however, constantly being in homes and places where he was too big to get comfortable. "It's just an instinct for me. I go into animus form, I tend to lean toward small, tight corners. You?"

"Well, I can't sit still if I see a stick being thrown, or worse yet, a tennis ball. I'm a very domesticated coyote in animus form," Shoryu informed his companion. "Not much of a menace. More of a house pet than anything."

"I imagine that must be difficult with a boy like Toshiya around," Portenda commented.

As the brooding Bounty Hunter viewed a mental gag reel of Toshiya Tearfang throwing a tennis ball down the road for his father to chase, a slim, waspish woman entered from the kitchen, her frail-looking hands carrying a tray laden with teacups and sweets. The woman wore a humble brown housedress adorned with an emblem of a panther on the left shoulder. Her nails, which appeared to be coated in some sort of wax, scraped the bottom of the tray as she settled it on the coffee table between herself and her lycanthrope guests. She smiled wanly at them, and indicated two of the teacups, both of which steamed with freshly brewed tea.

The woman in question, Kelly Honok, had once been addressed as Kelly Svelk, prior to her filing for abandonment-class divorce. Now, thirty years after her husband had betrayed his country, his wife, and his people in general, she didn't appear to be holding up on her own so well. Elves normally aged with grace and ease, the flow of years passing over them like gently flowing waters through a woodland. The males of their proud and mystical Race usually showed signs of aging far before the females, and even then age lines only appeared after about eight standard centuries. An Elf's average life span in Tamalaria, if he or she passed of natural causes, was about twelve-hundred years, by far the longest-living of the humanoid Races.

This woman, however, appeared to be wasting away, and before Portenda or Shoryu could think to question why, she provided evidence in the form of lighting a cigarette for herself. Lycanthropes and Jafts smoked with impunity; their regenerative powers kept the harmful effects from getting to them. Elves, Half-Elves, Humans and Gnomes, however, often succumbed to the Black Rot when they indulged in tobacco for a number of years. Full blooded Elves usually took a while longer to contract the disease, but *sure enough*, both men thought, *she's going to show the first outward signs soon. She's already getting wrinkles at six hundred and some change.*

"Good Councilor," she said as she chuffed a cloud of cerulean fog. "Thee, I know well from your work here in the capital." She spoke with the accent and grammar of an old-world Elf. "I'm afraid, however, that yon large fellah with the trappin's of a one-man army be somethin' o' a mystery ta me." She refilled Portenda's teacup nevertheless.

"Thank you," Portenda said when she pulled the pot away.

"And my, what a voice you've got you as well lad," she commented, pulling away and taking another drag of her cigarette. "What do you do for a living?"

"I'm a Bounty Hunter, ma'am," Portenda said, deciding right away that being forthright with this woman would yield the best results. From listening to the way the woman spoke, he assumed she had been raised by a very traditional Elven family.

Shoryu knew for certain that this was so, for he'd had the opportunity to meet with most of the elder heads of families in the kingdom's capital. If one followed the family line of Ms. Honok back far enough, one would discover that her great-grandfather had been the head lecturer of Rollingwood Academy, an institution of higher learning that had burned to the ground back in the middle of Tamalaria's Third Age. He silently approved of Portenda's choice of tact in this matter, for the older families didn't truck with mind games and wasting time.

"I see," she said slowly, stubbing out her present cigarette and lighting a fresh one right away. "So what brings you ta my front door, then?"

"Myself and my associate here, Councilor Tearfang, have been charged with finding your ex-husband and bringing him back to answer for various crimes against the kingdom. The most recent is the theft of several Historical Society artifacts and documents. Some of these artifacts have been considered extremely important to the kingdom's history," Portenda said.

Ms. Honok shook her head and groaned low in her throat. "Doesn't surprise me in the least," she muttered. "Sugar or honey, Councilor?"

"Oh, no thank you," said the Cuyotai marksman. Strapped to his back were a standard bow that he had been using for a few years, and his mystic quiver, which never ran out of arrows. He never wanted to be short of ammunition, but had decided some years ago that unless war came to the kingdom again, his family bow could remain in the Historical Society's care. At the moment he felt incomplete, however, for he knew that there would be hostilities once he left the relative safety of Whitewood for the wilds of the forests and plains beyond the city walls. Without the power of the mystic bow, he would be reduced to relying on his marksmanship, which had diminished over the years, he assumed.

"Ms. Honok," Shoryu said. "We have a short list of known contacts your ex-husband may get in touch with. Do you recognize any of these names?"

On cue, Portenda produced a sheet from the file folder he had taken from his rucksack and started rattling off names from one of the lists. He said several names without effect, Kelly Honok shaking her head and squinting her eyes at each name, trying to think if she had ever met any of the men or women mentioned. One of the men Portenda named had served with James Svelk as a Border Guard lieutenant, taking the position of Svelk's right-hand man. She informed Shoryu and Portenda that the gentleman now ran a sundry goods store over on Orchard Avenue, so both men ruled him out.

Finally, after getting three-quarters of the way through the list, one of the names caused her eyes to widen and her thumb to stop just before she flicked her Gnome fire-maker to light a smoke. "What was that last one again," she whispered.

"Sean Browler," Shoryu said, repeating the name very slowly.

Portenda sat and stared at the woman, his refreshed tea untouched, his gray eyes boring into her own green sockets, searching for the flicker he thought he'd seen there a moment ago. Finally, her left hand started to quiver slightly and move up toward her thin, grim mouth. "Ma'am, what is it," the Cuyotai asked, ready to come around the coffee table and provide what comfort he could.

"I never told the police," she muttered, mostly to herself. Her eyes glimmered brightly, and her mouth set itself in a grimace. "That man showed up here about three weeks ago. He just barged right in to my den while I was dusting my collectibles, you see, and he hollered at me to give him James's records! I told him I didn't have any such thing, and he slapped me," she said.

Shoryu gasped, shocked that anyone would simply charge into a stranger's home and strike them, especially an innocent woman.

Portenda, more of a pragmatist, understood the sort of man this Browler was; small-minded and petty, choosing to pick on and oppress only those who stood little chance of fighting back. A bully, in short.

"But I repeated what I'd told him, that I didn't have his records. I didn't want his bloody records, the faithless sod that he was," she finished, coughing raggedly as she stubbed her smoke in the ashtray.

"Wait a moment," Shoryu said, leaning forward in his chair. "Miss, how did you recognize his name? Had you met him before, when James still lived with you?"

"Oh goodness no," she said, once more offering her glib smile. "I remember the name because on his way out, he warned me that I should give him the records if I had them. He said to give them up, because, and I quote, 'nobody holds out on the Browler Brothers'."

Portenda shot up out of his seat, muttered a brief thanks for the tea, and stormed out of Kelly Honok's two-story home, his heavy footsteps clomping as he exited.

Shoryu, dumbfounded by the Bounty Hunter's strange behavior, tried to apologize to the good Elven woman for his partner's abrupt disappearance.

Ms. Honok waved him off and smiled up at Shoryu, who didn't realize that he had risen to his own feet already to follow the Bounty Hunter. "Again, I'm very sorry for being so quick to leave," he said.

"Oh, no worries, lad," she said. "Remember, I'm accustomed now to the idea of men slipping away from me rather swiftly."

The Elf-Queen's Bounty

Shoryu dashed through the front hallway and out of the house, locating Portenda just a few dozen yards away to the north.

The Simpa appeared to be looking around for something, his eyes squinted in the early morning sunlight filtering through the forest canopy overhead.

Shoryu took in a deep, cleansing breath before approaching Portenda, as the air outside felt wonderful when compared to the dreary, smog-choked aura of Ms. Honok's living room.

Shoryu approached at an easy gait, raising his left hand to Portenda's eye level to catch his attention among the growing crowds of citizens heading toward the marketplace. The city was finally coming fully awake and alive, a process that usually took a while since Whitewood was sizable.

Portenda glared at him with dead eyes, and Shoryu felt certain then and there that before this quest of theirs was at an end, they would be at odds with one another at least once. The Simpa just seemed too confrontational for it to be avoided.

"What are you looking for," Shoryu asked as he side-stepped a Lizardman merchant leading his horse-drawn booth cart toward the market.

"Bounty office," Portenda said.

"Whitewood doesn't have one," Shoryu said, following the Simpa as he started away without seeming to really hear what the Cuyotai had said. "To tell you the truth, this isn't an official job that we're on."

Portenda did not reply, which infuriated Shoryu to no end. The big man simply led him south on Trade Street, passing the market on the right as they continued through the next few major intersections in silence.

"I mean, her majesty won't have this mission on record with the Unified Bounty Association. Are you listening to me?"

Portenda merely grunted and carried on, Shoryu tagging along behind and feeling rather foolish.

He turned west on an unmarked road, and as Shoryu caught up about fifty yards down the road, he saw that Portenda stood before a ramshackle red and gray brick building.

Shoryu looked up at the fish-shaped sign, which was painted in marble black letters, 'Goin' Fishing'.

"What is this place," Shoryu asked of the Bounty Hunter. "I've lived in this city for years, and I don't recall ever seeing this business. Of course, Whitewood is rather large, and every city has its secrets…" He stopped when he realized that Portenda probably wasn't listening anymore.

The Simpa gave Shoryu one of his patented glares that revealed nothing of his thoughts or motives, and pushed the door open on tortured hinges.

The metal shrieked from rust and age, sending shivers up Shoryu's spine as he winced at the sound. When the door stopped, he looked past Portenda at what might have passed for a small shop, if there had been any merchandise on the various assorted shelves around the walls. A gruff Half-Elf fellow sat on a stool across the purchase counter from them, and he didn't even look up from whatever tome he had on the counter.

Portenda walked up to the counter, Shoryu following behind, and leaned forward on it, his snout only inches to the right of the clerk's face.

"Whadaya want," the Half-Elf groused, keeping his eyes down.

Shoryu actually found himself rather surprised; in all of his years as a resident of Whitewood, he had never heard a Half-Elf sound as gruff as this gentleman, not even any of the military veterans. In his experience, the half-blood Elves tended to try even harder to be nice and mystical than their full-blooded relatives. They had to try harder due to their half-blood status, and because often their non-Elven blood was of an aggressive Human nature. The clerk, Shoryu thought, clearly didn't care either way.

The Simpa began wrapping on the counter, three times very softly and in rapid succession, and then four hard, loud thumps with a hammered fist. After that, he tapped the end of four fingers on his right hand on the counter, and took a step back.

"Very good, sir," said the clerk with a combatant's grin. "Got any particular breed you're fishing for?"

The Bounty Hunter took out one of his many small yellow steno pads, scribbled something on it with a pencil, and tore the sheet out. This he handed to the clerk, who exited the shop then through a side door, looking at what had been written.

Shoryu, head cocked at an angle with eyebrow raised, looked at Portenda with bald confusion. "What the hells was all that about," he blurted aloud, looking back to the side door to find the clerk if he could.

Portenda offered no reply, however. Instead, the enigmatic Bounty Hunter raised a single leonine finger to his lips, shushing the Cuyotai archer.

The clerk returned from the side room a minute later, a thick black binder under one arm. He flopped the binder on the counter, and pulled a lever on the counter that appeared to be hidden between two tackle boxes.

A section of the wall behind him parted, revealing a study of some sort with all manner of bottles of liquor at a bar set in the far wall. The clerk opened the flip-top part of his counter and led Portenda, who had grabbed the binder, and the confused Councilor into the back study.

"That's everything for the last two years," the clerk explained as Shoryu tried to think of the size of the interior of this fishing shop. "There's more, but that's what you'll want to see." The clerk stopped just short of the back wall and its various bottles of liquor. "Not too long, I take it?"

Portenda shook his head and, avoiding the bar altogether, headed directly to a comfortable chair that was sized for Bounty Hunters of his size or thereabouts. The clerk smiled, and left the study, closing the wall behind him.

"This is a Bounty Office, isn't it?" Shoryu finally asked, padding slowly to the booze as he looked around.

Portenda snapped his fingers and made a hand gesture at Shoryu, one he recognized as being shot at with a pistol—the proverbial 'bingo'.

"The building doesn't look big enough on the outside to contain this all. Enchanted interior?"

Portenda nodded, opened the binder, and took half of the contents out, holding them out without a word toward the Councilor.

Shoryu went first to the back wall, poured himself a scotch, and then returned to the Bounty Hunter to take his part of the binder's contents.

Shoryu took a good long look at the Bounty Hunter, and realized that he had already reassessed his impression of Portenda. The Simpa still sat armed to the teeth and ready for war for all intents and purposes, radiating an aura of power and potential violence. However, as Shoryu took the papers in one hand, he saw that the big man was wearing reading glasses and handling his own papers rather gently. He appeared more like a detective than a hardened, seasoned hunter of men in moments such as this.

"What am I looking for?" Shoryu asked, sitting across from the Simpa.

"Relevant facts and references. This is Sean Browler's bounty file and most recent criminal record. He's our primary target's lackey."

"You sure? Couldn't it be that Svelk is Browler's lackey," Shoryu asked.

"No," Portenda said confidently, looking away from Shoryu and down at a sheet that catalogued the number of Sean Browler's criminal offenses. "Browler came for Svelk's records, which means he was sent for them. "Here." Portenda tapped the second sheet of paper from his half of the binder. "Standard statistics. 'Known to act as a hired hand for criminal enterprises'. City of Sharken Central Guard report."

Quietly the two men rifled through the records for Sean Browler.

After a few minutes of digging, Shoryu whistled between his front teeth. "Got something I think you'll want to know." The Cuyotai archer shuffled four pages from his portion of the file with attached sketch portraits.

He stood and crossed to Portenda, handing him the sheets one at a time so that Portenda could get a look at the men drawn on the sketch paper. "There's four of these guys: Sean, Dean, Benjamin and Reggie. Something doesn't look right about the last one, either. These aren't Mage's Eye images, but whoever drew these men had a keen eye, and Reggie Browler looks to be somehow, I don't know, wrong," Shoryu said with a shiver.

Portenda looked at the picture on the last sketch sheet, which was attached to a copy of a sheet from the United Bounty Association's records on the man pictured. Something indeed appeared off about Reggie Browler, a deadness that mirrored his own in the eyes. In addition, there appeared to be some sort of metallic covering over Reggie Browler's arms, but it didn't resemble bracers or armor of any sort. There was almost an air of wicked intent about the picture itself, as though whomever had drawn Reggie Browler had put a bit of the man's essence into his portrait.

"I concur, Shoryu, that there is something, well, off about him," Portenda said, looking up at the Cuyotai over the rims of his reading glasses. "However, I can't finger what that is, precisely. For now, I guess we'll have to wait and see." He handed the sheets back to the Councilor.

Shoryu returned to his seat and finished his drink, cycling through several more sheets of criminal activity information.

"Here we go," he said aloud after another minute. "A list of warrants. Wanted in the Dwarven Territories, Ja-Wen, the Kingdom of Suromy, Desanadron, Palen, and the Fiefdom of Lemago." He whistled once again. "That covers just about seventy-five percent of Tamalaria. You got anything?"

Portenda nodded. "Official bounty offers from all over, a lot of them police precincts in the regions you just mentioned. Government sanctioned contracts mostly, with a handful of private bounties. List here of contracted Bounty Hunters for the private contracts, too." He scanned the names and stopping on one near the bottom of the sheet.

Collin Caulkins, Red Draconus. "I've worked with this fellow before." Portenda removed his glasses and tucked the sheets back into the binder.

Shoryu handed back his sheets, and Portenda tucked the binder into his bag.

"So where do we go from here?" Shoryu asked, standing up and stretching.

"We contact Collin, find out what he knows. If we can find the henchmen, we can locate Svelk from there," Portenda said.

Together the Simpa and Cuyotai made their way out of the secret bounty office, and headed toward the Tearfang home. Portenda decided that they had made enough progress for the day, and Shoryu was heartened by the fact that they'd finished their day's work just after noon. They agreed to meet the next day in the evening, when they would head north through the forest and make their way toward Desanadron. There they could look for more thorough information and hopefully use Jonah Staples' teleportation service to get them across the continent to Caulkins's neck of the woods.

From there, they would begin the hunt in earnest.

Chapter Four
The Road to Desanadron

Late the following evening, after Shoryu said his last farewells, Portenda led the way north through the city to the small gates that opened on the forest north of the Elven Kingdom's capital. The light of the half moon shimmered ethereally through the canopy of the treetops high overhead, illuminating the well-beaten path that they would follow for most of the night.

Both men were dressed as they had been the day before, with the exception for Shoryu that he had donned his light leather armor vest and brigandine pants. Portenda nodded his silent approval; his sleeveless vest was also brigandine, a layer of light leather sewn shut around flexible metal sheets of armor. Shoryu's upper leather armor, however, had no such inner lining, but he preferred ease of movement to thicker protection. "Besides," he reasoned as they began their long march. "I'm not exactly used to fighting in close quarters. I tend to range about."

"In other words you run or leap to a safe position and open fire with your bow," Portenda said as they walked between the rows of elms that flanked the path before them. "That's your way of fighting, and that's just fine. I do that myself from time to time," Portenda patted the mecha weapon on his right hip. His enormous revolver sat in its holster, recently broken down and oiled to ensure proper function by the Bounty Hunter. He had run low on ammunition once again, another reason for the two men to take the trip to Desanadron. He could purchase more ammo from a mecha dealer in the metropolitan city-state, the only place he could find the appropriate caliber bullets.

"Do you use that thing often?" Shoryu indicated the mecha weapon.

"Not as much as you might think," Portenda replied, for once in the mood to make conversation. "I don't entirely trust the damned thing, and for good reason. You see," he said, quick drawing the revolver from his hip, pointing the barrel skyward. He rested the end of it in the hollow of his shoulder as he walked a few feet to Shoryu's left. "I found it in a set of ruins while pursuing a target. I knew what it was, even had a vague notion of how it worked," Portenda said, his blank countenance softened briefly with a small grin. "Well, I cornered my target, and when he drew his weapon, I pointed the revolver at him and opened fire."

"Did you hit him?" Shoryu asked, hands behind his head as he walked along.

The Elf-Queen's Bounty

"Oh, you could say that. You see, this is a revolver of the forty-fifth caliber," Portenda explained, holstering the mecha weapon. "Essentially, it's a hand cannon. It blew a hole the size of my fist through the target's chest. He died almost instantly." Portenda's eyes glazed over slightly as he thought back to that fatal moment. He could remember the smell of charred flesh, the acrid underlying odor of spraying blood. His tongue could still taste the gun smoke, and every time he fired the mecha weapon, the sensation that his arm was going to be ripped out of its socket reminded him of that first shot.

His target had been a Wererat on the lamb from one of Ja-Wen's correctional facilities. Charged and convicted of seventy-three counts of larceny, the rat looked forward to forty years of hard labor. After only four of those years had been served, the target had discovered a way to remove the artifact device that Ja-Wen placed on all lycanthrope prisoners' wrists, thus preventing them from shifting form. Once he removed the device, the prisoner had shifted into the shape of a rat, and made his way out of the prison via its sewer system network.

He'd been gone three days before the guards finally finished searching the entire prison grounds for him. In his cell, they discovered the bracer that had been removed, set into the tank of his toilet to remain unseen. Hours later, the warden had placed the bounty order, and Portenda had signed on, chasing down the lingering scent of his prey. The warden had asked that the Wererat be brought back dead or alive, and Portenda usually preferred alive. Standing over the ruined body of the target, however, he'd had to settle with dead as he dragged the corpse back to the surface from the underground ruins.

None of this, however, did the Bounty Hunter relate to Shoryu. Somehow he didn't think the Cuyotai would want to hear it, for his had been a life of peace and politics for the last three decades.

"We should shift into animus soon if we're going to make any progress at all," Shoryu suddenly said, interrupting Portenda's thoughts.

The Bounty Hunter agreed, and both men began the transformation into their animal forms, their equipment and belongings wavering to the spirit realm where they would remain safe and attached to them until they returned to their bestial forms.

After a minute, the path held not two lycanthrope men, but from the looks of it, a long, tan coyote, and a gray-striped lion with the long and low body that almost showed Portenda's Khan blood.

In this way they began to lope along, running north into the night.

* * * *

The time approached dawn when finally the Bounty Hunter and the Councilor silently agreed to stop traveling and get a few hours' rest. They both padded a short distance off of the path, into a knot of spruce trees, where they transformed into their bestial state.

Returned to the upright form of a half-man, half-beast, Shoryu stretched his arms and legs, rubbing feeling back into his hands. "That's the one drawback, if you ask me. I always lose the feeling in my hands right after I shift back, no matter how little running around I do," he complained, sitting down with his back to a tree and removing his rucksack.

Despite the late start they had the evening before, running along in their animus state, or animal forms, had cut down severely on both the danger they faced in traveling through the forest and the amount of time they would take getting to Desanadron. They had effectively reduced their distance to about two more days of steady jogging along in animal forms to reach the northern border of the Elven Kingdom.

Shoryu thought back to the forced march that he had gone on with Byron and his troops, from the Elven Kingdom all the way east to Mount Toane. With the aide of Q magic, the entire army had made the trip in only a few days, but he and Portenda had no such assistance in their own journey. They had their own wit and strength to work with, and for the first time in many years, Shoryu was forced to wonder if his own strength would be enough to keep him going.

As Shoryu pulled out the few things he needed to make himself a cup of tea, Portenda sat down heavily a few feet away from him. The Bounty Hunter, with his cold, gray eyes, searched the Cuyotai's face for a sign of the archer's endurance. "You should get some rest after your drink," Portenda said, abruptly breaking the eye contact and rising to his feet. "I will stand a watch."

"Is that really even necessary," Shoryu asked, looking around and out into the surrounding woodland. He could see no signs of anything hostile, could not smell anything but trees and moss and some other forms of plant life. His keen archer's eyes could not detect any visible threat for nearly a half-mile in all directions, so he did not understand why Portenda would want to remain awake. "This is a relatively safe area of the forest, you know."

"No place is safe enough to remain without a guard," Portenda replied flatly, his tone filled with icy indifference. "And I do not have the necessary equipment to set up warning traps for a camp perimeter."

Shoryu realized that what he was now seeing was the Bounty Hunter as he truly behaved most of the time: cold and businesslike. Back in

Whitewood, surrounded by Elves and Cuyotai and a smattering of Humans, he had been forced to behave more like a citizen. Now that he sought his target, however, Shoryu could tell that Portenda the Quiet would start to act more in line with his reputation and his given title.

"As a result, I shall remain on guard for now," the Bounty Hunter started to stalk in a slow circle around their two-man, makeshift camp.

Portenda knew full well what he was doing. As he widened his perimeter around Shoryu and his own pack of supplies, the adamant loner let out a sigh of frustration. When he worked alone, he didn't have trouble like this, he thought. He had total control of his emotions and his mouth when he worked alone, and most times if he worked with someone else. Twice now, however, he found himself reaching out, trying to open himself up to the possibility of having actual friends outside of the realm of other Bounty Hunters.

The first time had been with Jonah Staples, a little less than a year before. As Portenda slowed his pace, sniffing the air northwest of the Cuyotai archer for unseen threats or anything out of the ordinary, his thoughts turned to that crafty Alchemist boy. For a Human, Jonah had impressed Portenda during their time together on the road. He had turned out to be resourceful and cunning when he needed to be, much to his benefit. Since the boy couldn't fight in hand-to-hand combat for squat, and since he probably couldn't handle a bow very well, he relied instead on the power of Focus and his sciences. He had also turned out to be crafty, another bonus in his favor.

Portenda had been slow to like Jonah, but when he decided the boy was worth being around and working with, he had become very protective, stupidly so he often thought since the return of Jonah's sister to her family. Portenda had worked well for years without any close friends; he could continue to do so if he kept things in order. Shoryu Tearfang bothered him as a result, because the man was pretty friendly and his people were hard, in general, not to like. Portenda also found himself disturbed by a single fact that had previously not occurred to him, arising now out of the depths of his mind.

He owed Shoryu a measure of respect, for though the Councilor was young at heart and acted boyish sometimes, he was older than Portenda. Factor in as well that he had been one of the few to personally travel and fight with Byron of Sidius in his crusade against Richard Vandross. As a result of those two facts, Portenda had reason to bow his head in respect and listen patiently to just about anything that the man had to say.

Suddenly, he wanted to avoid as much conversation as possible.

* * * *

At around noon, Portenda lightly shrugged Shoryu awake.

The Cuyotai opened his eyes, his vision blurred from sleep, and yawned expansively, stretching his arms and legs on the ground. He cracked his neck and his back as he stood up, hoisting his rucksack onto his back. "You want to catch a couple of hours," he asked.

"Negative," was Portenda's only reply.

The Bounty Hunter led the way back to the main road leading north, and Shoryu followed dutifully behind. He expected Portenda to want to walk a nice and easy pace for a while, but instead the Simpa shifted down into his animus form once on the path, loping easily ahead. Shoryu shrugged his shoulders, and followed suit.

For several hours they ran on in this fashion, fueled by rest and a small meal they partook of in the late afternoon. Shortly after their respite, light rain started to fall, gray clouds blocking out the sunlight of the day, and Portenda quickly led them off of the beaten track when it turned west toward the township of Marrow. He continued north, though at a slower pace as the rich soil of the forest floor soaked up the falling rain, creating puddles and muck that they had to trudge through at a more cautious pace.

The smaller woodland animals along their route gave them a wide berth, which left a slight pang in Shoryu's heart. He loved the animals of the wild, looking on them as kindred spirits, much as his wife did. Clearly, however, the animals did not trust him in return, especially not with a long and muscular lion leading the way.

Resigning himself to only the company of the Simpa and his own thoughts, Shoryu continued on, staying a short pace back from the gray striped Portenda.

As night fell on the forest, Portenda found the way back to a main road and shifted up into his bestial state.

Shoryu did the same, and came up alongside the Bounty Hunter, who had stopped his northward progress and was looking around the path, his nose twitching up and down.

"What is it?" Shoryu asked.

Portenda merely held up a hand to silence him, still sniffing the air, both ears pricked slightly upward to listen intently to the sounds of the forest around him.

Portenda used his heightened senses to filter out the sound of the pattering rain on the forest floor and underbrush, listening for the thing that had caused him to stop jogging along and prepare himself for battle. The various animal and plant odors, along with the strong scent of the wet soil beneath his feet, combined to betray his olfactory senses.

Ignoring this and concentrating on his hearing, the Simpa Bounty Hunter listened intently to the sounds of the woodland around him.

There, he thought, north and slightly east of the path. He could hear several small sets of feet, slapping about in the thick mud. The quality and volume of the splashing feet allowed him to identify the number of his quarry, which measured five sets of feet. He heard one of the sets of feet scrape lightly against a tree, which told him that whoever was out there, they were trying to remain hidden.

Cloth, he thought, *probably leather boots. No metal, so they aren't that heavily armed, whoever they are.*

Another sound mixed in with the small, shuffling movements reached his ears: a short sword clearing a scabbard. Portenda closed his eyes, shutting off his sense of vision, and covered his ears with his hands, blocking out all noise. Now he concentrated as hard as he could on his sense of smell, trying to filter through the plant life odors and the various animal aromas that interfered with his detection.

After a full minute of this concentration, he finally identified the scent of the five foreign bodies as belonging to Goblins. *No serious threat,* he thought, *especially in such small numbers.*

He opened his eyes and brought his hands to his sides, looking at Shoryu. "What is it already?" Shoryu asked impatiently.

Portenda saw that the Cuyotai had not wasted his time, however, drawing out his bow and an arrow from his mystical quiver.

"Goblins," Portenda said quietly, his tone devoid of inflection as usual. "Five of them. No large threat."

"Goblins," Shoryu asked, looking north along the path. "Well that doesn't make much sense." Now it was Portenda's turn to raise an inquisitive eyebrow at the Cuyotai archer. "We haven't had any troubles with Greenskins in the kingdom in years. Most of them pulled back to the Greenskin Nation a while back, and the ones that didn't mostly live in the townships peacefully, working in the mills and farmlands."

"Apparently that doesn't apply universally." Portenda drew his spear from his assorted weaponry. "Come on. If they give us any trouble, we'll just have to kill one of them and send the rest packing. Shouldn't be too difficult, hmm?"

Shoryu nodded and followed a few yards behind Portenda, his bow at the ready, one arrow already notched on the string.

Four minutes later, walking along in the light rainfall, Portenda and Shoryu both heard the twang of a sling strap before they saw the Goblins come out from hiding. Both men ducked the hefty stone that had been launched at them, and with a battle cry the Goblins sprang from the bushes to the right of the path, short swords in the hands of three of them, slingshots in the hands of the two Goblins furthest away. Dressed in drab gray leathers and tunics, with long brown caps flapping from their heads, the Goblins stepped into the path and stopped, their battle cries forgotten when they finally got a good look at their intended pray.

The following should be noted about Tamalarian Goblins—while they are usually overconfident when attacking in greater numbers, they aren't stupid to the point of getting themselves killed when it can be avoided. They are cowardly little misers who would sooner run away than stay and fight a losing battle. As a result, it came as little surprise to either Portenda or Shoryu when one of the little green-fleshed men was pushed from behind toward them while the remaining four Goblins fled screaming back into the woods to hide from the 'big people'.

The unfortunate Goblin pushed at them dropped his sword as he stumbled toward them, slipping in the mud and falling flat on his face.

Portenda shook his head and sheathed his spear on his back, reaching down and plucking the quivering little man up out of the mud by the back of his leather jerkin. Portenda held him dangling several feet up off of the ground, and the Goblin craned his head up, giving them an awkward smile. What it lacked in teeth it made up for in genuine, boot-shaking fear.

"What are you doing out here, little man?" Portenda asked, staring into the wide brown eyes of the Goblin in his hand.

"Na puchak mina meshna, suru paltowel nima coodoo," came the Goblin's reply through a shit-eating grin.

"Did you catch any of that?" Shoryu asked the Bounty Hunter, who shook his head slightly. "Do you speak Common at all," he asked the Goblin directly, but the little Greenskin man merely looked at him with a blank stare.

"I'm not sure he understands our questions," the Cuyotai said.

"Well, he won't mind then when I ask him if he'd like to be talking around his balls." Portenda gave the Goblin a look of such ferocity that the Goblin began trembling anew. "Because if he does understand us, and is just screwing around, then I'm going to rip them off and stuff them in his foul, rotting little mouth." Portenda moved his free hand forward slowly.

"No, wait! No need for that," the Goblin shrieked, suddenly very fluent in the Common tongue. "Heh heh, I was just, uh, testing you guys! Yeah, that's it!"

"Just answer my question and you can go rejoin your comrades," Portenda said. "What were you five doing out here?"

"Well, there was supposed to be a caravan coming from Marrow toward Soreton," the Goblin said, his words escaping him in a rush. "We were going to spring on them, take some stuff from their carts, and hightail it back to our hideout. Honest, we wouldn't have hurt anybody!"

"Sure, that's why you're armed with swords and slings," huffed Shoryu. "We should carry you to Soreton ourselves and turn you over to the town guards!" Shoryu put the arrow back in his quiver, his left hand still gripping his bow tightly. "But you did answer our question, so we'll let you go for now. Right?"

"Right." Portenda dropped the Goblin into the mud.

Muck splashed around as the Goblin thrashed to his feet and scrambled away, scampering off into the woods and out of sight.

"Come on," he said, moving ahead. "There should be an inn somewhere nearby for us to hole up in. We don't need you falling ill too early on in the chase."

As they trudged on, neither man saying much of anything, night fell upon them in earnest. An hour after moonrise, they came upon a long, one-story building with a humble look to it. A sign along the road pronounced it to be the Nighty-Night Inn, a sappy name by both men's estimation, but quaint and warm from the look of it. Portenda led the way inside, through a tall oak door, into a central check-in office.

A tired-looking Gnome dressed in a white button shirt and beige slacks sat in a tall swivel chair at the front desk, thick bifocals slid halfway down his nose, eyes focused intently on a book before him. He looked up as Portenda approached, sliding the glasses up the bridge of his nose with a practiced motion and smiling dutifully at his potential customer. "Oy, welcome to the Nighty-Night Inn. What can I do for you gentlemen," he asked in a cheery voice.

"Two rooms, beds sized for men of our stature," Portenda said.

The Gnome reached under the desk for a register book, and thumbed through the pages and a sheet of parchment to the left of his book.

"Here we are, rooms seven and twelve," the Gnome said. "Just sign the register here, sirs, and I'll get the keys for you. It'll be four gold pieces altogether." He hopped down out of his chair.

Portenda signed the register with a pen, then handed it to Shoryu to sign as well.

The Gnome returned with two brass keys, writing down the room number next to each of their names and handing them the keys as he took Portenda's money.

"Right. There's coffee over there if you'd like any." The Gnome pointed behind the two of them to a battery-operated coffee machine.

Candles and lanterns provided the lighting in the Nighty-Night, like most businesses throughout the Elven Kingdom. The Elves' natural dislike and distrust of anything mechanical made things difficult for many Gnome businessmen, but most adapted as they could, like this fellow.

Portenda took the key to his room and marched off without another word to either the innkeeper or Shoryu.

"Friendly fellow, isn't he," the innkeeper whispered as Portenda slammed his room door down the hall.

"He's just tired I'm sure," Shoryu replied, surprised that his words came out sounding somewhat defensive. He didn't care much for the Simpa's gruff demeanor, true, but part of him did sympathize with his mannerisms. Few of the members of Byron's company had been the kindest or most levelheaded either, and he had traveled with them for a couple of months. Something about being on the road again, he thought, being out in the wilds after so many years of peace and quiet and family rearing, reminded him of who he used to be. A Hunter, one of the best in his tribe, he thought as he sauntered past Portenda's room toward his own.

He had faced down great dangers in those days, from rampaging Lizardmen, Orcs, and Ogres to demons. He had even been involved in standing against a Dreadnaught, an undead creature made from various bits and pieces of dead warriors and mages alike. He had fought and survived through all of that, and now he was with the Bounty Hunter, chasing after a man who had directly affected the course of that struggle and had come back into his life, stealing his ancestral bow.

As Shoryu opened the door to his room, taking in the welcome sight of a quaint hotel room with a more than generously sized bed for him to sleep on, he wondered what possible threat could be more dangerous to him now than he had faced back in those days.

* * * *

Reggie Browler operated in three different cycles, and each cycle came with a degree of queerness that big brother Sean could only gauge qualitatively. Usually, Sean preferred working with hard numbers. For example, he liked to know how much money the gang had pulled in during a job, so he could appropriately divvy up their earnings. He liked to know how many constables or police officers were pursuing him at any given time, so he could adjust for his escape. He liked to get a firm count of the cards in a dealer's deck in a gaming hall, so he could properly swindle the house for a grand sum.

The Elf-Queen's Bounty

Numbers simply didn't work very well where his brother Reggie was concerned, however. For starters, the amount of money that little Reggie spent on parts and ancient mecha schematics, books and equipment was very high indeed. Numbers that were high should only be marked as 'incoming monies', Sean thought, not 'outgoing monies'. Next, there came all of the complicated mathematical formulae that Reggie muttered on and on about as he systematically 'bettered' himself. When Sean attempted to grasp the math concepts involved, his brain did a funny little jig that warned him that too much more of that and blood would shoot out of his nose.

Lastly, the number involving Reggie that nagged at Sean the most, the one that popped into his head at that moment as he watched Reggie spin a new foot into place. That particular number came in the form of a percentage, and Reggie often grinned his soft, boyish grin as he quoted it with pride to big brother Sean. He grinned with pride each time he said the number, because each time the number got higher.

The evening that Portenda the Quiet and Shoryu Tearfang spent in the hotel in the woods, Sean winced as he heard the latest update.

"Sixty-five percent, brother," Reggie said in his gentle half-whisper.

Reggie stood and kicked his left leg out, holding it at head height a few feet away from Sean.

Several whirring blades shot out of the sides of the foot, and the foot then rotated around at high velocity, a deadly saw attached to the bottom of an artificial leg.

"Sixty-five, eh?" Sean asked. "I'm not sure I want to know how you came up with that number, but okay. Now, you've finished your foot like you asked, so hurry up and pack your things, Reg." He reached up and patted his little brother on the head. "We've got to make tracks."

"Yes, brother." Reggie darted off to his temporary room to pack up those things he would need to take with him on the road.

Sixty-five percent, Sean thought. *My littlest brother's body is sixty-five percent artificial.*

"What a wonderful world," Sean Browler said rather sarcastically, and spat.

* * * *

The late night hours came, and with them arose the grumbling, groaning and stretching form of Portenda the Quiet. Being a lycanthrope, he was prone to the occasional tug of nighttime wanderlust, and he felt the alluring call of the dim moonlight out in the forest around the hotel. However, being of a mixed nature, he knew that the best time for him to make progress toward his real goals was during the daylight hours, when the sun's rays could energize him via the Khan blood he carried in his veins.

Undressed from the waist up, he swiveled his legs over the side of the enormous bed he lay in and made his way to the window across from his sleeping place, peering out into the woodland. As happened to him so often during these quiet times of night, the hours of pre-dawn, he leaned against the windowsill and thought about his heritage. His body had a predominantly Simpa appearance to it in terms of his musculature, his torso arrangement, and his head. The only physical signs of Khan blood in his family line were the charcoal gray stripes of fur mixed with his golden mien, the slightly shorter and slimmer claws in his hands, and the fact that he took energy from sunlight. That, of course, was not obvious, however. Only he knew of the effects of the sun for himself.

It's the subtle things, though, he thought with a grunt, stretching his arms and the muscles in his back. Portenda suffered from having a Khan's slower regenerative healing pace, and as a result, did everything he could to avoid injury in battle. That wasn't always an option, especially when combating someone like the Red Tribe Werewolf in Desanadron a few months back, but most times he could escape confrontation with minimal wounds. He also worried about the number of injuries he would sustain, however, when dealing with groups like the Browler Brothers Gang.

Without lighting any of the candles in the hotel chamber, relying entirely on his heightened sense of sight, Portenda moved away from the window into the deeper shadows of the room, toward a small card table on which sat several manila folders. He eased himself down into a sturdy oak chair designed for use by Minotaurs and picked up one of the folders, opening it and pulling out the papers within. "James Svelk," he whispered to the shadows, himself, and the four walls. "What makes you tick, you rodent? Why risk being hauled in by the authorities by returning to the capital, hmm?"

James Svelk's service record sat in Portenda's hand, and once more he pulled his reading glasses out of his sleeveless vest, which he had hung on a coat rack just behind his chair. He adjusted the spectacles on his wide nose, feeling silly at having enhanced vision at medium and long range but being unable to help himself at close range. It wasn't faces or details, but only printed words that tended to elude his sight without optical help.

Everything in Svelk's command file indicated that he had been a hard-nosed major in the Elven Kingdom's military forces, not very well liked by his men but well respected for his ability to lead and get things done for his majesty. It made sense to Portenda that he would hire the Browler brothers to assist him in his tasks, but something about what he had done didn't seem within his scope. Svelk was a fugitive from justice in the Kingdom, and because of the Queen's diplomatic prowess, many other kingdoms and city-states throughout the continent of Tamalaria were on the lookout for Svelk.

To the Simpa Bounty Hunter, this would indicate that Svelk had received instructions to do what he had done at the Historical Society building from someone else. Whether or not that someone else had hired him as he had hired the Browlers, however, remained to be seen. Svelk had given up everything when he betrayed the kingdom to Richard Vandross: his military career, his pension, his wife, his home, all of it gone in the blink of an eye. Why then, Portenda wondered again, would the man risk coming all the way to Whitewood to break into a government building and steal a handful of artifacts and documents?

"A distraction," Portenda said, answering his own question. "But to what end?" As he pored over the file before him, the sun rose over the forest, and its vitalizing rays shone through the window and onto his bare chest, filling him with solar energy. Portenda smiled, and rose from his seat to meet the new day.

* * * *

Shoryu rolled over in his rented bed and cracked his eyes slowly open, snuffling the stale air of the room. He found his heart already sinking at the realization that his wife lay not with him, but in an empty bed of her own back in their cottage home in Whitewood.

Throwing back the sheets and hopping to his feet, the Cuyotai Hunter made his way to the bathroom, using the facilities and preparing for the day ahead. With any luck, and a good running pace, he and the Bounty Hunter could make the border of the kingdom by late evening, and then be well on their way to Desanadron. Shoryu had been to the sprawling metropolis fairly recently, six months almost to the day prior to that morning. The Queen had dispatched him to the city-state to finish collecting signatures on a new trade accord between the Elven Kingdom and Desanadron. During his week-long stay in the city, speaking with the regional governmental heads of state, Shoryu had been struck by the idea that Desanadron's stability was truly a testament to the military police forces and the citizenry of the city itself. Desanadron had a High Council, much like the Elven Kingdom did. However, the High Council of Desanadron had surprisingly little actual authority over the city-state. Bills were brought up for vote, and were passed into law or rejected. Then, the Councilors left things up to the military police to enforce the laws, and that was that.

Shoryu stepped out of the bathroom and nearly jumped back in when he lifted his head to look toward his gear. Portenda stood throat-to-nose with the Cuyotai, looming over him like the shadow of Death. "Oh," Shoryu squeaked like a mouse. "Good morning, Portenda."

The Bounty Hunter flashed him a smile full of teeth and a hint of what might be madness, and then let his expression fade immediately back into a flat, icy glare. He stepped back and to one side, and shook his head slightly.

"I'm amazed you let yourself be snuck up on like that," said Portenda evenly as Shoryu fairly dashed past him to his bag.

The Cuyotai archer dressed in fresh clothes and adorned his light armor, his bow and his mystical quiver. Hitching his bag up on his shoulders, he turned and shot Portenda a venomous stare.

"If we'd been out in the wild, someone or something would've torn you apart."

"Now see here," Shoryu spat, finally fed up with the cryptic mannerisms and straight business-like demeanor of his companion. "It has been a long time since I was out in the world, you know! I'm fully aware that I've gotten a little soft due to having a nice, cozy life from day to day." He gained momentum and fury with each moment that he spent speaking at what he essentially thought of as a brick wall.

Portenda, arms crossed and eyes ashen, dead, stood and stared at the Cuyotai without reply.

"I've lost a little of my savage touch, it's true. But I refuse to become something that I am not," Shoryu growled, pointing a single clawed finger at the Simpa Bounty Hunter. "I am a civilized man nowadays, you know. I don't see why you had to, to," he sputtered, trying to think of the right words.

"Test you?" Portenda asked, raising an eyebrow at the flurry of fur and words his traveling companion had made himself into. Before Shoryu could continue, Portenda raised one hand to stay his words. "Councilor, please, just hold off for a minute and let me explain. The people we're going to be running into on our way to Svelk aren't exactly the nicest bunch of fellows you could meet."

"Yes well, I imagine not," Shoryu said, flustered still but gradually regaining his calm. That was bad, he thought, feeling his blood slow in his veins, the tension in his back ease. Portenda had appeared so suddenly before him, between Shoryu and his armor and weapons, that for a moment the Cuyotai archer had panicked, nearly thrusting his own mind and body into a brief lycanthrope rage. His temper was so short sometimes that it frightened him, for he didn't want to lose control of his dark tendencies as he had so many years ago, up in the Dwarven Territories. The years had given him a nice buffer since then, putting politics and his loving family into his life to ease him away from his random 'black moments' as he termed them.

"This morning was merely a test of your early morning readiness," Portenda said flatly, stepping out of the room and into the hallway. "Think of it as a way for me to gauge just how much preparation I'm going to have to do along the way."

"Are you insinuating that I'm possibly going to be a handicap to you," Shoryu spat, restraining himself as best he could as he followed Portenda past the check-in desk, both men depositing their keys on the way outside.

"No, but if that's what you take from it, be my guest." Portenda stepped out of the hotel and into the warm, welcome shafts of sunlight that beamed down through the forest canopy overhead to give heat and illumination to the woodland and all of its inhabitants. Without another word to the infuriated Councilor, the Bounty Hunter shape-shifted down into his animus form, and started to saunter away north, leading the way.

Shoryu followed suit, and soon the two animals were dashing away north, staying mostly on the trail but straying here and there where it turned slightly east or west for a while. They didn't bother following the road at those turns and twists, opting instead to dart and dash between the trees and foliage, avoiding the other predators and prey in the forest as they came near.

The morning and most of the afternoon passed swiftly in this fashion, with both men stopping at the interval tree now and again to take care of their toilet business. In the late afternoon, with the border of the forest in sight, Portenda brought their progress to a halt and shape-shifted up into his bestial form. As he made the change as well, Shoryu gave pause for a moment to wonder, as he often did, just what happened to his belongings in the spirit realm when he changed himself into his animus form. He shook the thought off and followed the Simpa Bounty Hunter to a small clearing, where Portenda started a cooking fire.

The Simpa's rucksack made for another point of mystery for Shoryu. Every time the big man went to open it, he closed his eyes for a moment and thwacked the buckle on top before opening the bag.

Before Portenda reached into the bag, Shoryu put one finger up near his nose to gain the Simpa's attention. "Why do you do that?"

The Bounty Hunter continued through his action, pulling a medium sized pot out of the sack.

"Do what?" he asked in return, reaching in once more and pulling out a plastic container of some sort with what appeared to be a brownish muck inside.

"That little whacking of the buckle on your bag," Shoryu asked as Portenda pulled the lid off of the container and poured the contents into the pot, which he then set on the fire after placing a metal cover on it, also taken from the bag.

"It's a bag of displacement," Portenda said by way of explanation. When silence met his answer, the Simpa looked up into Shoryu's eyes, and saw the unasked question there. "There are actually multiple holding spaces in the bag, but each must be summoned forth by thinking on the particular items needed. You divide up your belongings into the various spaces by a category. For instance, I concentrated on my food and pot, and then struck the buckle. That activated the specific holding space currently accessible in my bag. The file folders we got in Whitewood are in another space of their own, and so on."

"Fascinating," Shoryu said, genuinely interested for once and not merely being conversational. "Where did you get it?"

"Palen," Portenda said, and Shoryu grunted and threw up his hands to say, of course. An item such as a displacement bag, after all, wouldn't be hard to come across in the city known the realm over as 'The Capital of Magic'.

The odors coming from whatever slop Portenda had placed in the pot became rather tantalizing after a short bit, the scent of sweet meats, carrots, potatoes and peas all boiling and roasting together in a stew. Portenda grabbed the rucksack once again, concentrated, and tapped the buckle. This time when he reached into the bag, his hand came back out bearing two earthenware bowls and two heavy duty spoons. One bowl and one spoon he handed to Shoryu, who accepted them with a mumbled thanks and a salivating glance at the steaming pot.

What Portenda did next Shoryu would remember for quite some time, because the action itself took little time, effort, or thought. Without gloves or any sort of protective material, the Simpa grabbed the side handles of the pot, took it from the fire, and removed the lid with the claws of his left hand. Next, he poured a healthy portion of the stew into Shoryu's bowl, then the rest into his own, and set the pot on the soft grass next to him. The fire he put out by merely tossing some soil on it, which he dug up with his bare hands. After wiping his dirty hands on his trousers, the Simpa snatched up his spoon, and scooped up a bit of the stew, blowing on it to cool it.

The Cuyotai worried that perhaps Portenda had scalded or badly singed the fur on his hands, but on second look and smell, he could see that no damage appeared to have been done. Shoryu contemplated what he saw and smelled at that moment, trying to figure out how Portenda had managed not to harm himself throughout the process. Fortunately, he didn't have to wait long, for his own nose finally picked up what Portenda must have scented when he led the Cuyotai over to this small clearing to make the meal.

The section of turf that Portenda had dug up to put out the fire appeared to be shot through with grass that held a vibrant red and white hue. Shoryu recognized the herbs immediately for what they were, for Ellen had used them many times before on Toshiya in the boy's youth. The herb was referred to as angel grass by members of those Classes familiar with the plant, which included Gaiamancers, Alchemists, Scholars and Hunters. How Portenda had known the stuff grew wild through the soil in this one particular clearing, Shoryu couldn't guess.

Angel grass could be used as a medicinal aid on its own without processing, if one knew where to get it fresh from the ground. Most times, however, those few individuals with information on the location of the herb purchased tracts of land where it grew, in order to hoard the stuff for their own private sales. Shoryu wondered if perhaps he should gather up some of the angel grass and dry it out, so that he might process it later for various uses. Or rather, so that he might get an Alchemist to process it.

"You knew that stuff was there," Shoryu blurted aloud. "You knew, so you didn't worry about burning yourself. Am I right?"

Portenda said nothing in reply, but nodded as he finished off the last of his meal.

"How did you know? I mean, angel grass can hardly be detected by its scent, because it grows just beneath the soil. How then," he began.

"I've been through this area before," Portenda said in a clipped voice. He packed up the pot, the bowls and the spoons after using some of his canteen water to wash them off. "I use it when I need it, and then I cover it back up. No point in tearing the stuff up when I don't need it that often. I'm a Simpa. My regenerative abilities should suffice most times to keep me alive. Now come on," he said, hitching up his bag and heading north once more as the sun made it to the horizon, preparing to plunge down out of sight and bring night chasing behind it. "We've little time to waste by chatting right now."

Though the swiftness and evasiveness of Portenda's reply unbalanced Shoryu, he nonetheless followed after the Bounty Hunter. They remained in their man-beast, or bestial, forms, making easy progress toward the edge of the great forest that was the Elven Kingdom and approaching the Border Guard on their way toward Desanadron and its protectorates.

When they exited the woodlands at last, twilight had fallen in earnest over the lands of Tamalaria. The main trade road they traveled upon gained a look of heavy traffic, which more often than not had to slow its pace as merchants and traders prepared to lead their caravans in single file down the narrower roads throughout the forest kingdom of the Elves. The moon had not yet become visible in the twilight sky, but it would in about an hour, and when it shone this night, it would shine full.

A full moon, Shoryu thought with a mental grin. For reasons that he never looked into or researched, a Cuyotai's body became more powerful during the light of a full moon. A Cuyotai also gained incredible alacrity during the full moon, and Shoryu knew that he was already one of the fastest archers in the lands. Under the glare of the full moon, he might even be able to fire an arrow faster than the strange mecha weapon that Portenda kept holstered on his hip.

Marching along in relative silence, both Cuyotai and Simpa saw the first of the Border Patrol officers approaching with a torch held at head height.

An Elven man from the smell of him, Portenda thought, *wearing half plate armor and a broadsword at his left hip.*

Shoryu tried to guess the man's rank from the distance, but the flare of the torchlight obscured his view of the man's rank insignia button, located on the collar of his armor.

"Good eve, gentle sirs," the guard hailed to them from twenty yards away.

Knowing the routine for these situations, both men came to a complete halt next to one another, and left their empty hands hanging at their sides.

Thus stopped, the guard appeared to hold no apprehension of them, as they would for all intents and purposes appear to be merely peaceful travelers who wished to exhibit no hostile thoughts. The Elven Border Patrol officer came to within five yards of them, and lowered his torch slightly, revealing the visage of a military man whose past in the service included at least several major breaks of his nose and cheekbones.

"Good eve, sergeant," Shoryu said after spotting the triangle shaped tag on the man's collar. The Elven sergeant gave Shoryu a small smile at the recognition of his rank, and nodded to him.

"T'is good to see that you are familiar with our military forces, sir. I assume then that you are a citizen of the great Elven Kingdom?"

"Indeed." Shoryu moved his right hand slowly and easily into one of his trouser pockets. He withdrew his billfold, and handed it to the sergeant, who flipped it open with his free hand to look at the identification papers within.

The sergeant's eyes widened for a moment before he smiled once again, with more honest mirth than before, and handed the billfold back.

"Sorry for the intrusion, Councilor Tearfang," the Elven guard said. "Routine procedure to ask who you are and where you're going, you know," the man said, a trace of nervousness in his voice. As a Councilor of the capital of the kingdom, Shoryu had just enough authority to strip the man of his rank and, ultimately, his job. Only officers of the rank of major or higher were safe from such judgment, though Shoryu hadn't once in his many years of service exercised this right.

"I understand completely," Shoryu said, dismissing the apology with a wave of his hand. "Myself and my companion are heading north, to Desanadron. We have urgent business there."

At this point, two corporals from the nearby unit had come up behind the sergeant, and both troopers maintained a close eye on the Bounty Hunter. The sergeant joined his glare to theirs for a moment, and turned his attention back to the Councilor.

"And who is thy companion, lordship," the Elven man asked.

An old world Elf, Shoryu thought, listening to the man speak. Though a military man for some years, by the look of him, the sergeant had retained a portion of his aristocratic upbringing in the kingdom. Many of the older families in cities like Edgewood and Arboria maintained the old world ways, and a military career didn't really factor into their upbringing of their children. However, his background as a member of an upstanding family would explain the nervousness and the seeming need to apologize. After all, in Elven high society, it is usually taught that one should always respect one's betters.

"He is Portenda the Quiet." Shoryu watched the flare of recognition ignite behind the eyes of both lower-ranking patrolmen. They edged a step or two backward, their chain shirts clinking softly in the background. "He is a Bounty Hunter on hire by Her Majesty the Queen. The specifics of his assignment are to remain confidential, however, sergeant." Though he had not seen a flicker of recognition in the sergeant's eyes at the mention of Portenda's name, the term 'Bounty Hunter' seemed to have wiped the smile off of the officer's face. Instead, the sergeant now sneered slightly at the Simpa, and Shoryu's overactive imagination sent him a rather horrid mental play-by-play of what might happen as a result of that look.

In his mind's eye, Shoryu saw the towering Simpa take a step toward the Elven sergeant. He saw the sergeant guffaw at Portenda, and stare indignantly at him before telling him to remove himself from the sergeant's presence. We don't mix with ruffians, he could hear the sergeant saying just before Portenda grabbed the sides of the man's head and twisted quick and hard, spinning the man's head around until he faced the troops behind him. Then, the body would simply crumble to the ground without the benefit of life still being in it.

Shoryu shook his head violently, bringing himself crashing back to reality. Returned to the moment, he turned and saw that Portenda had walked on, north along the trade route, past the Border Patrol unit. Shoryu smiled and bowed to the sergeant, and sprinted after the Simpa Bounty Hunter, huffing and puffing as he did so to let the elusive Portenda know who was charging up behind him.

When the two men could look back and barely discern the officers in the fields south of them, Portenda gave Shoryu a curious look. "What happened to you back there," he asked, facing forward once more.

"I had a lovely daydream," was Shoryu's reply.

* * * *

The next day, at around noon, reminded Shoryu why he preferred the rainfall in the forest. In the woodlands of the Elven Kingdom when the rain fell, even if it fell hard, a walk in the woods could still be made in relative peace. The mud and muck only got a couple of inches deep, and where the water pooled together, the puddles remained small and shallow.

Out here on the plains and grasslands, however, Shoryu plunged his left leg a third time in a sinkhole up to his knee. Portenda ranged ahead, much to Shoryu's chagrin, somehow avoiding every deep spot of mud or water. Shoryu was a Hunter by Class, and should have been able to seek out such pitfalls with ease. Once again, however, he had to remind himself that he hadn't been really out in the world in many years.

As he struggled to pull himself out, the soaking wet Cuyotai howled over the rain, "Oh, no! I'm just fine, no need to come back and help me out you giant prick!"

His words went unheeded, and once more he got himself up out of the mud and jogged along to catch up to the subdued Simpa. "Did anybody ever tell you you're a jerk?"

Nothing from the Simpa, which seemed pretty much par for course this day. Since waking earlier in the day, Shoryu noticed that Portenda had refused to partake of any sort of conversation, as if he was holding his words back for some reason.

Unbeknownst to Shoryu, Portenda focused on hearing through the rain, beyond the rain and thunder and lightning. His nostrils flared, and he retained his silence in order to further heighten his observation senses, a trade-off he had long since mastered. One of the mysterious benefits of his taboo birth (likely endowed, he often suspected, by Death or Fate) was his ability to make his senses even more powerful than they naturally were.

Due to the constant conversation with Shoryu since accepting this assignment, Portenda had only been able to build up a little of this power from time to time. Right now, he suspected that someone or something hostile was on their trail, and until he could identify it and lure it out of hiding, the Bounty Hunter refused to be goaded into replying to any of the good Councilor's prompts. He had to pinpoint the source of his own suspicions.

The source itself followed after them, staying about a mile behind.

* * * *

Sean had made things pretty plain to him before Dean Browler departed on his assignment. "Remember, don't attack them, just find out where they're going, and what sort of progress they make in a few days. Then use the scroll to get back to us, okay?"

Dean had agreed quickly enough, but the damnable streak of rebellion kept ripping up his spine, urging him to strike while he had the opportunity.

Spying the Simpa and the Cuyotai from about a mile south of their position through a long-barreled spyglass, Dean Browler wondered what sort of man this Portenda the Quiet was. As a Ninja of moderate skill, Dean worried only about three types of men or women, those being Monks, Samurai and more experienced Ninjas. However, Sean had seemed fairly certain that the Bounty Hunter could and would do him some serious damage if he engaged him, even in ranged combat. "Just stay away and observe," Sean cautioned. "Stay away and observe."

Using the network of informants available to them, Sean discovered that the Councilor and the Bounty Hunter had checked into the Nighty-Night Inn on their way north, out of the Elven Kingdom. Since the information had only been a day old, Sean had immediately dispatched Dean with a pair of teleportation scrolls, the first one depositing the Ninja of the Browler Brothers Gang at a hideout near the Nighty-Night. Since then, he'd been following and watching the two men at a distance.

Following them during their runs as animals had proven marginally more difficult for Dean than he suspected it might be. The reason for that was that the Elven Kingdom was host to more creatures and monsters of a hostile nature than one might know if they traveled on the well-established routes. Dean had been forced to deal with tree-dwelling serpents, hungry wolves, a rashum in the form of a half-eagle/half-dog, and a single Wraith. The last of the aforementioned creatures, of course, he had dealt with by running away from it through the treetops. Dean knew of no way to defeat their kind.

Thusly harried and worked, Dean took a small measure of relief from his quarry's current pace, slowed by the rain and weather conditions. The rain didn't bother him one bit. His uniform was waterproof, and he kept a pair of magic sutras on the bottoms of his boots that allowed him to walk atop the surface of any puddle or sinkhole. So long as he kept himself out of any such pitfalls deeper than a few feet, the sutras would continue to operate as intended, and he would remain on the trail of his targets.

Peering through the spyglass once more, Dean confirmed the Simpa and Cuyotai's pace, and moved swiftly through the rain and gathering mist to a position that would allow him to keep an eye on them with minimal movement and maximum coverage. Dean Browler shuffled along in a half-crouch, keeping his eyes locked on his destination until he arrived, then sprawling himself against the side of a large outcropping of rock like a spider that has just taken a leap of faith.

He took out the spyglass once more, and a secondary piece of copper tubing that was bent at an angle. This he attached to the end of the spyglass, and peered into the sight, which used the bent tubing and refracting mirrors to show him the magnified view above and beyond the rock outcropping without exposing his head to anyone looking in his direction.

Once more he spotted the Simpa and the Cuyotai, and Dean tried to calculate the progress they were making with the amount of time they were likely to spend traveling that day. They won't make it into Desanadron until mid-morning if they stop at around midnight, Dean thought. If they stop earlier than that and wake early, they'll be there in the early morning. I'll have to take an opportunity to delay them if I get one.

Dean Browler still had a rebellious streak, and it was shouting at him to make an opportunity of his own.

* * * *

As the afternoon drew on into early evening, the rainfall steadily increased, dropping visibility even further with the spreading of fog. Portenda could still feel someone watching him, spying on him even, but he couldn't identify who or what it was due to all the noise, fog and odors assaulting him. However, he didn't have to mime any warning to Shoryu, and for once, when the Councilor spoke, Portenda took heart from his words.

"We're being followed, you know," Shoryu said in a voice nearly drowned out by the world-ending thunder rumbling through the sky and the ground.

Portenda nodded, putting a thick finger to his lips to call for Shoryu's silence.

"We'll have to deal with them sooner or later, whoever they are," Shoryu said, leaning in closer to Portenda to convey his message. "Any idea how many or what they are?"

At this, Portenda merely shook his head, keeping his eyes forward, on the road ahead.

Shoryu took his cue from the lumbering Simpa, and simply continued to stare ahead as he moved.

The evening came closer without any further development in the situation, with the exception that the rain finally slowed, and the skies cleared a good deal. As they prepared to make camp for the night, only about seven or eight hours from Desanadron by Shoryu's estimation, both men sat at the fire for a silent meal.

Halfway through the meal, the first of their various troubles to come made its appearance.

* * * *

Dean Browler thought he might have a good shot at making some trouble for his targets that late evening. He assumed, during the hours preceding the halt of Portenda and Shoryu's march, that the decrease in rainfall and thunder and lightning served as a good omen for him. He assumed incorrectly, which seemed to be the case as often as not for the Ninja among the Browler clan.

Dean heard the creature's approach before he saw it, and what he heard gave him reason for pause in his observations of the two men making camp. He remained in hiding a half-mile away from their position, crouched in the last of many miles of rows of corn from nearby Vershak's farmlands. Before he put his spyglass down, after a peek at the Bounty Hunter and Councilor, he detected the slow, torturous thumping of something enormous moving along the murky, muddy road that traversed north and south.

Turning southward with his spyglass to his eye, sans attachments, Dean's night-trained vision helped him make out the outline of a creature that neither he nor many other men would want any part of on a dark and blustery night: a bladeron. Bladerons, not often seen outside of forests and woodlands, were among the most fearsome of Tamalaria's semi-intelligent monsters. Vaguely man-shaped, bladerons stood on two legs cast in bark-like flesh with hundreds of spiked protrusions hard and sharp enough to tear through steel full-plate armor. The limbs themselves, generally speaking, measured no more than a foot in circumference, which amazed most who survived an encounter with a bladeron, since they carried so much weight.

The monster's torso, like all of its kind, had a strangely glowing point of light in its broad chest, emerald in hue. The little bit of light given off proved enough for Dean to view the creature's head and face, the parts of its body that usually gave adventurers the willies or shakes when they spotted one, even at a distance. The bladeron's neck stretched a full foot and a half from its shoulders, a granite-like protrusion of muscle that supported a head that, for all intents and purposes, appeared to be nothing more than a floating bubble of water. Two wide, lidless eyes floated around in that water, and a black void filled a spot on the outer bulb of the head, the mouth with which the creature fed.

A third arm shot out of the back of this orb-head, an arm with no apparent bones in the joint. All three arms appeared as black as the granite throat, contrasting only slightly with the brown, bark-rough flesh of the torso and legs. Despite the dark hue of that flesh, however, the musculature could not be missed; bladerons had been known to break redwood trees to form makeshift clubs, after all.

As Dean Browler maintained his position, he watched through the spyglass as the creature approached the Cuyotai and Simpa. If the bladeron killed them, then his brothers' problems were mostly solved for now.

* * * *

Portenda had his spoon halfway to his mouth when he felt the first tremor issuing through the ground. Rather than stop eating and give Shoryu reason for pause, he started to chew his food.

As the light of the full moon shone down on them both, Shoryu surprised Portenda once more. "It's about half a mile away. Whatever it is, it's enormous," he commented, not looking away from the food he greedily shoveled down his gullet. "Preemptive strike?" he asked, standing up and drawing his bow from his back.

Risking losing some of his perceptive power by speaking, though not much on the scale of what he'd gained thus far, Portenda conjectured, "Might be a good idea, though I'm not sure what we can do at this range." The Bounty Hunter set his bowl on the grass and stood, drawing out his revolver and facing south with Shoryu.

The Elf-Queen's Bounty

"You get much range on that piece of machinery?" Shoryu asked condescendingly.

"You'd be surprised." Portenda squinted his left eye shut. Now that he was looking in the direction of the tremors, with his heightened sense of sight he spotted the threat. For a moment, his breath caught in his throat: a bladeron! Portenda had faced two of these creatures in his many years roaming the lands, and had only slain one of the two as it had been a young member of its species. The specimen marching its way slowly toward the Bounty Hunter and Councilor was a fully grown male of the species, and Portenda's immediate impulse was to retreat to a safe distance and develop a plan of attack.

The adult bladeron he'd faced ten years ago had nearly pulverized him, causing Portenda to retreat from the battle and plot a proper course of action to deal with it. Giving chase, the bladeron stumbled onto several explosives that Portenda left in his wake, which served only to slow it down and cause it some minor injuries. Running away in his animus form, Portenda got a couple hours' lead on the bladeron, enough time for him to enlist the aid of a group of adventurers on their way to Midden in the Fiefdom of Lemago. Together, he and the adventurers had ambushed the creature, and the female Aquamancer in the adventuring group had delivered the final blow, hurling a spear of ice through the creature's head.

Now, he had only himself and the Cuyotai Hunter, along with some of his technological weaponry.

Portenda heard the thwang of Shoryu's bow string release an arrow toward the bladeron.

His own abilities increased by the full moon's mysterious lunar glow, Shoryu had spotted his target only moments after Portenda, and had let fly with a single shot. Both men watched, Shoryu with satisfaction and Portenda with a hint of admiration, as the arrow struck true in the left shoulder of their oncoming foe.

The bladeron, struck in a nerve, stomped around in the flatlands and howled its terrible cry of pain, still a quarter of a mile away.

Portenda knew his revolver could not fire accurately at even this range, and he had to admit now that he had been right in bringing Shoryu Tearfang, Councilor of the Elven Kingdom, with him on his assignment. Portenda specialized mostly in melee combat and technological warfare. Shoryu, a true Hunter still, preferred ranged combat and old world tactics. Together, they complemented each other's skills quite nicely, the Simpa thought.

After a minute of stomping some of the flatlands even flatter, the bladeron faced them squarely, and began advancing on their position with frightening speed. Due to its sheer size, it made steady progress, forcing Shoryu to start beating a retreat, notching another arrow and letting fly as he backed away from the fire and his companion. Portenda watched as this second arrow lodged itself cleanly in the bladeron's left thigh, causing it to scream once more, but also to slow down.

Now, Portenda thought, raising the barrel of his revolver and taking aim. The creature was only three hundred yards away, and Portenda felt confident that he could make the shot at this range. Raising the barrel and shifting his site just to the left to adjust for the oncoming wind, Portenda fired a single shot at the monstrosity.

The slug struck home in the creature's right thigh, further incapacitating its ability to pursue them successfully. With a tremble following the outpour of blood from its leg, the bladeron shuddered and dropped to its knees.

Sensing that the time to make the killing strike had come, Shoryu drew three arrows from his mystic quiver, and took careful aim at the creature's chest. He fired all three arrows at once, his training and instincts serving him well as the first of the arrows thudded solidly into its left shoulder, the second arrow it its groin, and the third in its upper right chest area, just over the heart. This third arrow, however, seemed to only land in thick, muscular flesh. It had not struck the heart, and without the magical force of the Tearfang family bow, his normally fatal shot proved only to be wounding.

Portenda, however, never did mind taking the risk of getting up close and personal. Charging forward with almost reckless abandon, the Simpa Bounty Hunter sprinted to within the creature's melee range. He leaped as the creature took a hard swing at him with one of its normal arms, and planted a firm flying kick into the arrow in the bladeron's chest, shoving the arrow through the muscle and into its heart. Kicking off backward, Portenda flew back from the creature and landed in a three-point stance as it shivered, trembled, and then spewed blood from its strange, watery mouth. The head of the bladeron splashed to the ground, followed immediately by its main body. The monster was dead.

Shoryu let out a triumphant yip, jumping and pumping his free hand into the air, and Portenda gave him a slight smile. *Not over quite yet,* Portenda thought, listening to the air around him ripple and tear as something small and metallic flew toward him from the south.

Dropping into a shooter's kneel, the Bounty Hunter propped his revolver in the crook of his left arm and fired without turning his head.

The Elf-Queen's Bounty

There was a loud clang of metal striking metal, and Portenda watched a dented steel shuriken land a few feet from him, its momentum spent by the collision with the bullet.

Well, he thought, *that was kind of you to give me an idea of what you are.*

Portenda remained in a crouch for a full two minutes before Shoryu tapped him on the shoulder from behind.

"What's up?" Shoryu asked, to which Portenda replied by holstering his weapon and moving a few feet south. He retrieved something shiny from the ground, and tossed it to Shoryu.

"Ninja," Shoryu whispered mostly to himself, but Portenda grunted to confirm his suspicion. "Still doesn't tell us how many there are."

"No, but it does tell us that we are indeed being followed, watched," Portenda said. "Shoryu, draw your bow." Portenda felt suddenly inspired to take action against their unseen foe, whose identity he felt relatively certain of since mental review of the Browler brothers' files.

Shoryu did as he was asked, and Portenda gave him the exact line of sight that their tracker had to have attacked from, using a shuriken. "Do not fire yet," Portenda said as Shoryu notched an arrow and drew back on the bow.

Portenda drew out one of his pin grenades and lashed it to the arrow, propping one claw through the pull ring on the tab. "When I pull my finger away, let fly quickly, Shoryu Tearfang, lest you wish to test the true power of your lycanthrope regeneration."

Shoryu nodded his understanding, and Portenda counted to three. On three, he drew out the pin, and Shoryu let fly with his arrow at a slight upward angle, to allow for wind drift.

The grenade exploded almost a half-mile away, but neither man heard a scream or smelled any fresh blood. "Well, if nothing else, our foe will think twice about following us."

"Any idea who it was," Shoryu asked as the two men headed back to their camp, leaving the fallen bladeron out in the road for any merchant who could remove the highly prized leg flesh.

"Indeed," Portenda said with a half grin. "Dean Browler, of the Browler Brothers Gang. But don't worry, we're not going to go back for him," Portenda said, catching Shoryu by the wrist to stop him from sprinting back in the Ninja's direction. "He'll likely have used a sutra or scroll to teleport back to his brother Sean. For now, let us just pack our camp and head to Desanadron," Portenda said. "After all, it's only a few hours away."

Chapter Five
Criminal Elements

Well I'll be damned, Dean Browler thought as he watched his targets destroy the bladeron, seemingly with ease. Councilor Tearfang's accuracy with a bow had been frightening to watch, and the crack-boom explosion of the Simpa Bounty Hunter's mecha weapon had caused a quivering to kick up in Dean's heart. As the creature was falling to the ground, slain, Dean thought he saw an opportunity to strike, and he took it.

Sliding his hand down to his right hip, Dean grabbed a single star-shaped shuriken, and tossed it with lethal force at Portenda the Quiet. However, the Simpa had somehow predicted the course of the weapon's flight, shooting it down out of the air as it hurtled toward him.

As soon as Dean heard the connection of the bullet with his shuriken, he turned and fled through the rows of corn, reaching into his various pockets, trying to remember in which one lay the scroll Sean gave him before his observation mission.

Fully two minutes later, running along like a bat out of hell, Dean felt a wave of force blast him in the back as an explosion rocked the fields south of him. Dean had opted to flee west after the deflection of his shuriken, for he felt certain that if Shoryu knew the direction to fire in, he'd be brought down by an arrow. Misdirecting Portenda with the shuriken throw had apparently saved his life, he thought as he flattened himself on the ground among the corn.

Dean Browler rolled onto his back, found the scroll, and winked out of existence, back to his brothers.

* * * *

"Well, that was a bit sudden I'll give you that," Sean Browler said, rubbing his sore lower back. The second eldest of the Browler brothers had succeeded in escaping a conflict with Portenda and Shoryu, but only just barely. When he used the teleportation scroll, Dean had been deposited about ten feet in the air over Sean Browler's head. Hearing a loud 'poof' in the air overhead, Sean knew what had happened, and had the misfortune of falling forward when he tried to stand up from his seat in front of his tent. Dean landed squarely atop his older brother, and after a moment, the two brothers untangled themselves from one another.

"I'm very sorry about that Sean," Dean said, feeling the back of his head where the warmth of the blast had felt most heated. His black Ninja mask was partially singed from the heat, but this didn't cause him any worry. Indeed, Dean Browler smiled beneath the cloth mask as he wondered how the Bounty Hunter and Councilor would explain the burning destruction of those cornfields to the crops' owner. Always look for the positives, Mother had told him, and so he did.

"Well, not to worry, Dean. Tell us, what'd you find out about them," Sean asked.

The two eldest brothers headed about twenty yards away from Sean's tent to a fire pit, where Benjamin, the family Pickpocket, and Reggie, the family's young mecha prodigy, both sat around the fire, tending to the meal. Sean and Dean sat down on opposite sides of the cooking pit, Sean grabbing the plate that Ben offered him and Reggie setting Dean's meal down next to him to cool. For reasons unknown even to Dean himself, the Ninja of the Browler brothers preferred his food cold.

"Well, I can tell you a few things, though unfortunately, none of them is good for us," the Ninja began. He accepted a mug of coffee from Reggie, and this he began drinking immediately, pulling his mask down from his nose and mouth and tucking the material under his chin. Beneath the mask, Dean Browler's handsome features appeared almost academic and learned, like an educator's. Sean didn't understand why he adhered to the old rule about masks among Ninjas, seeing as Thaddeus Fly and Markus Trent never bothered, and they had been Dean's instructors. But Sean let the idea pass; after all, everyone was allowed their eccentricities.

Dean told his brothers about the Bounty Hunter and Councilor's speed and agility in their animus state first, trying to convey to them the feeling of futility he felt while trying to keep up with them in that shape. He wasn't certain that Benjamin or Reggie would understand, as Ben took little or nothing in life seriously (except the pursuit of other people's money), and Reggie spent most of his time wrapped in his own little world of nuts, bolts, and ancient technologies. They could be relied upon when called up to do the work that needed to be done: beyond that, however, intelligence reports mostly got absorbed by Sean for further plotting.

Dean told Sean about the Simpa Bounty Hunter's mecha weapon, the mention of which caused a light to flare behind Reggie's eyes. "Describe the weapon in full detail to me," the youngest Browler brother beseeched of him, and Dean did so. "That's a forty-five caliber revolver, from the sounds of it," Reggie said evenly, a small smile betraying his thoughts.

"Good weapon?" Sean asked.

"It's a hand cannon essentially," Reggie said, helping Ben divvy out the rest of the food from their assorted pots and pans over the low fire.

"Only way to get more power is to move up in weapon classification to a rifle."

Sean looked warily at Reggie, for this was a veritable speech for him, and outside of his workshops and lab areas, the youngest of the brothers seldom spoke at length, even if the subject interested him. Sean had known Reggie only to do such a thing once before; during the Bad Days.

The Bad Days, as all four of the Browler brothers thought of them, had been the eleven days it had taken for Mother to finally succumb to the last stage of The Black Rot. A heavy smoker all of her life, Victoria Browler ignored the warnings she had often gotten from friends and co-workers. "I don't care what they'll do to me," she informed many of them. "It's either this, or I start hitting people!" Though a Human, Victoria Browler had been a large woman, and few wanted to contend with her in a foul mood. As such, a lot of the complaints and warnings were offered after she'd left the room.

Sean decided to let the matter go for now, but he'd have to take his littlest brother aside while they traveled during the day and have a talk with him. If Reggie was thinking about Mother again, he might become erratic and take off, as he had done twice since her demise. And right now, with a high-price client on their hands, with a sensitive situation to work around, the last thing the eldest and leader of the Browler Brothers Gang needed was an extra task to take care of.

Dean proceeded to tell them about the encounter with the bladeron, and how handily the Simpa and Cuyotai had dealt with the monstrosity. Lastly, he told his brothers about his escape, leaving out no detail that might seem important.

Sean grumbled and silently processed everything as he ate, now and again looking from Dean to Reggie.

He never realized that Benjamin, meanwhile, had taken a few extra coins from one of his pouches out of habit.

* * * *

James Svelk waited in a corner booth of a tavern situated in the middle of a small village, just south of the Fiefdom of Lemago. The salty air wafting in through the open doors from the ocean and the fishermen steadily streaming in and out of the bar stung his nostrils and eyes, but he didn't complain. Complaining about the prearranged meeting place would have been a waste of his time and mental effort, so he instead turned his thoughts toward the future, and what it held for him.

Dressed in a dark green traveling cloak over an uncovered chain shirt and iron greaves, with the hood up over his head to conceal his face, he looked not unlike many other adventurers of his Race. He took the booth in the far corner, away from the door, and insisted upon sitting by himself despite the few offers of company he received. The locals were mostly Jafts, Minotaurs and Humans, and having no great love for any of those three Races, Svelk kept entirely to himself. Besides, he mused, it makes it easier to conduct my business.

The doors of the tavern swung open once again, and finally Svelk saw his contact. The man in the doorway had sent Svelk a letter many months before, offering him an opportunity that the former Elven military man simply couldn't refuse. Standing at around six and a half feet in height, with a brown travel cloak covering his half-plate armor rather well, the newcomer raised his hand toward the barkeep, who approached the bar as did the contact. "Elderberry wine, my good man," the contact said from the recesses of his hood, and the Human bartender obliged him.

Svelk grinned as the contact came directly to his table, seating himself across from the former major without preamble. Svelk cleared his throat and leaned forward slightly. "There are fine roses in my gardens," he said, the first part of the agreed-upon code to initiate any conversation between himself and his contact, or rather, employer.

"Which means there be fine thorns as well," the contact said, and Svelk relaxed, letting out a sigh of relief. After all, he had been pursued by several rather clever Elven and Half-Elven Bounty Hunters over the years, and a couple of them had approached him in much the same manner as his contact and employer.

"I must say, James, I was impressed by the good work you did in Whitewood," the employer whispered, sipping his wine lightly after. "All of those priceless items, spirited away from the kingdom. Tell me, however, that you got the one item I absolutely required of you."

"Of course, good sir," Svelk said in a mockery of a gentleman's manner. "Benjamin Browler took care of that whilst we were busy in the Historical Society building. With the attention drawn to the dead guards there, nobody has thought to look through the royal palace."

"The replacement," the employer asked, raising an eyebrow.

"Dean Browler took care of that, sir," Svelk said, now at ease, aloof. "Very talented young men, all four of them. Of course, the youngest of the brothers remained outside of the city, in case any of the other three brothers or myself had been apprehended. His job would have been to break us out of lock-up."

"Could he have done it," the employer asked, his face still hidden in the pockets of shadow in his hood.

James Svelk grinned from ear to ear in reply, letting the matter go unspoken.

"Very good. This Dean, how well versed is he in the forgery of documents?"

"Don't worry, sir." Svelk took a pull on his own drink. "As I said before, many times, I did my homework, and these boys are the best. My only concern lies with their loyalty," Svelk whispered, his tone shifting from light and easy to concerned and serious. "They could do us both a lot of damage if they decide to turn against us. Not that I think they will, but a little extra coin in their pouches might help smooth things over,"

The employer lifted his head a little, revealing the age-lined lower half of a once handsome Elven face. Years and years of hard work, servitude, and battle had hardened the lines that otherwise might be softer, caused by laughter or smiling on the man's Elven countenance. Even grizzled war veterans in the Elven Kingdom tended to have softer features than this man. As always when Svelk saw even a portion of the man's grimace of a smile, he shuddered. Skilled though Svelk was in combat, as clever and cunning in worldly affairs, he didn't stand a chance against his employer, and both men knew it.

"You shouldn't push your luck, James," the employer said with his grimace/grin. He lowered his head, and reached for a pouch at his hip, depositing it on the table in front of Svelk's glass. "However, these things often do get complicated by the greed of others. Let's lubricate every wheel and gear we need to until my plans reach fruition." The employer finished his drink and rose to his feet. "Don't worry, James. I won't forget about you when the time comes. I made you a promise, and gave you a trooper's word," the employer said, starting away.

And what, James Svelk wondered, *is a trooper's word worth?* He opened the pouch on the table, and therein discovered four green gems, each flawless to his untrained eye. He plucked one out of the group, and held it up to the dim light of the tavern, peering hard at the gem. *Well,* he thought, tucking the gem away, *a trooper's word I'm not sure of, but I should fetch a few degrees of loyalty for these.*

* * * *

"Well, they're probably in Desanadron by now, " Benjamin Browler said, making his first contribution to the conversation in a few days. The four Browler brothers were situated comfortably on a wagon that, four hours before, had belonged to a prosperous Lizardman traveling merchant. Now said merchant floated facedown in a stream with several dozen stab wounds in his body. His wagon and horses, however, belonged now to the Browlers, and they made good use of both. Sean sat in the driver's seat, and he kept the flaps behind him tied open to speak back and forth with his kin.

The goods that the merchant had on sale consisted mostly of standard weapons and chain shirts, along with several pairs of sturdy steel greaves, leggings, and a collection of odds and ends that, for the most part, had already been tossed unceremoniously out the back of the wagon. The brothers still had their own travel rations for several days, and as they continued eastward, away from the Elven Kingdom and Desanadron, Sean tried to use the map of Tamalaria that he had sketched over the years to plot their course.

Their work for James Svelk had pretty much reached its conclusion, with a single exception, and to this task the four brothers now traveled. Their destination was a small village in the northeastern flatlands, out near the city of Palen. There, Sean Browler would, with the help of his brothers and a goodly amount of skill in the art of disguise and deception, pretend to be James Svelk. He would commit a few felonies in the guise of his employer, and then make good an escape from the village, north to the Port of Arcade.

Law enforcement officers from the village, which stood as one of Palen's city-state protectorates, would immediately inform their superiors and describe the suspect. Palen, having an excellent trade arrangement with the Elven Kingdom, would swiftly send the information along to Her Majesty the Queen. She, in turn, would send a messenger of some sort to the Bounty Hunter and the Councilor, and thus, they would follow a false lead all the way across the continent and waste precious time and energy.

While Sean Browler had been impressed with the scope of Svelk's plan, he hadn't cared much for the inherent risk he and his brothers were taking on. After all, what if the authorities apprehended them? What if Palen sent elite guards to the village on a routine basis, and the four brothers had to deal with a group of highly trained, magic-wielding officers?

These concerns were not, however, his largest. Despite the overall jovial mood of his brothers in the back, Sean Browler couldn't help but think that somehow, some way, the Bounty Hunter would show up before they pulled off their end of the plan. If they finished their performance and made it up to the Port of Arcade, the Browlers were in the clear. After all, in a city full of thieves, brigands, and gangs, they stood almost as high and mighty as royalty.

"Just gonna have to hope we make it that far," he muttered to himself. "Momma, if you're listening, watch out for us. We need all the help we can get." He turned his head to look in on his younger siblings.

* * * *

A few hours had passed, and now Reggie Browler held the reins to the horses. The quiet, disturbing presence he exerted seemed to make the horses a little shy, and a tad more nervous in their cantering. However, with expert handling of the reins, tightening pressure here, relieving it there, and tapping his feet on the running board in time to their clomping hooves, he calmed them. "Impressive," Sean said to his littlest brother before heading back inside the wagon.

"Thank you," Reggie replied, keeping his eyes ahead on the flatlands and side roads they traversed. Evening approached as he took control of the wagon, and in the back of the wagon, he could hear his older brothers all settling in to grab a few hours of sleep. *Sleep,* Reggie thought with a tilt to his head and a faint smile. *What a waste of time.*

Reggie's trunk remained in the back with his older brothers, and when it came time for him to stop the wagon for the night, he would head back, retrieve it, and then take himself a ways from the group. He loved his brothers deeply, as Momma told him he should, but sometimes they acted funny when he field-tested his new equipment. So, to give his brothers a measure of comfort, and to ensure that he never disobeyed Momma, Reggie tried to test his equipment only when his brothers were asleep, or if Sean took an interest in his work.

Ah, Sean. Reggie's lips parted slightly as he gave the twinkling evening a full smile, one of the few he'd allowed himself in weeks. *Big brother,* he thought, *is the only one who ever takes an interest. He's the only one who comes close to understanding me and my work.* On occasion, Reginald Browler dared to imagine that some day his big brother would allow Reggie to give *him* some new equipment. Of course, the initial process was always painful, the removal of the original body part. *But,* Reggie thought, *I know how to lessen the pain and make the transfer so much faster these days! Yes, with these new arms of mine, and the ones I'm working on, I can perform the whole procedure in a few hours I'll bet!*

The Browler Brothers Gang rode on into the quiet evening, jouncing along comfortably in the back of the wagon. The only one awake, guiding the four of them with the horses at the end of the reins, wondered how it would be to make all three of his older brothers like himself.

* * * *

A few hours later, Reggie pulled the horses to a halt near a small creek, unlashed them, and led them down to the water to drink and graze on the tall grass near the bank. He returned to his brothers up in the wagon, and shrugged Sean gently to awaken him.

"What's up Reggie," he asked, his eyes still heavy with sleep.

"Just thought I'd let you know I've stopped for the night," Reggie informed Sean. He grabbed his large, long black trunk and his tool bag from their spot near the back of the wagon. "I'll be up a while, working. Is that all right, brother?"

"Course it is, kid, course it is," Sean mumbled as he rolled back over and returned to the lands of slumber.

Reggie pulled his trunk and bag down out of the wagon, and paced about twenty yards away from the wagon and his older brothers. In a patch of low grass, he sat down, opened the trunk, and began removing his latest creations. Reggie removed his cloak and overcoat, exposing his sleek, artificial arms to the lunar light of the night.

His left arm, an older model he'd completed the year before, felt odd and clunky as he utilized it to rummage through his tool bag. The right arm, his newest limb creation, thrummed softly with stored solar energy from the dragon scale installed in the forearm. Plucking a socket wrench from his bag, Reggie used his old left arm to reach into the solid trunk and remove the new replacement for it, setting it on his crossed legs. The scent of machine oil filled the air, and he took a deep, exhilarating breath of it into his lungs. Where his brothers would have gagged on the thick, cloying scent, he thrived upon it.

His right arm, a shining example of what mecha could accomplish, had nubs and wires dotting the interior of each finger, and these simulated nerves for Reggie Browler. While he could do a great deal with his left arm and the old right arm, he couldn't feel anything with them. As a result, he had taken extra care to install electronic nubs to create an artificial tactile sensation in the new set. That night, sitting under the moon as it stared blankly down upon the realm of Tamalaria, Reggie Browler made the finishing touches to the new artificial limb.

He would install the new hardware before dawn.

* * * *

A couple of hours before dawn, as the night sky began brightening, Portenda and Shoryu approached the southern outskirts of the city of Desanadron.

His nostrils hypersensitive for any threat that might befall them, Portenda caught the familiar odors of all-night diners and alehouses, scents he recognized well in the sprawling metropolis of Desanadron. His ears, too, picked up on the half-whispered conversation of the patrolmen who padded back and forth on the city's perimeter.

Even from a distance, without the aid of unusually heightened senses, Shoryu could smell one of the guards and identify him as a Jaft. The natural funk that escaped the pores in the man's flesh left no doubt of his Racial identity. The other guard he spoke with, however, could not be so quickly identified due to his full body plate armor. Shoryu had rarely seen such heavily armed guards in the sprawling city-state of Desanadron, but he knew that sometimes caution was the better part of valor. Combined with the sudden upsurge in the number of gangs in the city, perhaps the guards would do well to be more heavily armed.

As the two travelers approached to within fifty yards, the Jaft officer, wearing the chain mail armor and blue, sleeveless and open-sided coat of an enlisted man in the military police, called out to them. "Hail and well met, travelers." He pitched a cigarette off into the dirt.

"Hail and well met, goodly sirs," Shoryu replied, waving one hand high up over his head.

Shoryu and Portenda, walking side by side, stopped a few yards before the stout Jaft trooper and his fully covered companion.

Short for a Jaft, Shoryu thought, standing a full three inches over the blue-fleshed humanoid. Still, he's just as thick as any other gent of his Race. "What can we two do for you, officer," he asked, remaining polite and proper.

"Nothing much, Cuyotai," the Jaft said with a half grin. He popped a fresh cigarette in his mouth, lit it with a match, and tossed the spent item into the dirt. "We would only ask that you keep safe and get someplace indoors quickly. These last few hours before dawn tend to be when the smaller, pettier gangs come out to play."

"If they are small and petty, what risk are they to us?" Shoryu asked gently.

The Jaft gave a soft chuckle, and the guard in the full armor guffawed rather loudly. Shoryu still couldn't get the make of the man, though Portenda knew full well what the fully armored man was; an Illeck, or dark Elf.

When did they lower their standards to this? the Bounty Hunter thought.

"They feel they've got more to prove, you see," the Jaft guard explained, his tone harsh though his eyes held nothing beyond concern for these newcomer travelers. "You both look like big boys, can probably both handle yourselves just fine. But these street punks don't play by anyone's rules, ours, their own, or the Guilds'. Just watch your step while you're out, at least until sunup. There's only a few gangs that'll bother people in broad daylight."

"Like the Marrow Suckers," Portenda said, offering his first words since the encounter with the bladeron.

The guard's eyes widened a little, and the Jaft gave Portenda a quick up-and-down.

Portenda leaned toward Shoryu slightly and said, "Gang of adolescent and young adult Khan who've lived in the city all their lives. Upstarts, not too swift in the brains or judgment department."

Shoryu nodded and kept his thoughts to himself.

"You seem to know our city's goings-on pretty well, traveler. Come to Desanadron often," the Jaft asked.

"I'm a landlord over in the sixteenth district," Portenda said flatly.

That's news to me, Shoryu thought as he gave the Bounty Hunter an appraising look. *Landlord? This wandering Bounty Hunter is a property owner?*

"Ah, my apologies, sir," the Jaft said, pitching his cigarette and lighting another fresh one. "Please gentlemen, head on in. And don't hesitate to call for help if you need it." The officer turned and headed back over to his Illeck partner.

"Something tells me we won't need much of that, will we?" Shoryu offered when he and Portenda were out of earshot of the guards.

Portenda gave him a toothy grin, and led the way into the metropolis that served as his second home.

"What exactly are we doing here, if I might ask?"

"Desanadron has one of the best official bounty offices in the lands," Portenda said, leading Shoryu further into the residential area. "Collin Caulkins comes here quite a lot for information, and he keeps an apartment in his name here, in case he needs someplace to crash for a few days at a time."

"Wouldn't it be more efficient for him to just rent a hotel room when he stops in," Shoryu asked.

"Collin's been in this business a lot longer than me, Councilor. He can afford the apartment," Portenda said without inflection. Truth be told, the Red Draconus named Collin Caulkins had earned several times over what Portenda had. However, whereas Portenda invested his earnings in real estate and security accounts in those city-states that offered them, Collin spent a lot of his money on, well, things he didn't need. The Red Draconus drank quite liberally, and enjoyed the more expensive rice wines of the Fiefdom of Lemago. He purchased martial arts training equipment in large quantities, and trained heavily for a few hours every day. He kept equipment in each of his rented apartments throughout the cities of Tamalaria, and he also furnished all of his hideaways as lavishly as he could afford to. In short, he wasted his earnings on non-essential things.

"That's right, you had mentioned him as being posted on a bounty for the Browler brothers," Shoryu said, looking around at the mostly empty sidewalks and thoroughfares. He was reminded for a moment of his home, Whitewood, where the streets pretty much emptied hours before midnight.

As the two men continued down the road they'd entered the city on, the illusion wavered and broke as he saw packs of people roaming here and there, many of them drunk and still having a good time, being loud and generally obnoxious. Further distancing itself from his beloved capital, a window up on a third story of an apartment building opened, and a gruff-looking Storm Tribe Werewolf leaned out, bleary eyed. The man glared down at the revelers.

"It's almost five in the morning, assholes," the Werewolf screamed down at the jolly, drunken Humans. "Some of us need some sleep before we head off to work in a few hours!" The window slammed closed, and the revelers giggled and cajoled with one another as they continued onto a side street, singing drunken songs and wishing each other well as they dispersed for the day.

"This city never sleeps," Portenda commented as he continued, leaving Shoryu standing in the street, staring up at the Werewolf's apartment window. He'd seldom heard foul language in Whitewood, and certainly not bellowed loudly enough to echo into the surrounding neighborhood. That sort of thing earned citizens of Whitewood a writ for disturbance of the peace!

"Hey, Councilor. Falling behind."

Shoryu looked down, and saw that Portenda had actually stopped about twenty yards away to wait for him.

"Let's get a move on."

Shoryu looked up once more, took a deep breath, smelled the general filth of the residential district they stood in, and proceeded to catch up. He didn't remember coming to this part of the city, and in truth, probably had come through in a carriage. For some reason, however, despite the filth and the low-class residents, he found he liked this part of Desanadron. It spoke volumes to his humble beginnings.

Still, he wouldn't want to live here.

* * * *

As the sun started it's final ascent into the sky, bringing with it the warmth that promised to stay throughout the day, Reggie Browler undid the last holding clamp on his old left arm with an audible click. He twisted the arm counterclockwise, holding it by the wrist, and pulled away from his body, thus removing the artificial limb. Reggie took a moment as he tucked the old arm away in his trunk to look at his left arm from the elbow up to the shoulder. "Still have to get that replaced," he muttered aloud.

The youngest of the brothers then took his finished left arm, complete with a small fan-like object in the back of the palm to collect energy in the air itself, and attached it to its base. He turned it clockwise with a grunt of effort, and smiled as the servomotors whirred to life, and the artificial nerve synapses kicked in. He flexed the metallic fingers one by one, each one multi-jointed to adjust for functionality, and marveled at the feeling of control he had over this new arm.

"Reggie! Oi!" Sean Browler sauntered down the hill from the wagon, already having taken care of his morning business. The scent of motor oil and metal filled his nostrils as he approached Reggie, and the sound of clacking metal links set his teeth on edge. The soft grassland soil under his thin-soled boots gave him a wonderful springy feeling, but as his littlest brother turned toward him, the ground seemed to tremble under him, threatening to swallow him whole. "Oh, gods above," he whispered to himself, staring at the new artificial left arm.

In order to give himself more functionality and range of movement, Reggie had made the structure of the artificial limb skeletal in design, with cables and wires guarded by iron casings and tubes made of hard but flexible materials. Each of the five fingers appeared to be more widely spaced than those on a normal Human hand, and each one was currently bent clean in half, exposing small tools tucked inside of the fingers. Despite all of the mechanical oddities, though, what frightened Sean Browler most was the fact that Reggie wanted his entire body to be made of such stuff.

Machinery, mecha, technology, Sean thought with as little venom as he could manage, for his distrust of all things mecha was great, but no greater than his care and concern for his brothers.

"What did you need, Sean," Reggie asked as he flexed the arm up and down, finally pulling on his overcoat. While his fake hand would still be exposed, it would be a blessing to have it hidden again. The right artificial arm had at least looked fairly simple, straightforward, and Sean could deal with that. But this new one? *All those wires,* he thought with a shudder.

"Dean and Ben are up, and we're going to get started on a small meal for the morning. I want you to take a look at the horses and the wagon, make sure the animals are healthy, make sure the wagon's still holding well, because we're going to try to get some better speed up today, make better time. Okay?"

"Yeah, sure thing big brother," Reggie said, his smile filled with genuine fellowship.

Sean thanked him, and stalked away. Some day, Sean thought with a pang of regret, we may need to take his tools and toys away from him.

* * * *

"Not a chance, not in all the seven hells," Benjamin Browler said to his Ninja brother Dean. "He's too good at what he does."

"Still, you have to admit that the possibility is there," Dean countered, stirring the eggs in the cast iron cooking pan suspended over the fire. "Besides, it's not even as though he'll see us. He's all the way in Desanadron, Ben," Dean said, scraping the eggs around to cook them more evenly.

"Maybe for now, but not for long. He's been following us too long to let the trail die. We've eluded him for a while, but just you watch! He'll be down on us when we try to pull off this stunt in that village. He'll recognize us, and he'll come after the lot of us. If anybody says they recognized James Svelk, he'll be right there to tell them otherwise."

"What are you two talking about," Sean Browler asked as he returned to his other younger siblings by the cooking pit. He looked down at the two young men, the Ninja clad all in black, his mask off for the time being, and the skilled Pickpocket clad in his plain traveler's tunics and jerkin.

"Collin Caulkins," Benjamin said after a moment's pause. "The Red Draconus, you know? The Bounty Hunter we've been on the lamb from for the last five months?"

Benjamin ducked his head and rooted around in one of his coat pockets, pulling out a small green apple to nosh on before the meal was complete.

"We've managed to run into him only three times, and we've always escaped with our necks intact and our wrists free of shackles, but I've got a funny feeling that he's going to catch up to us, and soon. If we run afoul of him in Shora and he sees us, he's not going to be fooled into thinking you're James Svelk. If that happens, the whole plan is shot to hell."

Sean Browler didn't often like to admit that Benjamin had a valid point, but this time, he did. They had managed to avoid capture for a while, though each of them had been imprisoned for periods of time each over the years. Caulkins, however, had been contracted to bring all four of them in, and through information contacts, Sean had learned that the contract Caulkins had taken was a dead or alive type. Even if he could not capture all four of them, he could simply kill three and arrest one. Or, he thought grimly, he could kill all four of the brothers and simply escort corpses to the Fiefdom of Lemago's capital.

"Even if he does find us," Sean said slowly, deliberately. "We are four, gentlemen. We can take him down, just like we've taken down a dozen or more of his kind. He always works alone, don't forget." Sean accepted a plate of eggs, bacon and lumpy pancakes from Benjamin. "And if he is still in Desanadron, he'll be on the road again in no time. The doesn't mean he'll know how to follow us, though."

"Um, I just had a disturbing thought," Dean said with a fork full of eggs halfway to his mouth. Ben and Sean both leaned in toward the Ninja, who set his plate down and brought his hands together in front of his face. "Guys, what if he meets up with those two I was tracking?"

Sean, chewing a piece of bacon, felt his jaw slow down and come to a complete stop after only a moment of thought. Suddenly, the smell of the fire and the food, the cool breeze blowing over the open plains, all seemed more real. The sound of songbirds filling the air with their happy music struck him as the most beautiful noise he'd ever heard.

"If he meets up with them," Sean said slowly, setting his plate down on the ground, no longer hungry. "We'll have a lot of preparation to do. It'll be for the last big brawl we ever see this side of life." With nothing more to say on the matter, Sean headed to the wagon, to check on Reggie's progress.

Chapter Six
Business

"**So,** now that we're here, are we going to get some rest?" Shoryu asked as the sun rose over the horizon. In the hour and a half since their arrival in the city, Portenda had remained fairly quiet, pointing out certain landmarks as they turned onto one side street after another, almost always avoiding the main thoroughfares. The Simpa Bounty Hunter seemed extremely knowledgeable as far as Desanadron went, and Shoryu appreciated the roundabout tour he was receiving. However, the daunting fact had come from Portenda's mouth ten minutes ago, when he informed the Councilor that the two of them had hardly covered one tenth of the city's layout.

Presently, Portenda was stopped a few dozen yards away from his apartment building. The scent of the dusky street, the sounds of tenants shouting at one another inside, the feel of the ground vibrating softly under his feet as dozens of passersby jogged along to whatever event they were running late for, all combined to make him feel once again at home. Though not as comfortable for him as Ja-Wen, the world's largest city offered him a nice second home.

"No, we're not heading in yet," he said in response to the Cuyotai's question. "We're heading to the nearby bounty office. They've got everybody's information here, so we can make some headway right off the bat. If Collin's in town, we'll find him and talk to him about the Browler brothers. If we can find them, we can find Svelk."

"I don't understand why we don't just go after the prick himself," Shoryu grumbled, remembering the insults hurled at him those many years ago by the Elven major. "Why go after his hired hands?"

"Because chances are, he'll have some hideouts that we won't uncover through conventional means." Portenda led the way away from his apartment building, turning down a narrow alley, where several Wererats played a game of chance with dice (most likely rigged, Shoryu thought) and several of the city's lesser known merchants peddled their less than legal wares.

"Also, through his employees, we may be able to get him to come to us, instead of the other way around."

At the end of the alley, Shoryu looked over his shoulder slightly and finally realized that he had walked an entire alley filled with Wererats, and none of them had tried to rob him or sell him something. *Most likely,* he thought, *they've all dealt with the big fellow in the past.* Following Portenda out into the next main road, Shoryu found himself delighted with the odors wafting in his direction from an open-front diner down the street.

As Portenda was about to head west down the road, Shoryu finally took charge of their course, grabbing the muscular right arm of the Bounty Hunter and turning him around.

Portenda did not react as Shoryu suspected he might; he didn't yell, didn't growl, and didn't take a swing at him. Instead, he merely raised one of those thick eyebrows of his.

"Food," Shoryu said simply, pointing back toward the diner. "I'm tired, I'm hungry, and I'm in desperate need of some sit down time. Besides," Shoryu said, looking away from Portenda's face. "I still don't know much about you."

"Well, we'll eat," Portenda said, motioning Shoryu to take the lead. "But I can't promise you'll learn anything new about me. I tend to talk business while on a contract."

Shoryu headed inside, with Portenda following closely behind.

They were seated quickly, and both travelers enjoyed the various aromas that came from the kitchen. The sounds of idle, early morning conversation around them gave the diner a quaint aura, which Shoryu enjoyed though Portenda could not.

"Could you wait here for a minute," he asked Shoryu, standing from his seat. "I gotta go take care of something."

"Ah, yes, taking a trip back to indoor plumbing," Shoryu said, nodding at the waitress as she poured him a cup of coffee. "No rush. I'll order without you."

"Go ahead," Portenda said. He headed toward the men's room, leaning toward the Human woman working the counter seats. "Hey Jenny," he said with a slight friendly inflection, bringing a smile to the middle-aged woman's face. "I'm over there with the Cuyotai. Just my usual if you could."

She gave him a nod and jotted down his order as he passed by to the men's room. Inside, he turned and locked the door, trying to ignore the stale urine smell of the one-person toilet room. "All right, what do you want?"

NOTHING MUCH, a familiar voice boomed. JUST THOUGHT I'D SAY HELLO. Death came out of the toilet stall, deigning to actually open the door for a hint of humor. HAD TO STOP IN HERE, SINCE IT SMELLED LIKE THE LAST CUSTOMER MIGHT HAVE LEFT SOMETHING DEAD IN THERE.

"Reducing yourself to toilet humor in the literal sense?" Portenda asked, folding his arms over his chest. "I never would have expected that from you. As for just stopping to say hello, you're the one who's full of shit now. Why are you here?"

WELL, TO BE QUITE HONEST, I HAVE BUSINESS IN THE AREA. NOT HERE, MIND YOU, BUT DOWN THE ROAD. Death turned his free left hand over, looking at a sundial on his wrist. I'VE ONLY GOT A FEW MINUTES, SO I'LL MAKE THIS QUICK. I JUST WANTED TO LET YOU KNOW THAT YOU ARE OFFICIALLY IN THE HISTORIES NOW.

"So, no need to worry about the gods being all pissed off about me, you know, breathing and all," Portenda asked, pouring as much sarcasm into his voice as he could.

THAT IS CORRECT. NOW, IF YOU'LL EXCUSE ME, I HAVE AN APPOINTMENT TO KEEP. Death swiped his scythe through the air, creating a void rift in mid-air, stepping through it and pulling it closed behind him.

Portenda flushed the toilet without having used it, washed his hands, and headed back out to his table. His meal was already sitting on the table in his spot.

"I'm assuming they know you here," Shoryu said with a wry grin, sipping his coffee.

Portenda grunted in reply, and started on his meal. Down the road, at a street performers' mobile stage, the sword swallower had a rather unfortunate accident, selecting one of the real swords instead of a prop.

* * * *

Desanadron, a city filled with various Guilds, organizations, and criminal syndicates, could be said to have no real news. The city was home to several newspapers, and a town crier or two, certainly, but there was no news. Instead, there was 'profitable information,' and whoever had the most agents in the know, or had the most thorough information available, usually had the edge over everyone else. The *Desanadron Daily Times* contracted out to multiple members of the Midnight Suns for the latest breaking stories within the city. *The City Ledger*, a slightly smaller city-wide publication, purchased its information from the Hoods, who often gathered information on regional and local politics for the exact purpose of selling the info to the paper.

Thus it came as little surprise to Ignatious Stockholm to discover that an enormous Simpa, armed to the teeth, had entered the city with a tan-furred Cuyotai that very morning. The Red Tribe Werewolf thanked the agent for the information (said agent had been instructed, as had many others, to keep a keen eye out for this man) and informed Anna, or rather William while still among their peers, that he would be heading up into the city.

Ten minutes later, he stood in the doorway of the diner in which Portenda the Quiet and Shoryu Tearfang sat. Though the agent hadn't recognized the Councilor from Whitewood, Stockholm kept himself familiar with most of the realm's movers and shakers. He adjusted his sleeveless green vest slightly, cleared his throat, and asked the young waitress who approached him if he could just get a cup of coffee. "I'll be with the Simpa and Cuyotai over there, by the window," he rumbled quietly.

Portenda smelled him as soon as the door to the diner opened, and his initial instinct was to leap from his booth seat, revolver in hand and open fire on the huge red menace. But he kept himself in check for several reasons; first and foremost, of course, being the number of innocents between himself and the Red Tribesman. The other primary reason was, of course, the fact that they were not enemies, and never really had been. However, Stockholm had bested him fairly in open combat, a feat not accomplished by any normal mortal that the Bounty Hunter had encountered.

As Stockholm approached their table, Shoryu Tearfang looked up into his eyes, and for a moment, the Red Tribe Werewolf saw the quiver of anticipation that came with anyone spotting him coming.

Hmm, Stockholm thought, handsome fellow. For a Cuyotai, he amended.

"Room for one more?" he asked Portenda as he stood at the head of their table. The Red Tribesman, not looking away from Portenda, held out his right hand, plucking his coffee from the startled waitress's hand.

The lumbering Simpa said nothing, shuffling himself over closer to the window.

"Many thanks, old friend," Stockholm said.

"You're not my old friend," Portenda grumbled, chewing on his sausage with renewed interest. "We are acquaintances and little more, Ignatious." Gods, Portenda thought, the man uses some expensive shampoo for all that hair. In a way, the Simpa Bounty Hunter thought, he smells almost sort of, well, feminine.

"You two seem to know one another fairly well," Shoryu commented as he finished the last of his meal, slurping the last drops from his coffee cup before raising it for a refresher.

"We've done battle once," Stockholm said jovially, smiling broadly at the Cuyotai and revealing a large array of teeth.

Shoryu wasn't certain he liked where this encounter might be heading, but he tried to show no fear of the thickly muscled Werewolf.

"Oh, no worries, Councilor Tearfang," Stockholm said, shocking the fear out of Shoryu and replacing it with intrigue. "I've no intention of starting a brawl here. I'm in this diner a little too often to mess the place up."

"Oh," Shoryu said, silently nodding to the waitress as he took back his refilled mug. "If I might ask, then, what do you want with us? And more importantly to me, how do you know who I am?"

"It's a little thing known as world history," Stockholm said, swiping a piece of Portenda's bacon. "I know who you are because of the War of Vandross. Plus, I keep up on most things political." As he said this, Stockholm felt something hard and metallic pressing into his ribs under the tabletop.

"Put it back on my plate or I'll blow a hole in your side," Portenda growled, keeping his head down and his teeth bared.

Stockholm smiled warmly at the Bounty Hunter, and placed the strip of meat back on his plate.

Portenda holstered his revolver once more, and finished his meal quickly.

"You should learn to keep less savage company, Councilor," Stockholm said with his usual cynical grin. "As it happens, though, I'm here because I heard you were in town and decided to help you if I could. What're you guys looking for here in Desanadron?"

Shoryu and Portenda both finished their coffee, and remained silent for a minute, each man lost in his own thoughts. Shoryu still wasn't entirely certain they could trust this Red Tribe Werewolf, who more and more gave the impression to the good Councilor that when he had done battle with Portenda, he had bested the Bounty Hunter.

"We're looking for an associate of mine," Portenda said finally, breaking the awkward silence between them. His tone was once more flat, toneless, lacking in inflection and emotion.

Back to business, Shoryu thought with a sigh. *And just when things were getting interesting again!*

"Red Draconus, a Bounty Hunter like me, but he used to be a Monk. Name of Collin Caulkins," Portenda reported. "Six feet eight inches in height, weighs approximately three hundred pounds. Right handed, but he prefers to fight southpaw. His primary martial art style is Haprika, an art that concentrates primarily on kicking attacks and hard-line defense techniques." Finished with the basics, Portenda finally cooled off enough to realize that he had fresh coffee, probably the last of his refills.

"Well, while that's an impressive resume, I'm not sure I can say I've seen him myself. I can put some folks on it, if you'd like," the Werewolf offered.

"No need," Portenda said. "We're heading over to the bounty office to check on him. He's official, so he'll be easy to track down if he's in the city. If he isn't, then maybe we'll come talk to you."

Stockholm finished his second cup of coffee, and rose to leave.

"Is Lee hanging around anywhere in town?"

"No," Stockholm said, a faint scowl forming on his face. "The little troublemaker is out east, I think in Ja-Wen or thereabouts. If you really need to contact him, I can talk to William about it."

"No, there's no need," Portenda said. "He's just usually handy to have around when I need something that's hard to find. In any event," Portenda pulled out several gold coins and depositing them on the table to pay the bill, "take care of yourself, Ignatious Stockholm."

"Likewise, Portenda." The Red Tribesman waved over his shoulder as he sauntered out of the diner.

The Bounty Hunter and Councilor only waited a minute to leave, but when they exited the diner, Shoryu searched north and south along the road. He didn't see any trace of the huge Werewolf.

"Like a ghost," Shoryu commented, sniffing the air for a trace of Stockholm. Nothing there, either. "How did he manage to disappear like that?"

"Trade secret I'd bet." Portenda led the way north. "Now come on. We're going to hit the bounty office, and if we turn up Collin's location, we'll zip on over to him. If he isn't in town, we'll find a vacancy at a hotel. Either way, we'll be getting some rest soon, so don't worry." That, of course, was the best thing Shoryu had heard since the fight with the bladeron.

* * * *

The official bounty office in the southwest region of the city stood two stories tall, and appeared on the outside to be a place of business, just like the office in Whitewood. The primary difference on the exterior, however, was that instead of a fishing store front, this office had a sign outside that clearly named the building- Desanadron Bounty Office Station #2. Two well-armed Humans stood guard out front, both men dressed in scale mail armor, some of the strongest and most durable protection available.

"Is it just me, or are they becoming the most prevalent Race in the world?" Shoryu whispered as Portenda swung the waist-height gate open, stepping onto the front walkway that led to the double doors between the guards.

"It's not just you," Portenda replied, his voice still devoid of emotion or interest. "It's been happening for about two centuries. It isn't the first time in history that it's happened, either."

Portenda and Shoryu approached the guards and the doors, and Portenda halted for a moment just outside of the entrance. "Gentlemen, I am Portenda the Quiet, Bounty Hunter. I am registered with the International Bounty Alliance, and give permission to you and your colleagues to perform any investigative procedure you feel necessary while I am within, or without. Nod if you understand."

Both Human guards nodded, keeping their eyes forward, though a hint of perspiration had cropped up on their foreheads, a briny odor that Shoryu would have appreciated if he hadn't felt the day to be relatively cool. *Nervous sweat*, he wondered?

Portenda opened the door to the main entrance, and Shoryu followed him inside, giving the left hand guard a quick look as he passed him by. He thought he'd heard a sigh of relief escape from the man when Portenda passed inside.

In the main lobby of the bounty office, several dozen men of various Races and apparent Classes sat in comfortable lounge chairs or at a bar in the far left corner, opposite the door. Open hallway entrances stood at both ends of the lobby, giving the impression that business could be conducted anywhere in the building. Shoryu craned his head around to take in all of his surroundings. "Now this is impressive," he said aloud.

The two men approached the bar in the corner, and Portenda raised one finger toward the Jaft barkeep.

"Greetings again to you, Portenda the Quiet," the barkeep said, filling a glass mug with some scum-colored fluid, passing it down the bar with a skilled flick of his wrist.

A half-Troll at the far end caught the drink and began to swiftly consume it, and as Shoryu watched the vile liquid disappear down the man's throat, he wondered what could possibly be in the drink that appealed to one such as that man.

"What can we do for you," the Jaft asked as flatly as he could.

"Bob in?" Portenda asked, casting his gaze about the room.

"Yeah, he's in the billiards hall," replied the barkeep. "Want a drink before you go talk to him?"

"No, thanks. The good Councilor might need one, though," the Simpa said, pointing over his shoulder at the Cuyotai with his thick thumb.

The Jaft poured a shot of bourbon for Shoryu, and handed it to Portenda, who turned with the glass to the Councilor. "Bottoms up, Shoryu," Portenda said.

"Isn't it a bit early for that?" Shoryu protested, waving his hands before him to reject the drink.

Portenda downed the shot with one tip of his head, handing it back to the Jaft barkeep. "I mean, don't get me wrong, I like a stiff drink now and again same as anyone, but at this hour?"

"We haven't been to sleep yet, so it's not early, Councilor. It's late," Portenda reasoned, leading the way through the entryway that had been to the left when they first entered the main lobby.

Shoryu saw the wisdom in this, and now regretted having rejected the drink.

The sound of mixed voices and laughter dimly filled the hallway they walked down, echoing off of the fine pine walls and barren concrete floor. A tinge of oily gray mist flowed into the hallway from the end they approached, thick cigarette smoke that never really quite made its way out of the building. The scent of the smoke led Shoryu to believe that nearly everyone in the billiards hall was puffing away on the cheapest available brand, and when he entered the room behind Portenda, his eyes confirmed what his nostrils had already reported.

Whether by dislike of the habit or concern for his own health, it appeared that Portenda was the only Bounty Hunter in the room that wasn't puffing away on a cigarette or pipe, as a few of the older Humans in the billiards hall were. Ten individual pool tables had been arranged about six yards away from those in any direction and the wall for the outer tables, and nearly every table was occupied by four players, each man armed heavily and wearing a fair amount of protective gear. Only one man stood out in this respect, wearing a sharp-looking brown suit jacket over a tan vest, white shirt, black tie and brown slacks.

The well-dressed man stood out in other ways to Shoryu, who realized that this stranger among the flock was probably Bob, the man that Portenda had asked the barkeep about. Bob stood only five and a half feet in height, and appeared to weigh about twenty to thirty pounds over the median weight for a man of his apparent age and height. A calm, subtle look of wisdom graced his handsome features, and his slicked-back hair lent itself to the overall look of a businessman rather than a brute. The man lit a fresh cigarette, and chuffed smoke up into the air as he looked up at the approaching lycanthropes.

Looks like a Human, Shoryu said, though he could not be certain exactly of that. He could not detect the man's scent through all of the smoke and the various other distinct Racial odors wafting through the air. However, as he came to a stop beside Portenda only a few feet from Bob, Shoryu could feel a distinct aura of strangeness.

"Portenda," the man said, his voice a smooth baritone to match his slick appearance. "It's good to see you're well. And who may I ask is your companion?" Bob nodded his head to Shoryu.

"This is Shoryu Tearfang, Councilor of Whitewood in the Elven Kingdom," Portenda said by way of introduction. He turned slightly to Shoryu, and said, "Shoryu, this is Robert Keynorth, but everybody calls him Bob. Bob's a highly respected member of the bounty hunting community, and one of the proudest Sidalis you'll ever meet."

Sidalis, Shoryu thought, *a mutant. That would explain why he smells mostly Human but not entirely.*

"It's a pleasure to meet you, Bob." Shoryu extended one paw.

Bob accepted, and the two men shook hands.

To Shoryu, the mutant's grip felt firm and warm enough, but there was a subtle and constant vibration in the man's very bones, it seemed. "Bob, if I might be so bold as to ask, what is your mutant power?"

"Oh, that?" Bob said with a smile. "I can create sonic concussion waves by clapping my hands together." He took a puff of his cigarette. "Also, if I place my hand against a solid surface or a person, I can generate force waves that way through the ground or a bounty-head themselves. It's handy, but then there's my deformity," Bob said uncomfortably.

Shoryu had forgotten momentarily, fascinated by the man's mutant power, that as a Sidalis he would invariably have a physical deformity to go along with the powers.

"What's your deformity," Shoryu asked before he could think of how rude a question that must be to ask a Sidalis. "Oh my, look, I didn't mean anything by it," he blurted, but Bob was already shaking one hand to wave the apology off.

"It's not a problem, Mr. Tearfang," Bob said.

Portenda had remained silent during the entire exchange, as he knew exactly how it would progress. After all, this was almost word-for-word how his first exchange with Bob had gone.

Bob reached down, cigarette held in his mouth, and brought his left foot up onto his right knee, leaning back against one of the pool tables for support. He removed his shoe, which revealed a black silk sock, and Shoryu couldn't see what the problem was. Then Bob removed the sock, and Shoryu understood quite well. "You see, Mr. Tearfang, I have no feet," Bob said, wiggling his appendage. "But sometimes it is very useful to have four hands instead."

Bob used his 'foot' to point a finger up at Shoryu, who took an impulsive step back, both fascinated and horrified at the prospect of having to walk around on hands all the time.

Bob laughed aloud at the Councilor's reaction, as did several of the Bounty Hunters around them, and put his sock and shoe back on.

Finally, Portenda spoke once again, bringing Shoryu's attention into sharper focus. "Bob hears most of the information that goes through this office. He has since he established it about twenty years ago," the Simpa rumbled in his flat monotone. "Bob, I need to get down to business, because the Councilor and I need to get some rest soon. We're looking for Collin Caulkins. He been through lately?"

Bob stubbed out his cigarette in an ashtray and scratched his chin. "You know, he passed through not two days ago, actually. He's probably still in town, checking out information on a contract he's on. Mind if I ask why you're looking for him?"

"Well, I'm on a job myself, and the target happens to be employing Collin's targets in his business. So we're hoping that we might find my target through Collin's quarry," Portenda said. "Is there any way we could contact him, or find out where he's at right now?"

"No need," a gravely voice said from behind the Simpa Bounty Hunter.

Shoryu and Portenda turned, and found, standing in the entryway a tall, brutal-looking Red Draconus. The dragon-man wore heavy iron half-plate armor, complete with armored sleeves and shoulder plates. The iron was tinted red, just like his scales, and aside from this armoring, he wore no protective gear. For a Draconus, regardless of sub-species, armor wasn't much of a necessity since their scales usually provided good protection. The only exception in Tamalaria were the Yellow Draconus, whose scales were generally much softer and thinner than the other sub-species.

"Ah, Collin, it's good to see you," Portenda said, for once breaking with his usual expressionless demeanor and offering a grin. He stepped forward, as did the Red Draconus, and both men extended a hand to one another. "I trust business has been well for you?"

"As well as can be expected," replied the former Monk Draconus. Collin peered around Portenda's broad shoulder at Shoryu. "Who's the Cuyotai?"

"My partner on my current job," Portenda said flatly. "Collin, this is Shoryu Tearfang. He is a Councilor in the city of Whitewood. My contract is government-issued, so he's along for the work."

"To say nothing of the fact that my family bow was taken," Shoryu added with a hint of indignity. "A pleasure to meet you, Mr. Caulkins." Shoryu offered his own paw for the Red Draconus.

When Collin took it, Shoryu nearly cried out, as the Red Draconus didn't apparently know the meaning of the word 'restraint'. The grip was solid, and ground down on Shoryu's hand quickly and sharply.

"Likewise," the Draconus replied with a smile, letting go of the Councilor's hand.

Shoryu did not rub his hand as he might have at home, or in other circumstances; showing any weakness in a place like the bounty office didn't seem like a good idea.

"So, what're you fellows looking for me for?"

Bob excused himself to take his turn at one of the pool tables, and Portenda led the way back toward the main lobby, speaking to Collin as Shoryu followed behind.

"You're on the Browler brothers contract, right?" Portenda skipped right to the matter at hand.

"Yeah, I am. You're lucky I'm still in town, because I finally got a lead on them," the Red Draconus said. "If I didn't need to make some preparations first, I'd be long gone already. Don't tell me you're trying to muscle in on my work." He waggled one gnarled, scaly finger at the Simpa. "That's never been your style."

"Actually, my contract is for a man who's presently using the Browler brothers as hired hands," Portenda said. "I'm hoping to piggyback off of your work in a way."

That brought a smile to the Draconus' lips. "You want to find the Browlers and interrogate them about your man, eh? Not a problem." Collin stepped ahead of Portenda and led the way outside.

In the brisk mid-morning air, Shoryu caught a brief second wind, waking himself up just enough to realize how desperately tired he was.

"When do you want to get going?"

"We both need some sleep. Is it all right if we crash at your place?" Portenda asked.

"Not a problem. We can head out after you've got your beauty rest," the Red Draconus chided. "My place isn't but a few minutes from here. While you guys settle in for a bit, I'll get the last of my supplies."

"So, where are the Browler brothers now?" Shoryu asked from behind the two lumbering Bounty Hunters.

"They're in the south-central plains, just west of the Fiefdom of Lemago," Collin said. "I've got a reserved teleportation through Jonah Staples to the town of Menwa in the Fiefdom. It'll put us about a full day ahead of them east."

"Any idea where they're heading," Portenda asked as the trio headed across the busy street toward an apartment building.

"I suspect they're heading back to their favorite hidey-hole in the Port of Arcade." Collin plucked a key from one of his various pouches and handed it to Portenda. "I don't see why you don't go sleep at your place," the Red Draconus noted.

"Because it's across town, and your place is right here," Portenda said. He handed the key to Shoryu, who shrugged his shoulders and headed inside.

Safely out of earshot, the Simpa Bounty Hunter whispered to his colleague, "And I think the Councilor could use a nice fluffy bed for a while instead of the ground or a cot. He's married after all."

"Ah, pampering wife," asked Collin.

"Not entirely certain about that. But I'll tell you this, my friend," Portenda said with a wicked grin that showed off his pearly whites. "Attractive and attentive she may be, but a push-over she is not. I'd hate to imagine what a domestic dispute might look like in that house."

With a hearty chuckle, Collin shook Portenda's hand once more, and the two men parted ways for a while. They would be traveling together when Shoryu and Portenda awoke, and nothing more needed to be said for the time being.

When Portenda arrived at Collin's place, the good Councilor was dead asleep on the Draconus's pillow-topped bed, facedown and snoring.

* * * *

Sean sat in the back of the wagon, thinking over the group's plans for the near future. Benjamin drove the horses ably, and for the most part without complaint. Reggie appeared to be fast asleep, tucked into one of his blankets with his head on his tool bag, his eyes tightly closed. Dean sat with his back to the opposite wall to Sean, and now and again the Ninja rose to check behind the brothers and their wagon, keeping a keen eye out for any sign of pursuit.

"What do you think, big brother?" Dean said after a while, his back against the wall of the wagon, checking his equipment.

"About what?" asked Sean irritably, his train of thought broken. The pervasive odor of his own sweat was starting to bother him, along with the fact that they hadn't eaten food that they hadn't had to cook in many days. Sean didn't mind eating the food that Dean and Ben cooked, but it did leave him wishing that they had better supplies. The stuff they purchased usually had good longevity, but the taste was almost always sub-par. *And besides,* he thought, *my brothers and I shouldn't have to make all of our own meals. When was the last time we ate out at a diner? Of course,* he mused, *that's part of the problem when one lives life with a collection of warrants out against them.*

"About our chances of evading both Bounty Hunters," Dean said. "I am confident that we could take down one of them, if he were to come at us alone. They can make all of the preparations they want, but we would defeat them. Both at one time, however." He looking away from Sean, out the back of the wagon, and shook his head gently from side to side.

"We don't have to evade them," Sean finally said, breaking an awkward silence that brewed between them for a full minute. "Ben and I are the only ones that are on the bounty lists. You and Reggie could break away clean and try to make something better for yourselves."

"You know I can't do that," Dean rasped back, his eyes squinting close together, his brows furrowed in heated frustration with his older brother. "I will not leave you and Ben to your fates. You know that big brother." The Ninja once more looked away. "What would Momma think?"

"Momma would know that I was just doing what's best for you and Reggie," Sean retorted hotly, raising his voice without meaning to. "She told me to take care of you boys, and that's my intention! We both know that there isn't a cell in the world that could hold Benjamin for more than a few days, so he'd get out without a problem. Or, we could get some documents forged, get you guys out of the watchlists, so long as you'd lay low for a while. Besides, Ben's bounty is for some relatively petty stuff."

"About a hundred charges of petty stuff," Ben said from the driver's seat. "Hey Sean, you got a smoke I could bum off of you?"

Sean produced a pack of cigarettes and tossed it up to Ben, who fumbled with the airborne pack for a moment, pulling it close at last and drawing one out. He inhaled deeply as he lit it with a match, and tossed the pack back. "They'd have me in the clink for a while with so many charges."

"Still, that's not the overall point, guys," Sean said, addressing Reggie as well, whose eyes had fluttered open during his last outburst. "The point is, the Draconus is after Ben and I, and it'd be easy enough for Ben to take off with you guys and lay low. We don't have to go through with this plan of Svelk's just because he wants us to."

"But big brother, we already told him we would. "And besides," Reggie added with a hint of worry in his voice, "we all agreed that we'd stick together, always. You aren't really thinking of leaving us, are you big brother?"

Oh gods, Sean thought, I hate that big soulful eyes routine of his. Still, it worked well, and Sean shook his head slightly, folding his arms over his chest. After a few minutes, he finally spoke again to his brothers.

"All right, we'll go through with the plan," he said, keeping his head down. "However, if the both Bounty Hunters show up, you guys have to pull a quick hit-and-run on one of them, then get the hell out of town. Dean, you said that the Simpa still had the Councilor with him, right?"

"Indeed, though he appeared quite skilled in combat as well," Dean said. "At least, as an archer. Cuyotai are not generally the best melee fighters."

"Good," Sean said. "That's good to know. Let's formulate a plan, guys, and let's make it work. We can use the Cuyotai as a quick getaway, if we need to. Dean, if you got in close, you think you could immobilize him?"

"Certainly," replied the Ninja, who already knew where this was going.

"Very good. If all three of them come at us, we'll do what we do best. We'll be ruthless criminals, as everyone thinks of us, and we'll take the good Councilor as a hostage," Sean Browler said. Finally, he felt they all had a chance of surviving an assault by both Portenda the Quiet and Collin Caulkins.

Chapter Seven
Mistakes

Well, it's good to see you again, Portenda." Jonah Staples came out of his back storage room.

Shoryu detected various spices and herbs, most with an acrid, bitter smell, and the air itself tasted of chemicals. The Cuyotai Hunter could also hear someone else in the back room, muttering to herself angrily. He couldn't make out the exact words the woman was saying, but he could tell the words were of the Elven language.

When the Elf came out of the back room, Shoryu understood distinctly why she seemed so irritated; her brow had a sheen of sweat on it, and her blouse wasn't properly buttoned. They had apparently interrupted the couple during their 'inventory check.'

"As it is to see you, Jonah," Portenda said, shocking Shoryu and Collin both by offering the tiny Human Alchemist an embrace. They hugged briefly, and pulled away from one another with a sort of familiarity that spoke of trials shared.

"Are you a father yet, Jonah? It would appear that we have interrupted your practice run at making the child."

Portenda's chiding brought a flush to both Jonah and Elisa's cheeks.

"No, not yet," Jonah said, finally looking away from the Simpa and spotting his client. "Ah, Mr. Caulkins! I've got almost everything prepared for your departure! Will these gentlemen be accompanying you?"

"Yes they will, Mr. Staples," Collin said plainly, putting a strange glass obelisk back on its shelf. He had forgotten he was holding onto it when Portenda had shown momentary warmth toward the Human, who appeared to barely be of a man's age. "Will there be any additional charge?"

"For Portenda? No, no extra charge," Jonah said with a smile. "I'll just pop on over into the Site chamber and finish the last of the inscriptions." He pulled a nub of chalk from a pocket. "Dear, could you bring them some tea or something to drink?"

Elisa shot her husband a look, and the Alchemist bounded off to the Site chamber.

"You haven't changed much, Elisa," Portenda said to the Elven woman, who finished fixing her blouse.

Shoryu couldn't believe the lack of modesty in this woman, but she didn't appear to be like most Elves. After all, he thought, she was with a man whose Class was among the Scientist types, and a Human at that. Elves tended to sneer at Scientists, or at least most of them, with the exception of the Psychics, whom they felt belonged to the Mage classification.

"Nor have you, Portenda," she said pointedly.

While she was a beautiful specimen of Elf, her harsh, city-born tone of voice, her mannerisms, and her gruff stance all belied the usual impression got of the sylvan folk of the woods. She almost reminded Shoryu more of an Illeck than of the first-born Elves. "Oh, by the way Mr. Caulkins, you still haven't paid for this service." She addressed the Red Draconus with voice and brilliant eyes. "You will have to pay before using the teleportation site." She crossed her arms over her ample chest and flicked one hand to indicate he should place the money directly into it.

Collin pulled a pouch from his belt, stalked forward, and grinned blithely at her, setting the money in her hand. "All there, Mrs. Staples," he said. "You can count it if you don't trust me."

"He's good for it, Elisa," Portenda said on his fellow Bounty Hunter's behalf, but the Elven Alchemist poured the money on a nearby workbench anyway, counting out the coins. She plucked two from the total, and came back to Collin with them, holding them out to him.

"You miscalculated, Mr. Caulkins," she said in an even tone. "Two over." She dropped the coins into his open claw. "When he's ready for you, Jonah will call. Did any of you want tea, or something else to drink while you wait?"

"No thanks," Portenda and Collin said in unison. "Councilor Tearfang may want some tea, however," Portenda suggested. Shoryu nodded at Elisa Staples, and she gave him a quick up-and-down.

"Very good. I'll bring you some directly," she said to Shoryu.

"Um, if you've any melong tea, that'd be great," he said without a thought.

Elisa Staples halted in her steps, however, at the Councilor's words.

"What? Did I say something wrong," he asked, looking at the wide eyes of Jonah's bride.

"You spend a lot of time around Elves, Councilor," she asked.

"Well, yes," Shoryu replied, trying hard to keep the sarcastic edge out of his voice. "I'm a Councilor of Whitewood, capital of the Elven Kingdom. And, like your husband, I too have an Elven wife."

Elisa then gave him an 'ah, that explains it' look, and hustled out of the room, returning quickly with a piping cup of tea.

Shoryu could smell the sweet aroma of melong leaves in the brew, and he took a greedy gulp of the hot liquid. "Thank you very much. We've only had a few hours of rest, and the caffeine is much appreciated." He finished the drink with a second pull and handed her the cup back.

Jonah called for them from the site chamber, and all three men departed from the main room of the Alchemy shop. Soon, Elisa saw a flash of light under the curtain in the doorway, and Jonah returned to the main room, flipping the sign on the front door to 'closed' once again. He gave her a single look, and she grinned and nodded. While Portenda, Shoryu and Collin flew through the time-space vortex of Alchemical teleportation, Jonah Staples got back to practice.

* * * *

It had happened before, Portenda thought, and he guessed it couldn't always be avoided. Sometimes, even in magic, practitioners made minor mistakes. They rushed the incantations of a spell, or used the wrong ingredients in a long, involved ritual, and things went to hell and back pretty quick. Distractions sometimes got in the way, or the magic user could be mentally addled by drink or drugs, and get a few words wrong in the casting of a spell. It wasn't entirely unheard of.

The same could be said of science, and he would be one of the first people to tell you that this was so. While Collin Caulkins was uttering as many curse words as he could in his native tongue, and Shoryu was looking around with a decided expression of confusion, Portenda merely sighed and sagged a little. He knew where they were, and knew that only a small miscalculation had been made. The trio had arrived not in the small township that Jonah had intended to send them to, but instead in a vast expanse of woodland about thirty miles south of it. They weren't as bad off as they could have been, Portenda thought, thinking back to the little side trip that he'd been forced to take with Jonah and Elisa to the Dwarven Territories.

"I'm getting my money back just as soon as I get back to Desanadron again," Collin grumbled, looking around the woods they stood in. "Do either of you have any idea where in the seven hells we are?"

"Calm down, Collin." Portenda took a deep whiff of the air. He could detect the scents of woodland wildlife around them, along with several other odors, mostly plant life. "We're about thirty miles south of the original destination, nothing more. It was a small miscalculation, perfectly acceptable. Shoryu, you smell anything out of the ordinary?"

"Not really," reported the Cuyotai, who'd taken his bow off of his back. "But there's signs of people having passed through here." Shoryu moved slowly in a half-crouch east, toward where the trees grew thicker together.

Portenda scanned the ground for tracks, and found nothing but animal footprints.

Shoryu looked back at the Simpa, and for once, felt he had an advantage over the lumbering bruiser. "You're looking in the wrong place." Shoryu pointed up into the trees. He had spotted the signs of climbers and tree-moving peoples almost immediately upon arriving in a flash of light and smoke from Desanadron. Added into this observation was the fact that he had lived in the forest for many years and knew that the behavior of the animals of these woods was far from normal.

For starters, the birds kept their nests in branches far lower in this area than they did in the forests of the Elven Kingdom. There was a sense of nervousness, tension, in those birds that he spotted and smelled living higher up, as though they expected their homes to be dashed aside at any given moment. That told him right away that there were either very traditional Elves living in these woods, most likely in a rope village up among the upper reaches of the trees themselves, or creatures that preferred moving from tree to tree. There was one other explanation, and the creatures and this third possibility caused him to draw his weapon out. The third possibility was a resident Ninja clan.

Normally, he wouldn't have known how to look for signs of a Ninja's passing, as they were usually good about hiding their tracks. However, even in the fair woodlands of the Elves, Shoryu didn't have to sniff too hard to locate the trace odor of a snake or other poisonous creature. Here, he smelled nothing of the sort, which might indicate that the animals were hunted or maintained in a secure location, where the shinobi warriors could extract the venom and poisons directly from their natural sources. He'd known little or nothing about Ninjas before residing in Whitewood. A local Guild in Whitewood, however, employed a large number of such warriors, and in dealing with the local heads of the Guilds, Councilor Tearfang had learned a great deal about the many Classes of Tamalaria, and their respective ways of life.

"All right, let's just head north and avoid any potentially hostile encounters," Collin spat. He was still furious about the miscalculation that had dropped him and his companions here in these woods instead of the intended town, but he wasn't just going to stand around and do nothing about it.

"Agreed," said Portenda. "Tearfang, let's go," he said to Shoryu, who kept his eyes directed skyward.

Though he lowered his right hand, he didn't put his bow back in its place. He had the distinct impression that even at that moment, eyes other than those of the local animals were upon them, keeping tabs on their movements and actions. He didn't dare be caught unawares.

As the trio marched north, Portenda sensed the movements behind them, up in the trees, while Shoryu visually caught the movements when he looked back for them. Only Collin seemed to remain completely in the dark, but in truth he knew the risk to the group better than either of the lycanthropes. He'd been in these woods before, just like Portenda. Unlike the Simpa, however, he'd been forced to deal with the clan of Ninjas who made this wooded region their home.

Collin Caulkins was all too familiar with the Tokusa Ninja Clan.

* * * *

The first shuriken flew, when the trio had about five hundred yards before they would be clear of the woods. As with Dean Browler, Portenda heard the multi-pointed star fly from its owner's hand, and he turned back to fire his pistol up, deflecting the projectile. Unlike Dean Browler, however, who'd been trained in the Obura style of ninjitsu, their present assailant hadn't thrown only one shuriken. A second and third followed closely behind, one sinking home in Portenda's exposed forearm, and the other sticking harmlessly into Collin's shoulder plate.

"You know, this could be interesting," the Simpa Bounty Hunter remarked.

Shoryu Tearfang, his nerves standing on end, peered around the area, his eyes directed skyward. *There,* he thought, spotting one of the Ninjas as he, she or it made a quick leap from one treetop to another.

Shoryu took careful aim at the tree where his target had been, and just before releasing his arrow, he pivoted on his heels and let fly. The thin shaft of mystical wood, tipped with solid steel, made almost no noise as it tore through a few leaves on its way to the Ninja's throat. There was a strangled gurgling noise, and then a loud thump and rustling of leaves.

Portenda and Collin had both seen the Ninja fall from the tree in full uniform, his body limp and his legs flapping about. Shoryu's single shot had pierced the man's throat, effectively delivering them from one of their assailants. With the Ninja down, Shoryu bound up for the reaches of the lower branches of the trees around them.

"Interesting," Collin said as Portenda assumed an exotic fighting stance. "The Ninja clan that rules these woods is not to be trifled with, my fine furry friend."

Another shuriken flew at the Bounty Hunters, swifter than the first projectile but only accompanied by one other shot. Portenda managed to duck and roll away from danger, while Collin leaped backward, snatching the shuriken up between two of his clawed fingers.

"I thought you said these guys are good," Portenda said flatly, looking around for the Councilor from Whitewood. Though he hadn't said as much, he felt terribly responsible for the Cuyotai's well-being, especially after assuring his wife Ellen Daires-Tearfang that her husband would be just fine upon his return. The Simpa sincerely hoped that Shoryu wasn't off somewhere, chasing down their adversaries up in the treetops. After all, one slip, and Shoryu would make Portenda into a liar. He worried more about Shoryu's nimbleness than the quality of Ninja up in the trees, because thus far, they hadn't proven very efficient shinobi.

"They are," Collin said, a little perplexed. "Or at least, they used to be. The Tokusa are ruthless speed-type Ninja, using projectile combat and swift hit-and-run tactics on their foes. But these shinobi don't seem very, well, effective," the Red Draconus said quietly.

Shoryu, meanwhile, was bounding from tree branch to tree branch, hot on the heels of two Ninjas in black uniforms and masks, both men looking back now and then to see how close the archer was to them. When he judged the distance and speed of the Ninja as best he could, Shoryu finally stopped atop a branch, took quick aim, and fired another arrow.

As one of the Ninja landed on his next perch, the arrow struck him in the leg, and he fell screaming to the forest floor some fifty feet below.

There was a sickening crunch upon impact, and Shoryu knew for certain that the black-clad Ninja was dead.

The other quarry appeared to have vanished however. *They're fast,* Shoryu thought, his breath hitching slightly in his chest. *They're fast, and I'm getting older.* At a little less than one hundred years of age, Shoryu had plenty of years ahead of him. However, even he knew that a Cuyotai's prime had passed him about twenty years ago. Still, he had managed to keep up with the escaping Ninjas for a while, and he had two victims to his name for this encounter.

Scanning the area briefly, Shoryu started back toward the Bounty Hunters.

Several kunei flew at Portenda, but this time he managed to dodge each weapon successfully. As the last of the knives stuck in the ground, he knelt down and fired up into the trees without looking at his target.

A loud, "Guh" followed the whip-crack report of his revolver. Another Ninja fell from his perch up in the tree branches. "How many of these pajama-wearing cretins could there be in one team," he asked Collin.

"Usually, they work in teams of three to ten. Judging by our distance from the border, they probably assume we're intruders into their territory." Collin caught one of the kunei and darted it back at his unseen foe.

Another sharp noise of pain came from the upper boughs of the trees, and yet another body fell to the forest floor. "Which would be correct, in an odd way."

"Well, we didn't mean to intrude," Portenda grumbled, thinking of how many ways he could curse at Jonah when he saw the young Human Alchemist again. "I don't suppose these Ninjas listen to reason though, do they?"

As he posed this question, four Ninjas in full uniform dashed out of the trees further into the forest toward them, weapons drawn. Four men of roughly the same size and shape, Humans all by the smell of them.

Portenda took one look at their pattern of movement, and brought his revolver up to eye level. He opened fire twice, dropping two of the agents instantly. The remaining two took refuge behind separate trees, and for that the Simpa was grateful. After all, he was out of bullets in the chamber.

As he began reloading, keeping his eyes on the two trees behind which his enemies lay, Collin smiled brightly. Shoryu landed with a heavy thud a few feet away, and the Red Draconus nearly launched a thrust kick at him in his surprise. "You know, you could have yelled or something," Collin complained at the smiling Cuyotai.

"I know. How many left right here?" Shoryu sniffed the air and quickly identifying two more Humans.

"Just the two that we're aware of. They're hiding." Portenda snapped his revolver shut with a full load of eight rounds.

"Not for long." Collin stepped in front of his two companions. "Keep behind me for a minute. Things are going to get very warm around here."

Crimson light flared behind his reptilian eyes, and a low rumbling began in his throat.

Portenda grabbed Shoryu by the shoulder and pulled him further away from the Red Draconus.

"What's going on?" Shoryu whispered.

"Barbecue," was the Simpa's only reply.

As Shoryu watched, Collin Caulkins reared back and then bent forward sharply, opening his mouth and blowing a stream of fire at one of the trees a Ninja was using for cover.

A huge scorched hole was left in the tree, and there appeared to be something wobbling back and forth in front of the hole on the other side. The scent of burned flesh filled the air, and there came a retching sound as the dying Ninja fell over, blood spuming up from his throat.

Before the other Ninja could run away, Collin breathed another jet of flames at him, igniting his black uniform and also setting the poor man's hair on fire.

Screaming and gibbering like a madman, the Ninja fell dead after only twenty or so yards.

"That was rather gruesome," Shoryu commented, watching the second burning Ninja with a hint of pity in his heart. "I feel kind of sorry for him."

"Don't," Collin said, spitting in the Ninja's direction. "They know the risks of their way of life, Councilor. Now, how many have we taken out thus far?"

"I tagged two thus far, but one got away from me," Shoryu reported.

"I've shot three," Portenda said flatly. "Collin, you hit one with his own weapon, and breathed fire on two. That brings our total to eight. How many more might there be?"

"One or two, no more than that I'd imagine." Collin pulled a metallic object from one of his pouches, and pressed a small button on top of it. He breathed on the object, then held it toward Shoryu, who raised an eyebrow at him.

"Go ahead, blow on it," Collin said, looking around the woodland, checking for signs of attack.

Shoryu did as he was asked, and Portenda followed suit.

Collin tapped the glass surface of the trinket, which looked a lot like a compass with a black background.

Shoryu looked at the object, which now showed three green dots in the center, two red dots a short distance off, and several blue arrows around the edges of the circular surface. Two red arrows then appeared, and Shoryu, puzzled, looked up at the Red Draconus.

"What is that thing," Shoryu asked, looking in the direction of one of the red moving dots.

"It's an artifact I picked up in Ja-Wen," Collin said, looking down at the compass artifact and then up toward the same red dot. "You, Portenda and I are all indicated by the green dots. Unknown humanoid or lycanthrope targets are indicated by red dots. Unknown large sized animals or monsters are indicated as blue dots. An arrow means that the detected type of creature is just outside of the compass's radius."

"Magic," Shoryu asked.

"You bet," Collin said, handing the compass to Portenda.

Portenda looked at the device, looked up, and took aim into the trees. He fired once, the boom of his revolver echoing through the forest. After a moment, one of the red dots on the compass faded, vanishing completely in a minute. "You see? With this, you don't have to second guess where your enemies might be."

"What if he just shot an innocent traveler," Shoryu asked, bringing a frightened look to Collin's countenance.

"No, that was one of those Ninjas," Portenda said confidently, sniffing the air. "There *is* another traveler around here, however. The other Ninjas should be distracted by whoever it is by now, so we should get moving." The Simpa Bounty Hunter handed the artifact back to Collin and holstered the mecha weapon.

Without another word, but keeping themselves ready in mind for confrontation, the trio headed north once more, exiting the woods after five minutes of walking carefully along.

* * * *

"We've got a sighting," said one of the border guards to his commanding officer. "Sir, if I might see the portrait of the criminals again?" The guard, like all of his fellow border patrolmen, was dressed in the traditional garb for his post, simple half plate armor arranged in a unique fashion. The armor on his upper body consisted of several interchangeable plates of iron, each approximately three inches in radius. Spring clips kept the plates together, and provided another layer of protection. The armor plates on the shoulders were cylindrical, and fitted over the individual troopers' shoulders quite nicely. The overall effect of the upper armor was a fully customizable upper armor, to provide protection and ease of movement.

The armored leggings and greaves were another matter altogether, and most often were personalized to each trooper, guard, and constable in the Fiefdom of Lemago. The captain of the squad that had the Browler brothers in their sights wore a simple set of blue steel chain pants, which were lightweight and flexible. His subordinates had on the traditional heavy plate leggings customary to the southern districts and townships of the Fiefdom, and he couldn't understand for the life of him why they would choose to reduce their own speed in such a fashion.

Despite the differences in equipment, the men under the captain's command all were of a like mind to him. The captain of the unit handed over a group of artists' sketches to the trooper who'd requested them, and the man peered at the papers and then up through his spyglass once more. "Captain Jugura, it is them for certain, sir. It is the Browler Brothers Gang."

"It was foolish of them to come back through our glorious empire," Captain Jugura, commented. At six and a half feet in height, and weighing approximately three hundred pounds, the captain was certainly not a small man like most of his Human and Elven countrymen. He was a half-Jaft, bred by his Jaft mother and his Human father. Of the two, he took mostly after his father in his ways of life. His father had been a noble Samurai guard in the Emperor's court, and had lived a life of honor and duty. His mother had been a bit wilder, and only achieved a position as a constable for the township of Fong after several years of hard work.

Captain Jugura shook off the thoughts of his heritage, and tried to focus on the task at hand. He had before him a reasonably manageable situation; the gang of four criminals, brothers all, was traveling in a covered wagon that was being drawn by two excellent chargers in prime condition. The brother in the driver's seat had been identified by the trooper with the spyglass as Benjamin Browler, who was wanted in the Fiefdom of Lemago for suspicion of armed robbery, a crime that in the empire could be punished by life imprisonment. Since the Fiefdom's acceptance of metal coins as currency, robbery had become a common crime, and no longer carried the sentence of death that it once held.

Inside the covered wagon then would also be Sean Browler, who was wanted not only in the Fiefdom of Lemago, but in several other territories that the Fiefdom had good relations with as well. If he captured all four brothers here, in the empire's borders, Jugura would have to process all four of them, and eventually hand Sean Browler over to another territory, most likely the Elven Kingdom to the west. Benjamin Browler was also wanted in Palen, but that city-state had the Greenskin Nation and several hundred square miles of free lands between itself and the Fiefdom. They would not ask for the Pickpocket.

As for the other two known Browler brothers, Reginald and Dean, well, they could not be held on charges without some sort of evidence. However, captain Jugura knew that the one called Dean had trained with a Ninja in Desanadron, and followed the olden ways of the Obura Ninja Clan, one of the eldest of the clans still operating in the empire. As a Ninja not recorded on that clan's student roster, however, Dean Browler did not carry the weight of a wanted man in any capacity. He could not even be suspected of a crime, but he could be held for forty-eight hours while the constables and guards of the Fiefdom looked for a crime to assign to the Ninja.

As for Reginald, all Jugura knew was that the boy had an unhealthy fascination with mecha. It had been rumored among some of the troopers, including his own command, that Reginald Browler had replaced more than half of his own body with ancient mecha and technology, known as 'cybernetics'. Jugura shuddered at the thought, both as a citizen of the empire, and a half-Jaft. The blue-fleshed humanoids had never done well with adapting to technologies dead or otherwise. They didn't even feel comfortable most times with indoor plumbing, and Jugura himself owned a house and some property upon which stood an outhouse. He refused to believe that even the Dwarves could make anything reliable from mecha.

"Give me the glass," he said to the private with the spyglass, taking the object and placing it to his eye. He peered out at the wagon, still about a mile and a half away. *Yes,* he thought, looking hard at Benjamin Browler. *Yes, the day for justice has come at last! We will pound you into the ground, outsiders, and you will receive the full brunt of the empire's righteous fist!*

"Captain, what are your orders?" asked another guard, a bow in his left hand.

"Ready the archers, sergeant," the captain said without looking away from Benjamin Browler. "Unleash the volley when they are within a hundred yards. Then," he said, drawing out not his katana, but his long tonfa. "Then the rest of us will charge them, and bring them down for an arrest. We will not kill them," he said pointedly, looking back at the sixteen capable Samurai and Soldiers at his command. "But we are going to make them remember that no crime goes unpunished in our great Emperor's lands! Now, everybody, to your positions!"

Captain Jugura's men prepared for battle.

* * * *

"How much longer before we take another pit stop, big bro'," Ben Browler asked Sean over his shoulder as he guided the horses along at an even clip, conserving the chargers' energy.

Sean looked up from his hand, looking away from the collection of cards that constantly shifted back and forth on the floorboards of the wagon. Dean, Reggie and he were playing a game of rummy, and Sean didn't like too many distractions when he played his card games. He gave Ben a sour look.

"Probably a couple of hours. Why, do you need to take a piss or something," he grumbled, turning his attention back to his hand. He picked up the queen of diamonds that Reggie had just discarded, and laid it down with the matching ten, jack and king.

"No, I just thought I'd ask," Ben replied, turning back toward the road. Something, he realized almost too late, didn't seem right about the road ahead. He had thus far led them along the route that big brother had requested he guide the horses down, but something about the small foothills they were approaching said to him 'ambush'.

He reined in the horses sharply, scattering his brothers' cards across the floor of the wagon as the chargers came to an abrupt halt.

"What the hells are you doing," Sean shouted just as the first arrows hit one of the horses dead-on in the chest. *Oh cripes and criminy,* Sean thought as he leaped out of the back of the wagon, followed closely by Dean, Reggie and finally Benjamin.

The four brothers stood at the back opening of the wagon, listening and waiting as the horse whinnied, kicked and tromped around, falling to the ground and pulling its partner down with it. Both horses were now braying loudly in pain, and the wagon against which their backs stood started bucking with their death throes.

"A border patrol," Dean conjectured, drawing out a set of shuriken. "I thought we were far enough east to be beyond all of them! Why would they have men this far east on a day like this?" His question went unanswered for the moment as another barrage of arrows started hitting the ground all around them. None of the arrows pierced the canvas top of the wagon, however; the Fiefdom border patrolmen didn't want to risk hitting any possible hostages.

"Who gives a shit why they're here, Dean," Sean shouted above the thudding rain of arrows. "The better question right now is, how do we get away from this?"

"There are men coming on horses," Reggie said matter-of-factly as he peered around the corner of the wagon.

This simple statement snapped Sean's attention away from his Ninja brother, and he felt himself tensing up. If the troopers were coming too fast and in too great a number, Sean and his brothers didn't stand much chance of standing their ground and fighting them.

"I can take care of most of them," Reggie said suddenly, and Sean, Ben and Dean all looked at him with disbelief clearly displayed on their faces.

Reggie looked at Sean, who was standing closest to him. He gave big brother a lopsided smile, and brought up his right arm.

Reggie pressed several buttons on his arm, and a low thrumming noise started up in it, originating around the elbow joint. "I've been storing up a lot of solar energy into my battery packs, Sean, so a few blasts should be just fine, right?"

Sean had zero idea what his littlest brother was talking about, so he just made a hurry-up gesture with his hands.

"Very well, big brother," Reggie said. He stepped out from behind the wagon, facing the charging Soldiers and Samurai, almost all of whom were astride horses.

Sean, Dean and Ben watched with bated breath, trying not to reach out and pluck their youngest kinsman back into the safety behind the wagon.

On the side of Reggie's left arm was a strange blue panel of glass, which was lighting with brilliant white light. He raised the arm, pointing his open palm at the oncoming assailants.

There issued from the hole in his palm a thick booming sound, followed immediately by a thick shaft of white light, which streaked toward their adversaries.

There was a brief scream of pain from the Soldiers and Samurai, and frightened nagging by their horses, but after a moment, there came only the sound of hissing steam and exclamations in the Fiefdom's native language.

Sean risked a quick peek around the corner of the wagon, and what he saw both amazed and stunned him. The beam of light that had erupted from Reggie's arm was apparently a weapon of some sort, because about a dozen corpses smoldered in the midday sun. Most of the troopers' horses had also received fatal wounds from the beam, huge sections of their bodies blasted out of existence.

Sean took a few steps toward his youngest sibling, and put one hand on his left shoulder, which felt strangely hot. "What was that you just did," Sean asked, watching as two troopers finally made good their escape over the hill about one hundred yards away.

"It's a lost technology, big brother." Reggie pushed a switch on his arm that ejected the battery pack he'd had in it. The pack was smoking as well, and instead of putting it among his bags and belongings, Reggie just tossed it over his shoulder to smoke on the grass. "You see, if you focus a strong enough shaft of light, it becomes a weapon that can do a lot of damage. I only stunned those two horses," he said, pointing toward two roans that were slowly trying to get to their hooves. "Their riders are dead, but I knew we'd have to replace the chargers. They won't be as fast, but we're not exactly in too much of a rush, right?" Reggie jammed a fresh battery pack into his limp left arm, then flexing the fingers.

"Right." Sean took another look at the corpses of their would-be jailers, and actually managed a stiff smile. "Ben, come out here and get these horses unhitched, then get the new ones arranged! Dean, you help him! Reggie and I are going to have a light lunch while you two get things squared away. Now," he said, draping a brotherly arm over his brother's shoulders. "Tell me all about this light beam technology."

While Reggie may have given him the willies before, Sean Browler was always willing to listen to someone talk about things that could turn into an advantage for the Browler Brothers Gang.

* * * *

Captain Jugura realized he'd badly underestimated the resources and abilities of the Browler brothers as he led the last remnants of his border patrol a short way north, to their guardhouse. He would have to send a letter to the local magistrate, and explain the situation. The mecha-obsessed Reggie Browler had used some sort of blasted technology on his troops and thirteen men and horses had been slain as a result. Had he known that a single man without the aid of magic could work such devastation, he would never have attacked the Browler brothers when he did. Now he had to get the few men he had left under his command back to their post, and request reinforcements.

He would also have to find a way to contact the Bounty Hunter who'd been in the region recently, chasing down Ben and Sean Browler. He would have to get in touch with Collin Caulkins, and warn the former Monk that neither of his contracted targets was the largest threat to his well being.

Chapter Eight
Heritage

When evening rolled around, Portenda, Shoryu and Collin all sighed with relief at the sight of Pombook, a small township in the Fiefdom of Lemago. None of the men wanted to camp outside this night, not when there might still be Ninjas following and stalking their trail. None would have slept well out of doors, if at all. *Also*, Shoryu thought privately, *I don't want to eat rations again.*

The outskirts of the town didn't appear to hold any guards at first glance, but all three men spotted the cleverly concealed troopers here and there, standing in shop windows and the darkened doorways of private homes around the perimeter of the town. Shoryu didn't feel the severity of the gazes he and his companions were receiving, but it took Portenda only a moment to realize why the intensity of the guards seemed to rise with their approach. *Here came marching a Simpa, a Cuyotai, and a Red Draconus*, he thought, *and none of the guards is larger than the average Human or half-Elf.*

His sensitive nostrils could not detect a single lycanthrope within a mile of him other than himself and Shoryu. Nor did he detect the odor of a reptilian humanoid other than Collin, and that did not behoove them well. They might have trouble locating decent lodging, he thought, and they might not even be accepted into the township. Yet all three passed between the first few buildings without incident, and from there he could feel himself and the nearby townsfolk relax a little.

What gives, he thought, sniffing the air once again, deeply.

Shoryu had noticed as well, and decided to voice his observation. "We're the largest creatures around, other than their livestock," he whispered as he walked behind the Simpa and Red Draconus.

Collin nodded knowingly, and reached into one of his pouches, extracting a thick oak pipe. He tamped some tobacco into it, and struck a match, puffing lightly on the mouthpiece.

"Indeed, we are." He smiled at one of the guards standing in his own doorway. "Pombook has never been home to anything larger than a Jaft now and again, and the townsfolk tend to like it that way. There's a hostel that puts up big folks like myself and Portenda when they come through, though you could probably fit on a normal sized bed," he said to the Councilor, who shrugged. "You're only a Cuyotai, and you're not too much broader than their largest guards I'd imagine. No offense," Collin added with a grin.

"None taken," Shoryu replied as Portenda led the way down the town's main street. The homes and businesses in this township did not get larger, Shoryu saw, than perhaps two floors, with only one exception. As the trio approached the center of the small town, he spotted what was probably their guardhouse, which most likely doubled as the local jail. It was a four-story stone building, and appeared much more solid than the homes and shops around it. It also appeared to be much older than the surrounding structures, which had a cobbled-together look to them. He could smell rats around the area, but he knew they weren't of the lycanthrope variety. Shoryu silently wondered about the quality of the commoners' lives in such a town.

"Is that the place?" Portenda asked, bringing Shoryu back around to his senses.

He looked at the building that the Simpa was pointing at, a two-story wooden manor with slat shingle roofing. He could hear some boisterous conversation and drunken laughter coming from the building's direction, and wondered what sort of guests would be within the hostel, as he was certain that was what Portenda was seeking to confirm.

"Yes it is." Collin chuffed blue smoke before he tapped out the pipe on the street. The ashes glowed on the dirt street, and a guard standing about ten feet away cleared his throat meaningfully. He was dressed in standard Fiefdom armor, and didn't appear intimidated in the least by the size difference between himself and the three out-of-towners.

Collin gave him a smile filled with razor-like teeth, and stamped on the glowering ashes from his pipe. "No harm no foul, right?" he asked the guard, who just grunted and looked away.

"Yes, Portenda, that's the hostel. Sounds like they've actually got a crowd in there tonight. We'll have to see if there's any rooms left available. If there aren't, we'll have to rough it in the little people inn," the Red Draconus said, still grinning. "Come on." He stepped past Portenda, now leading the way.

The front doors of the hostel stood open, and to the right of the check-in desk was a doorway that led to a smallish tavern. As Shoryu had suspected, there were several large lycanthropes inside, and all four of them appeared to be Khan.

Not good, he thought, recalling the natural distaste that Simpa and Khan shared for one another. In addition, Shoryu had seldom had good experiences to associate with the tiger-men.

"Can I help you?" a kind voice asked.

Shoryu turned his head to the left and saw that Portenda was leaning down to speak to a bespectacled old Human who apparently ran the hostel at night.

Portenda negotiated the rental of three single-man rooms, paid for the rental, and was handed three black steel keys.

Shoryu could overhear the elderly Human's last parting words before heading into the back as well, despite his whispering tone. "A word to the wise, sir; just head on up to your rooms. Those four have been getting a little rowdy in the bar."

"Understood," came the flat reply from the Simpa Bounty Hunter. He turned and handed a key to Collin, and another to Shoryu. "Rooms seven, eight and nine. They're up on the second floor. I'm going straight up right now. You two go ahead and do what you need to," he said evenly. "I'm tired and need some rest. I'll meet you guys at the diner across the street in the morning. Good night," he said, closing off any further conversation with his companions. He turned swiftly and headed directly for the stairs opposite the open bar, which Collin was already heading for.

Shoryu stood in the check-in lobby for a moment before deciding that he would head outside for a short walk and take in some fresh air. He'd had plenty for the majority of the day, but he enjoyed walking without a real purpose, and he decided it'd been too long since he'd taken the opportunity to do just that.

He stepped outside, and almost walked blindly into the back of a lumbering Khan, one of the gentlemen from the hostel's attached tavern.

The striped tiger-man stepped aside, and blew a cloud of smoke from his cigarette. Shoryu looked behind him, and above the tavern's doorway saw a 'no smoking' sign in red paint.

"Evening," the Khan said pleasantly enough to him.

"Good evening," Shoryu said in kind. He turned then and headed off up the street, hoping that the Khan wouldn't follow.

He sniffed the air lightly, and found that he was out of luck on that point. "Not heading back in?" Shoryu asked the Khan as the wandering tiger-man took up stride alongside him.

"What, back in with them?" The Khan tipped his feline head back toward the hostel as they walked further from it. "Nah, not tonight. One of us has to keep a clear head, and tonight it's my turn. So, what's you guys' story?" The Khan pitched his spent cigarette and propped his hands behind his head, walking with his arms arranged like he was sleeping out under the stars.

"Well, to tell you the truth, it's sort of a business trip," Shoryu said, taking a quick liking to the offhand manner of this particular Khan. "The name's Shoryu, by the way. And you?"

"Dennis," the Khan said, extending one clawed hand to Shoryu, who accepted it and shook. "Business, eh? Mercenaries? Bounty Hunters?"

"Well, those two are Bounty Hunters," Shoryu said with a hint of scorn. "Myself, I'm a bit of an official tagging along for the trip. You know, just overseeing things," he said, trying to play down his own role in the trip thus far.

"Most overseeing officials don't keep a bow, quiver, and short sword on hand," the Khan said with a leering grin. "So what's your Class? Soldier? Knight? Hunter?"

"Hunter," Shoryu said, remembering that he was still fully armed and equipped. He took a brief moment to give his temporary companion a once-over. "Yourself?"

"Boxer and Pyromancer." The Khan reached into his thick jeans pockets for his cigarette case. He produced a cigarette, placed his thumb under the end, and made a small flicker of flame spout from the tip of his nail to light the smoke. "My friends and I are heading for Ja-Wen ourselves, taking the scenic route. It's safer for us that way." He blew smoke away from Shoryu.

Hmm, Shoryu thought, *a polite Khan. Will wonders never cease?*

"Why do you say that?" Shoryu inquired, keeping his racist commentary to himself.

"Well, we're sort of leaving behind the tribal life of the Allenians." The Khan blew another cloud of smoke. "You see, each of us refused to take the traditional test of manhood for our tribe." The Khan turned with Shoryu onto a different street. "In our tribe, like most others in the Allenian Hills, the test of manhood requires defeating a Simpa warrior in combat. We don't have to kill them, though that's the most commonly accepted way of passing the test. So long as we injure them more than they injure us, we're considered worthy of the title of a man. We didn't really buy into all that, though."

"Why not, if I might be so bold as to ask?" Shoryu inquired.

"Well, my friends and I, we've been to Trapperstown, the free settlement in the middle of the Allenians," the Khan named Dennis said, smiling at his own private memory. "What we saw there really changed things for us, put everything in perspective. We saw people of all the Races, from the tiny Kobolds to the tallest civilized Orcs and even Troke. Can you imagine that? A real Troke, with a sense of civility and a law-abiding citizen to boot. That's the sort of thing you never expect to actually see when you're raised with the sort of beliefs we were brought up with. We even met a few Simpa youths who didn't want to tear our heads off. They were pretty nice guys, to tell the truth."

"So you saw a lot of contradictions to what you'd learned as kids." Shoryu nodded his head absently, looking up at the stars in the sky. "I can understand that pretty well, actually."

"You from a tribal village too?" The Khan pitched yet another spent cigarette.

Shoryu looked down from the stars, and realized that they were about to walk out of the township north, but he didn't stop walking straight ahead. After a few minutes of silent walking, the two men sat atop a small hill facing the town, taking in the sights of the quiet burb.

"Yes, I'm from a small village." Shoryu looked down at the township and pictured his village in its place. It hadn't been much larger than perhaps half the size of the town of Pombook. But the tents that had comprised his hometown had been spaced farther apart, and the organization of the families into their own little areas had been much more thorough than this township before his eyes. "It was a quiet Cuyotai tribal village, and we were the last of our particular tribe, you see." Shoryu's mind's eye starting to cloud over his physical sense of vision. "We lived a simple life, all of us. We had true Hunters, who gathered fresh meat from the woods that surrounded our valley and staved off the Lizardmen who came around, seeking to take our lands from us. We had the gatherers, who collected the fruits and herbs that grew wild in the woods. And we had small vegetable fields, in which we worked and toiled season after season, growing what we could when the soil allowed it."

Shoryu took his travel canteen and swallowed a long draught of cool water to ease his throat, and give himself time to steel himself against an emotional outburst. "My birth father had been taken from me when I was young, as had my birth mother, though both different circumstances. My mother had been slain during a Lizardman assault on our valley when I was but a pup. My father was felled during the Battle of the Final Push, when the free peoples of the land struck back at the warlock Tanarak of Sidius. It was not a good battle, and many thousands were lost, my father among them. So, our tribe's Chieftain, who survived the battle, took me in upon his return.

"I lived, learned, and grew up in his care, and for a while, things were good. I was in line to become one of the honored Hunters of my tribe, and then things went to hell for my tribe on the whole," Shoryu said.

Dennis gave him an inquiring look, and Shoryu returned to him an awkward smile. "It's best to be blunt about it, because what happened was no good. A new warlock invaded my valley with an army of the Lizardman tribe that had been our enemies for so long, and new forces. Greenskins, led by the warlock Richard Vandross."

At the dropping of that name, the Khan's eyes went wide.

"You survived the onslaught of Richard Vandross?" Dennis asked, mouth agape. "How many other survived?"

"Not many," Shoryu replied after another swig of water. He stood up, deciding silently that it was time to start heading back to the hostel. "Those that did headed all the way to the Elven Kingdom, where they integrated with other tribes to survive. I alone survived entirely intact, with the knowledge of my tribe's history and customs. I had help in surviving the battle, however. You see, near the end of the devastation, the Dread Knight Byron of Sidius came upon the valley, and he aided in my defense."

"You met him," Dennis asked, flabbergasted. "You met the great Byron?"

"More than that." Shoryu patted Dennis on the back. "I traveled with him, fought alongside him. So you see," he said with a grin, looking at the houses and shops as they reentered the town of Pombook. "This little business trip really isn't all that bad for a fellow like myself."

The two got back to the hostel, and found the bar emptied with the exception of Collin Caulkins, who was nursing only his second drink.

Dennis bade Shoryu a good night, and the Cuyotai Hunter headed over to take a seat next to the Red Draconus.

"You know," Shoryu said, accepting a mug of ale from the barkeep. "This whole trip isn't really turning out that bad," he said to the confused Draconus. "Not that bad at all."

* * * *

Portenda sat on the edge of his bed, facing the door, expecting trouble from the drunken Khan youths who passed by his room entirely and headed to their own lodgings. The room he'd rented wasn't exactly luxurious, but it met his needs. A single bed, a low dresser to put his belongings on or in (for an extended stay), a lamp, and a writing desk. All in all, not too bad considering the alternative of camping out.

When none of the drunken, slurred speaking tiger-men barged into his room spoiling for a fight, Portenda was at first skeptical. He didn't honestly expect them to just pass by an opportunity to take on a Simpa with uneven odds in their favor, but that was exactly what they'd done. Perplexed but not willing to pass up an opportunity such as this,

Portenda tapped the buckle on his bag, opened it, and withdrew his reading glasses case and a novel entitled *The Four Winds*. He lay down on the bed, propping his head up on a couple of pillows, and started on the forth chapter, where he'd last left off.

Portenda managed to get through two more chapters before midnight, when he took the glasses off, set them and the book aside, and found himself pondering Councilor Tearfang's personal history. The Cuyotai Hunter had proven himself a competent and capable archer during their two skirmishes, both with the bladeron and the Ninjas to the south. He'd traveled and battled with Byron of Sidius in the War of Vandross, and that too was no small feat. Perhaps he'd been wrong to be wary of bringing the Cuyotai along on his mission. Perhaps the Cuyotai would even save the Simpa's hide during a skirmish. Who knew?

Then there was Collin Caulkins, the Red Draconus Bounty Hunter. Portenda smiled at the thought of his old colleague. Since he'd been only a few years in the business, Collin had been there, offering advice, tips and tricks aplenty, and lots of good conversation. *But I've surpassed him,* Portenda thought to himself.

This assessment was not merely ego on the part of the Simpa: he had truly gotten better than Caulkins, who had become older and slower than the lycanthrope. But being older and less agile were only two factors in the grand equation, and Portenda knew it. There was also the fact that Collin had more of a capacity for emotion, and as such, the Red Draconus couldn't always do the quickest, most professional thing.

"Hasn't always been this way?" Portenda said aloud, rolling onto his side to look out the window of his rented room. "Doesn't have to stay this way, either," he reminded himself as well, envisioning the laid back, relaxed future he might have as a landlord. The rent money he was presently making wasn't the best, but he'd had precious little time to actually work on the buildings he owned. He had the financial backing he needed to invest in all of the renovations he needed to have performed, but in the case of the building in Ja-Wen, the scale of renovations would require that he remove several of his tenants. For some reason, however, he couldn't bring himself to do it, not just yet. He had his eye on another building in the city, a more up-to-date, five-story complex that would easily hold all of his current tenants from the twelve-story property. He could snap up the newer property, move his tenants temporarily, and hire a crew to work on the old building.

Portenda was internally cataloguing all the labor costs when he finally fell asleep. His dreams were filled with scenes of Dwarven carpenters and masons doing the renovation work as he supervised from the ground floor, a simple yellow hard hat on his head, a cup of coffee in hand. It was the most peaceful rest he'd had in a while.

* * * *

Collin awoke in his rented bed with a hangover that seemed to have a physical presence and body. *Take things easy, boss*, it seemed to buzz in his ears, *take things easy*. The Red Draconus couldn't remember drinking all that much, but he seldom indulged in hard liquor like he had the night before. "Ale's fast, but liquor's quicker," he said, reciting a bit of wisdom he'd not had to recall in some time.

He sat up and stretched, his scaled arms stiff from sleeping in a bad position. *Hope Portenda got some rest*, he thought, well aware of the Simpa's little sleeping problem. He'd known Portenda a good number of years, and knew that the Simpa didn't often get the kind of sleep he should, for reasons neither man could readily identify. Sometimes, he also knew, the Simpa talked in his sleep, and the sound of his voice took on an otherworldly quality. Collin imagined Death might have the same sort of voice in those moments.

He hopped down off the bed, and headed to the small, attached bathroom, splashing cold water on his face. He looked into the mirror after drying his face with a hand towel, and smiled. *Draconus*, he thought, *dragon-man*. The Draconus Race had been around for a very long time, and Collin's family lineage in particular had been fascinating to research.

He'd found a copy of his family's genealogy in the library of Palen about ten years prior to that morning, and had become engrossed in the thick tome's contents. His people's progenitor had been the great Red Dragon Unitenbo, who had metamorphed his body into the form of a Human. Unitenbo mated with various Human women, and the children they bore nearly a year later were all the first of the Red Draconus, the first of the family clans. Collin's family history led all the way back to the great Red Dragon, and included this first member of the family clan, Servius Coles. Servius had managed to meet one of the female Draconus born by Unitenbo's seed, and together they had nearly a dozen children.

Servius's first-born son took the name Caulkins as his surname, supposedly from a character in a famous novel of the time. That had been during Tamalaria's Second Age, so novels in general had tended to be hard to come by copies of, and the son had been rather proud. His name had been Jarvis, and he had served as one of the land's first Dragoons. Jarvis himself found a Red Draconus mate, and together they'd had five children.

It should be noted that Draconus are among the longest-living of all the humanoid species, with life spans lasting from around eight hundred to twelve hundred years. Only a few generations separated the current crop of adult Draconus from their ancestors in most cases, and Collin was no exception. Jarvis's first-born, his only son, had been Newton Howard Caulkins. Newton had mated later in life and had three sons and two daughters, the oldest of whom was Newton Howard Caulkins the Second. And the Second had three sons, Newton Everett, Collin Christopher, and Joshua Caulkins. All three sons knew with some degree of pride that they were not only fifth-generation Draconus, but they were pureblood Red Draconus.

As Collin hopped in the shower, he also made a mental side note of the fact that, as a result of being a purebred Red Draconus, he had a good deal more control over his fiery breath than did those Draconus with impurities in their bloodline. He could channel it into a single narrow cone, or spread it out into a widening fan. Unfortunately, he thought in addition, it also meant that the fire was always there in his belly, ready to burn and consume. As a result, he was almost constantly feeling either ill or hungry, and as his stomach growled in the shower, he knew he'd wind up paying for a meal before he and his companions left the town of Pombook.

Collin toweled off, got dressed, and donned his equipment. He stepped out into the hallway, and breathed in the air as best he could. Before he could venture up the hall to see if either of the other two men had awoken, Portenda approached from the stairwell.

"Morning, Collin," the Simpa said.

"Good morning, sunshine. I see you're as awake as ever," Collin said.

Portenda tipped his head back and drained the mug of coffee in his hand, twirling it around his pointer finger by the handle after finishing its contents.

"More so," the Simpa said, feeling vaguely chipper now that he'd had a good night's sleep. "The Councilor's already checked out. I figure he's at the diner across the street, just waiting for us. There's free coffee downstairs, so grab your mug."

Collin rummaged quickly in his bag for his own ceramic cup, grabbed it, and followed the lumbering Simpa downstairs.

In the lobby, the innkeeper had arranged several tureens of coffee, from which Portenda grabbed his third cup this morning, and Collin his first.

"So, you did get some rest last night after all," Collin said, noticing the small grin the Simpa wore.

"Yeah, that I did. Oh, sugar and creamer are over there." The Simpa pointed to the canisters of each item.

Collin readied his coffee and drank with Portenda at one of the small tables in the check-in lobby, and they seemed content for the moment to drink in silence.

"He's pretty good, you know. For a politician," Collin remarked.

"He's been through a lot in his time, Collin," Portenda said, his normal, business-like voice returning to him as he steeled himself for the days ahead. "Now, the town we're heading to. How many days away is it from here?"

"Oh, only about a day and a half east," the Red Draconus said. "Young master Staples got the longitude and latitude both wrong, but I suppose it's better than having to hoof it all the way from Desanadron. My contact should have some more information on the Browlers when we talk to him." Collin drained his mug and then led the way across the street where Shoryu had already secured them an outdoor table for breakfast.

"Good morning Councilor," Collin said to the Cuyotai.

"Good morning," Shoryu said. Shoryu knew he probably looked both shabby and miserable to his companions, but not without good reason. He'd had the same bad old dream the night before, the dream wherein another threat like Richard Vandross came crashing into his new home with his wife and children. The dream that mimicked the destruction of his home village so accurately. This morning, however, there hadn't been a good woman in the bed with him to give him comfort and the confirmation of her vitality and existence. "How are you two doing?" he asked, trying to maintain a neutral tone.

"Better than you, Shoryu," Portenda said bluntly. He and Collin seated themselves, making note of the way their wooden seats creaked as they gingerly settled their massive bodies down on them. "You look like something the cat dragged in."

When Collin gave a brief chuckle, Shoryu forgave the Draconus his laugh's implication. After all, what was a Simpa but a big cat on two legs?

"I'm fine, really." Shoryu raised a hand to get the only outdoor waitress's attention.

She smiled gently at the Cuyotai, and started over to the trio.

"I just didn't sleep very well last night."

"You still aren't used to sleeping in a bed without your wife," Portenda said, once more being blunt and cold in tone, though he didn't mean to seem impersonal. "When we find the Browler brothers, we'll get them to cough up Svelk. When we get Svelk, we'll pound him, gag and tie him, and then find a quick way back to Whitewood. It shouldn't really take all that long. By the way, Collin, any chance you could pick yourself up a horse from the local stables," Portenda asked suddenly. "We would make better time if you rode while the Councilor and I ran in animus form."

"Yeah, I've got the spare scratch to pick up a mount." Collin gave the waitress his order by simply pointing at his menu. "I just hope they've got one that's strong enough to carry me. I imagine they do, though. The Fiefdom's well known for its ability to breed strong animals."

Portenda and Shoryu ordered their food, and the three men ate their meal in a respectful and comfortable silence, each man mulling over their situation. At least, Collin and Shoryu were mulling it over. Portenda found himself thinking about his mother, as he sometimes did on bright mornings such as this, when the Khan blood in his veins was thrumming along at full power thanks to the rays of the sun.

Ah, mother, you would have loved to see a morning such as this, he thought. But his father, Telroke, had robbed his mother of the sight of another living morning. She was, he hoped, with Kagren, one of the many gods the Khan worshipped. She was with him, Portenda prayed, and she viewed every morning from the heavens themselves. She would be at peace forever in the loving embrace of the Khan god of peace and plenty, and Portenda could hope for nothing less for her.

For a moment, Portenda wondered what his life would be like if he had been born looking more like a Khan than like his accursed father, the drunkard and rapist. Almost all physical appearances pegged Portenda as a Simpa, and so as one of the noble lion-men he was known. Without the stripes on his arms and back in faded gray, he would never raise a single eyebrow. But he knew the differences between himself and other Simpa well enough to know that he had indeed inherited subtle signs of Khan lineage.

As Shoryu asked for another cup of coffee, Portenda automatically responded in kind. *The stripes,* he thought, *are the biggest outward sign. Then, there's the fact that I don't regenerate my wounds as swiftly as a Simpa. I have a Khan's regenerative qualities, a fact that very well may have lost me the fight with Ignatious Stockholm.* But that was a lie, and he knew as much as soon as the thought formed itself. There were two other subtle signs, and it amazed him how little anyone other than another Simpa might think of them.

Firstly, Portenda didn't have a tail in his bestial form. Almost all Simpa kept their tails combed and fluffed, trailing out behind them proudly, waggling back and forth with what seemed like minds of their own. A few Simpa tucked theirs into a pant leg, and Portenda benefited from this behavior, as it meant he never had to explain the absence of his own tail.

Secondly, and this one drew less suspicion than even the tail, was the fact that he had no mane of hair around his neck like most Simpa. But fur and hair could be styled in so many different ways, nobody ever thought twice about his lack of hair around the throat. Some Khan occasionally had a hard time ignoring this lack of mane and addition of stripes, but they more often than not had heard of Portenda the Quiet, and most knew of his taboo heritage. While the Allenian Simpa all thought of him as a twisted freak and outcast, most Khan thought of him as the potential destroyer of their people. They didn't understand how unlike his own father the son had become.

"Hey, are you still with us here in reality?" Collin snapped his scaly fingers in front of Portenda's blunted snout.

The Simpa Bounty Hunter grabbed Collin's wrist to cease his incessant snapping, and let him go right away.

The Red Draconus rubbed his wrist for a moment, and stuck his forked tongue out at Portenda. "Didn't have to be so rough about it."

"Don't complain. I could have been completely out of it and broken your arm," Portenda replied. "Come on, I'll leave money on the table. We've got to get going to the stables. Councilor?" Portenda dropped a pair of platinum coins, worth ten gold apiece, and shape-shifted down into his animus form, that of a tiger-striped lion.

Shoryu finished his cup of coffee and followed suit, taking the form of a tan-furred coyote with a thin summer coat.

Collin shook his head, never fully adjusting to the sight of a lycanthrope going from one of its three forms to the other.

Flanked on one side by a lion and on the other by a coyote, the Red Draconus had no trouble at all making a straight line for the stables, as everyone he encountered along the way was careful to stay a good fifteen meters to any side of him. "You know, this is useful," he said to the lion, who in animus still came almost up to his shoulder. "An entourage of vicious animals through a mostly Human town makes for quick travel." He guffawed.

The lion gave him a scowl and shook its proud head.

His face really isn't much different in this form, and neither is Shoryu's. I wonder what Portenda looks like in humanoid form, he wondered, unaware that the Simpa Bounty Hunter had no humanoid form. He could only go from bestial into animus and back.

Shoryu, on the other hand, may well have benefited from his humanoid form in a town such as Pombook. His humanoid form was that of an angular, handsome Human man in woodsman's cloaks. However, if he was going to be traveling long distance, he had to use his animus form. He didn't do well enough on a horse for extended periods of time.

The trio walked into the open doors of the barn-like stables on the eastern edge of the town, and immediately a half-Elven attendant approached Collin. "Good morning, sir," the attendant said, eyeballing the lion and the coyote suspiciously. "Might I ask that you leave the tamed animals outside? They might make some of the smaller horses nervous."

Collin looked back at the lion, Portenda, who simply nodded and had himself a seat at the door. Shoryu did the same, but he had what could best be described as an impish grin for a desert dog.

As Collin began negotiating a price for a large brown stallion in the attendant's stables, Shoryu started yipping and barking like a loon.

When Collin raised his voice to try to be heard, Shoryu started in with a high-pitched whining. So unnerving was it that the attendant asked the Red Draconus to follow him back into his office, further in the building, away from the dog.

When both men were out of sight, the coyote took a long look at the lion, who was grinning despite himself.

Twenty minutes later, the trio was heading east, with the lion and coyote running along at a decent clip, and Collin riding the stallion at a matching pace. He'd purchased the horse outright since he had the money, and the one he'd selected had been a brave animal indeed, for it did not balk at the sight or nearness of the two animals that often came close to its flanks. Considering the way things go around the Fiefdom, Collin thought, *it's probably seen a minor turf war or two in its time.*

As they loped along, Portenda spared enough time to have one more solid thought before he just let instinct take over. *Another reason it's good to have Khan blood. I'm a hell of a lot faster than the average Simpa.*

Chapter Nine
Playing Catch Up

After two days of being reprimanded by his superiors, Captain Jugura was pleased to still have a command. He was even more pleased when at around noon after a day and a few hours' travel from Pombook, Collin Caulkins came knocking at his front door. Jugura had been preparing to go and meet his new recruits when the knock sounded at his front door, and he set the razor down on the sink in his bathroom, using a wet towel to wipe away the soap from his face. He opened the door, and there stood the Red Draconus and two associates of his, a Simpa and a Cuyotai. "Collin-sama, it is good to see you," the captain said with a wide smile.

Portenda took a quick whiff of the man, because he thought his eyes might be playing tricks on him when he noticed the vaguely bluish tint to his skin. *Nope, he's a half-breed,* he thought, confirming that his eyes were not, in fact, going on him. He would have to spend a goodly amount of time remaining quiet, since he'd been talking since the day before. He needed to get his senses back to their usual sharpness, and he would use the Red Draconus's relationship with this man to remain respectfully quiet and regain his power.

"As it is to see you, Jugura." Collin gave the man a bow from the waist. He remained standing on the threshold of the captain's home, and after the customary time, the captain made a hand gesture to welcome him and his friends inside. "Good to see as well that you are holding to your father's ways."

"Tradition and custom are the backbone of a strong society," Jugura said, quoting the Fiefdom's first Emperor. "Can I get you and your friends anything? Tea? Perhaps some ale? I keep a few bottles in the ice box."

"That'll do just nicely for myself and the big fellow," Collin said, pointing back at Portenda. He looked over to Shoryu with a raised eyebrow.

"Tea will be just fine for me, thank you," the Councilor said, taking a look around the captain's living room. To say that it was spare would be an understatement; no couch, no coffee table, nothing decorating the walls. There were three chairs, all green leather numbers, with one chair facing the other two across the room from each other. Shoryu almost made a full circuit of the room, and then realized that there was something on the walls after all. On the wall opposite the front door, next to the entryway to the hall that led back to Jugura's bathroom and bedroom, was a sword stand with three blades sheathed on it.

Jugura came back into the room with the bottled ale, and grabbed the one chair that was apart from the others, placing the three chairs in a row and indicating that the three men who were his guests should seat themselves. All three did, though Portenda, as usual, had to squeeze a little to get into his seat. "Captain Jugura, may I introduce you to my companions?" Collin asked formally, indicating Portenda and Shoryu with a wave of his hands.

"Please," replied the captain as he buttoned up his uniform shirt. He didn't have a field assignment today, so he wouldn't be donning his armor. After all, for the next few weeks, he would be letting the sergeants who'd survived the assault of Reggie Browler do the instructing, while he took reports and wrote down information in personnel folders.

"This gentleman is Councilor Shoryu Tearfang, of the Elven Kingdom," Collin said. Jugura gave his last button a tweak, and then bowed from the waist to Shoryu, who was unaccustomed to such gestures.

He smiled and nodded in return.

"And this sour-looking chap is Portenda the Quiet, of, of," Collin said, stammering to think of something. He decided to go with the easiest route he knew to avoid awkward conversation between Portenda and the captain. "Of Desanadron."

The captain gave Portenda the same bow he'd given Shoryu, and smiled broadly as Portenda rose to his feet and returned the gesture in perfect form. The Simpa growled at himself as he squeezed his hips into the leather chair once again.

"It is a pleasure to make your acquaintance. Ah, the tea is ready," Jugura said as the whistle started piping from the kitchen. "Excuse me a moment."

He hurried from the room, and returned minutes later with a cup for Shoryu, and one for himself. Jugura stood in the middle of the room before his guests, and looked hard at Collin, still trying to smile. "I was hoping you would come by sometime soon, Mr. Caulkins," he said.

"Why's that?" Collin took a swig of his ale, and nearly spat it right out. Fiefdom ale had ever been of an inferior quality to the stuff the big cities got, but he'd forgotten how bad it actually was. He swallowed the bile, though, and smiled.

"My men and I encountered the Browler brothers a couple of days ago, out east near the border of our lands," the captain said, a statement that made all three visitors get immediately to their feet. "Please, please, be seated! We killed their horses, so they will not have made much time on you." The captain said needed to let Collin know exactly what he was up against in the form of Reginald Browler. The Bounty Hunter had to be informed of the devilry of Reginald's mecha!

"Were all four brothers together," Collin asked.

"Was there a fifth man with them, an Elf," Shoryu asked at the same exact moment.

"Please, gentlemen." The captain motioned them to take their seats again, and sure enough, Shoryu and Collin did.

Jugura looked at Portenda for a moment, and then at his chair. Jugura noticed now how warped the seat was starting to look. "I apologize for the size of the chair. Please, be seated on the floor if you will."

Portenda was willing to at least do that, but he made himself follow the Fiefdom custom, and sat with his legs tucked beneath his buttocks, sort of kneeling.

"You are well versed in our customs, I see," Jugura said, relaxing a little at the sight of a stranger showing such care and respect in his home. "You honor me by your efforts."

"He's got a knack for that sort of thing." Collin looked over at the Simpa. He and Shoryu both knew why Portenda was being so stoic, and so Collin decided to assume the role of Portenda's mouthpiece. "Now, were all four together," he asked once more of the captain.

"Yes, they were," Jugura said slowly, sipping his tea. He looked then to Shoryu. "However, there was no fifth man with them, no Elf that I observed. But one of them laid waste to almost my entire unit." He let the words sink in.

Collin knew Jugura's unit as a capable and competent group of trained Soldiers and Samurai. For one of the Browlers alone to do that seemed almost impossible!

"Only *one* of them? Was it the Ninja, Dean?"

"No," Jugura said, pleased despite the horrible memory of how close that beam had come to striking him in the head during his retreat. "It was the youngest of the four, Reginald Browler. He has strange arms made of mecha, and he used one of them as a weapon against us."

Portenda noted the slight shaking of the half-Jaft's hand as he lifted his teacup to his lips. *Composed, controlled*, Portenda thought. *The guy's good, and he knew when to get the hell out of harm's way. He'll be around for a while.*

"What did this weapon do, if I might ask," Shoryu asked, remembering Reggie Browler's record portrait. Now he knew for certain what had been wrong about the arms: they were artificial.

"He held his right hand out to us, fingers open to expose his palm. In the center of his palm, there was a tube of some sort." Jugura held his free hand out in the position that Reggie Browler had. "There was a thrumming noise coming from it, that I recall clearly, and I knew he was using some sort of technology or magic against us. I figured technology, since that is what he is known for. It fired a beam of light that tore holes in my men and their steeds." Jugura's entire body wracked with memory spasms. "If he did anything else, I did not see. I issued the order for retreat as soon as the first of my men fell, but by then it was too late to save everyone. Myself and a handful of my sergeants managed to get away."

"Did any of the horses survive?" Collin asked.

Jugura thought about this, and realized that two of the horses, a pair of roans, appearing to only be stunned by the beam from Reggie Browler's hand.

"If any, two of the roans," Jugura said. "But they were not as powerful as the chargers that the brothers were using to pull their wagon before we slew them. They will be slowed down."

Portenda silently cursed to himself. *They're using a wagon and horses to travel, so they may appear to be pilgrims or merchants,* he thought, *and that should get them past a good deal of town patrols and sentries. Probably jacked the wagon. If the roans are slower, though, we can catch up to them before they get to a big city where we might lose them.*

"Any idea what direction they were heading?" Shoryu finished his tea and bowed his head as Jugura collected the cup.

The captain headed back to the kitchen, and returned sans teacups. He had on his business tie now as well, ready for a day of paperwork and introductions. He checked the timepiece on the wall—he had to wrap this interview up quickly if he wanted to be early to meet the recruits.

"I am afraid my best guess is north and east," Jugura said in response to the Cuyotai's question. "I would believe they are heading for the lawless town of The Port of Arcade. They would be safe there from the long arm of justice," he said with a wicked smile. "Of course, the arm of Bounty Hunters is longer than that, isn't it?"

"Infinitely so." Collin topped off his swill-tasting ale. He rose, followed by Portenda and Shoryu. "So we have to watch for the mecha freak's hand cannon. And they're probably heading north and east until they can just turn north and get a straight shot toward Arcade. Okay, thank you very much, captain." Collin bowed deeply and meaningfully to the half-Jaft captain.

The Elf-Queen's Bounty

"You are all very welcome. Please, feel welcome to return in time and visit." Jugura ushered his guests toward the door, exited after them and locked the door. He gave them a brief bow, and headed off up the main road of his hometown, toward the guardhouse.

"Well, let's get a move on." Collin untied his horse from the nearby torch post and mounted up. "With any luck, we'll find some signs of the Browler's trail and be able to catch up. With a little more luck," he said, waiting for Portenda and Shoryu to take their animus forms before he kicked the horse into a trot. "They'll hit a snag along the road."

* * * *

Benjamin had shown himself more than competent when, after only a few hours with the roans pulling the wagon, he'd stopped the horses and started tossing the merchant's supplies and wares out the back, onto the grass. "They're not as strong as the chargers," he explained when Sean gave him a look of 'what the hell'?

Sean nodded, and together, the four brothers cleared the wagon of everything except their own supplies and the merchant's cash box.

The load lightened, the horses performed just as well as the chargers had, and they were rolling along at a good pace once more. Bumping along over the lesser used roads of the eastern flatlands, a question of some importance sprang up in Ben's head, and he decided it would be best to get an answer now. "Sean, we're heading northeast right now. Won't we wind up in the Greenskin Nation if we aren't careful?"

"Indeed we shall, but not to worry," Sean said with a smile, looking away from his rummy hand. "Dean here's got a forged document from the Ogre King granting us free passage. If any of those brutes or Goblins stop us, it won't be for long. When we're about halfway through the Greenskin Nation, we'll turn north."

"Won't we be passing close to Mount Toane then?" Ben asked, still worried.

"Why yes, we will. Don't tell me you believe those stories, Ben. You're not a little kid, so have some common sense." Sean spat, sick with his brother's superstitious fears.

"They're not just stories," Ben said defensively. "You know what happened back then. Vandross used demons, and he conjured them up from the hells themselves. That place has always been evil, so there might be something still hangin' about, you know?"

"Just shut your noise hole and direct the horses," Sean said curtly. "And don't bring up any more of this nonsense about demons! We're going to go by, maybe do a little sightseeing, and then we'll be gone, get it?"

Ben nodded, but he didn't believe a word of Sean's reassurances. Still, what could *he* do about it? Sean was big brother, and big brother had to be listened to, even if he was wrong. That was how mother would have wanted it.

So without another mention of demons he led the horses through most of the night, stopping only once to rest the horses, and awoke the next morning to Dean at the reins. Ben didn't mind much, but he did wish that Sean would let them stop for another cooked meal instead of a breakfast of cheese, bread and apple slices. He understood that they needed to make swift time toward their destination, but he thought Sean was being paranoid about the Bounty Hunters. Reggie had dealt with the Fiefdom's guards easily enough, so why would it be any different against the Draconus and a Simpa?

Well, let him worry about it, Ben thought as he chewed his bread slowly, groggily. *I'll worry about demons, and Sean can worry about Bounty Hunters.* After all, he's probably right, he reasoned. They were more likely to run into the Bounty Hunters than demons these days. *Still*, he pulled a charm out of his pocket and put it around his neck, *a little help never hurt.*

* * * *

"I think I know the route they're following." Collin took another look at the tracks leading away from the battlefield where Reginald Browler had destroyed a dozen or so Samurai and Soldiers. "There's a series of old trade routes and wanderer roads that winds up through the Greenskin Nation, past Mount Toane, and eventually terminates in Arcade. A lot of thieves use these paths and passages to minimize their chances of running into guards on patrol from towns and villages. Portenda, I'm surprised you don't know about these roads." The Red Draconus looked away from the tracks for a moment.

Portenda, in his bestial form, took out one of his yellow steno pads and scribbled something on the paper with a pencil. He handed the pad to Collin. 'I don't usually rely on that sort of thing' was written on the paper. Portenda snatched the pad back and jotted down something else. 'I've got Reggie's scent, and I think Shoryu does too'.

Collin looked over to Shoryu, who had remained in his animus form when they came upon the battlefield.

"Any idea how old the scent is?" Collin asked Portenda as he looked at Shoryu. The Cuyotai sniffed and poked his head around the bodies of the fallen warriors, though even the Councilor wasn't exactly certain what he was looking for. Portenda guessed right about him having caught Reggie's scent, a strange mix of metal and oils, but another odor clung to his sense of smell. He just couldn't tell what it was, but something nagged at him. Finally, after a solid ten minutes of searching, he found it, and it wasn't the smell of blood that bothered him. It was the smell of urine; one of the warriors still clung to life, but was too weak to even get up to relieve himself.

Shoryu started poking closer to the bodies, and Collin, not knowing why, felt a surge of anger well up inside. "Hey, leave them be! Have some respect for the dead!" Shoryu looked up at the Draconus and whined back in his throat, his ears turned down. He continued nudging along, and finally located the wounded but living Soldier, pinned by his own mount. Shoryu gently grabbed the man by his armored shoulder plate, and started to tug. "I said leave them be!"

"He's found a survivor," Portenda said aloud, breaking his code of silence for the sake of perceptive power momentarily. He dashed past the stunned Draconus to Shoryu, and knelt, getting his arms up under the man's armpits. He pulled gently, seeing how the Human Soldier was pinned under the dead horse. The man's body was limp, and when he got the Soldier out from under the horse, he saw that only part of his left leg had been pinned; the rest of the leg, from the knee down, was missing entirely.

Shoryu shifted into his bestial form, and immediately began rummaging around in his pack for a healing scroll. He found one swiftly, and read the simple incantation from it, directing the spell at the wounded man's lower body.

Green light flickered off of the scroll, which disintegrated in a brief cloud of smoke. The light remained, and filtered down onto the man's leg and lower body, stopping once it reached his upper abdomen. His eyes began to flutter open, and Shoryu thanked the gods for the scroll. Had it been of inferior quality, it might not have cured the infection that had worked its way to the Human's stomach. The spreading of the light had shown him that the damage had spread, but the scroll had done the job.

"Where, where am I?" the man said in thickly accented common. "I, I have to, get, out," he stammered.

"Well, good job guys," Collin said, clapping his hands slowly, letting the sarcasm drip from his voice. "You've stopped him from dying for now, but how are we going to get him to a safe place AND follow the Browlers, hmm? And we know they have a lead on us already, though we have no idea what kind of lead since you never answered my previous question, Portenda!"

If Portenda the Quiet hadn't been a thinking man, he would have risen and struck the Red Draconus silent. However, he thought a great deal before taking most actions, and his thought process worked rather much quicker than the average man's. He pulled out his notepad and his pencil, and he jotted down his message quickly, knowing that Collin would be able to read his chicken scratch writing. He thrust the notepad toward Collin, and then opened his rucksack, pulling out a coil of rope.

'We lash him to your horse. You will ride on my back. Wentin is only an hour out of our way, and the Browlers have a thirty-four hour lead on us. Do not question this.'

Well, Collin thought, *that makes things pretty clear, doesn't it?* He took the rope from Portenda, who was already carrying the unconscious Soldier to the horse. Together, they lashed the man in as comfortably as they could, being careful not to cut off circulation to any part of his body. Then, with Shoryu waiting a short distance in front of the horse and Portenda shifting into animus form behind it, the trio moved off once again to the north and east.

* * * *

"You got those papers handy," Ben asked as he slowed the wagon noticeably.

Sean stood, accustomed now to the movement and rocking of the wagon, and came toward the driver's seat of the wagon. He peered out beyond his little brother's shoulder, and saw that the road ahead was blocked by three rather bulky Orc troopers in official Greenskin Nation uniforms. Chain mail shirts protected their upper bodies, and were covered by serapes in green cloth with a yellow axe symbol embossed in the center of the field of green. Studded leather leggings protected their legs and provided warmth for the colder months, as the Greenskin Races tended to suffer from temperature changes more in their lower extremities than their upper bodies.

"Yeah, we got 'em," Sean replied as Ben reined the horses in to a full stop. Sean didn't even turn around as he stuck his hand back to Dean for the forged documents.

The Ninja of the Browler brothers placed the rolled up papers into his hand, and Sean handed them then forward to Ben. "Tell them there's four of us total if they ask. We don't want to bullshit a bunch of angry-looking Orcs out here where we haven't any friends."

"By what authority do you come barging into our grand territory, Human?" one of the Orcs asked as he approached the wagon, flanking the horse on Ben's left.

Ben smiled and kept his mouth shut, handing the papers to the tall, green warrior.

Like most Orcs, the trooper had a flat, almost ape-like face, and Ben had to really force his smile to stay on.

The Orc looked at the paper in his hand, and walked slowly back to the others. Sean watched with keen interest as they unrolled the papers and appeared to study them for a while.

Finally, the most stout of the three troopers approached the wagon with the papers in his hand. He handed them gently up to Ben, who continued to grin like an idiot. "You have our apologies for interrupting your travels, stranger. We have seen the seal of our leader, and have read the instructions in the letter. Keep the letter with you, and proceed unmolested." The Orc threw Ben an awkward salute.

Ben returned the gesture, and cracked the reins on the horses, who started forward with a lurch.

When the Browler Gang was well past the troopers, Sean seated himself and looked at his cards, tossing them on the floor of the wagon.

"You assholes switched my cards," was all he had to say as he smiled the smile of a man who's just conned a huge sucker.

* * * *

Back atop his horse, Collin held a new appreciation for the invention of the saddle. Riding bare astride Portenda in his animus form had turned out to be much more uncomfortable for the Red Draconus than for the Simpa. Portenda's spine had to be made of steel, Collin decided after only twenty minutes of riding atop the Simpa. His ass was so sore by the time he eased into the saddle that the hardened leather on the stallion felt like a down feather cushion.

"Well, we've lost another hour on the Browlers, though I'm sure we're making better time on them. Still have their scent?" he asked the lion, who nodded its huge head as it ran alongside the mounted Draconus.

Shoryu had the lead, as swift and fleet of foot as a coyote as he was in the form of a coyote-man.

Portenda ran a quick estimate in his head as he picked up the trail again, and put their time now as being only thirty-one hours behind the Browlers. Something had slowed them down, and a short while later, the trio passed an odd sight; various belongings scattered on the side of the road, in no particular order.

"They probably wised up and emptied the wagon when they noticed the roans were slower than their previous horses," Collin mused aloud. In the company of three animals, two of whom were still thinking in complex patterns, Collin rode on, content with the peace and quiet.

* * * *

A day later, as the Browlers continued on undeterred in their covered wagon, Benjamin said a silent prayer in his head when he spotted Mount Toane, its peak just visible as the wagon ascended another long hill. When the horses cleared the top of the rise, he had only to turn his eyes a little east, and he could see the dipping valley that fronted the demesne that once housed Tanarak of Sidius and Richard Vandross.

It's a wicked place, he thought, and for a moment, Benjamin Browler was convinced that he could see a thick purple aura radiating out around the base of the mountain.

"There is a foul odor in the air," Dean said from behind Ben, a comment that caught all three of his brothers' attention. "This place smells of death and decay."

Sean, Benjamin and Reggie all picked up the scent that Dean was talking about. The air had in fact taken on the scent of rotten meat, thick and pungent. Sean, who had previously balked at Ben's superstitious beliefs, now looked at his younger brother with an expression of alarm.

"Ben, how long has it been since we came across any Greenskins?" He pulled out his map of the continent and unrolling the cloth on the floor of the wagon, covering their rummy board. He no longer cared about the game. Ben's earlier worry might very well be valid: a demonic presence may well have caused the locals to vacate the area.

"Not for about an hour or two," came Ben's reply, which did Sean's heart and head no good. *They knew,* Sean thought. *The troopers all knew, and even if we have clearance to pass through untouched, they won't care if a demon or two decides to snatch us up! The bastards!* Not that he could complain to the troopers' superiors—too much of that and the documents they were carrying would eventually be taken to someone high up in their forces, high enough to tell them that the papers were forged. Orcs, Ogres and Trolls may have been dumb as bricks, but Goblins, Hobgoblins and the occasional Kobold willing to admit their heritage would see right through the forgery. They'd be caught up either way!

"Okay, we're still good." Sean tried to think of a way out of the area that wouldn't raise an alarm to the troopers, who would not expect them to stray from Mount Toane's radius. "We're just going to have to prepare ourselves for anything that might happen. Everybody, grab your weapons! Ben, slow the horses to a walk, but stay with them. We're going to walk past this area, and if we run across something we can't handle, we're hopping back in and getting out of here."

"And if we *can* handle it," Reggie asked, checking the readings on his current power cell for his right arm.

"Then we handle it and walk on. Protect the horses and the wagon, boys. It's our best mode of transportation for now." Sean stepped off of the moving wagon and onto the tough, brown grass of the plains near Mount Toane. The stench of decay struck him with such force once he was outside that he was amazed that Ben hadn't retched and passed out.

Dean jumped out next, followed lastly by Reggie. Sean made a hand signal to Dean, who headed to the right side of the wagon with Reggie in tow. Sean remained on the left side of the wagon, so that he could more easily talk to Ben and give him instructions, should they need to escape in a hurry.

The air in the area began then to thicken with a greenish mist, and the brothers' line of sight was cut down to about fifty meters in any direction.

"Crap," Sean heard Dean say on the other side of the horses. "This could mean big trouble, Sean. Whatever this stuff is, it isn't poisonous to us or the horses, but it doesn't look right either."

"I know what you mean," Sean said. "Everybody, put on your masks."

Each brother strapped a nuisance mask over their nose and mouth.

"Is it getting any thicker?"

"No," came Reggie's reply. "I'm going to run an analysis on the air with my arm sensors." His statement no longer mystified Sean. While talking with his brother several days before, Reggie had explained in layman's terms a great deal about the lost technology that he put to use for himself. Sensors, Sean knew, could take and observe a thing or substance, and then tell the user exactly what it was, so long as the information was available. Reggie had taken sensors from an ancient mecha man buried in a set of ruins in the Elven Kingdom while they'd been in the forest on Svelk's assignment. Now Sean sincerely hoped that the database attached to the sensors knew what this stuff hanging in the air was.

"Anything yet," Sean asked after five minutes. He didn't feel like he was making any real progress, but he could tell that the ground was at least passing under his feet.

"Nothing specific," Reggie replied, nearly shouting. A wind had kicked up, and was now blustering past them with ruthless volume. "All I'm getting just now is that it's some form of magic! I'm hoping I get something more detailed in a minute!"

Sean hoped so too, because so long as their field of vision was so limited, he couldn't tell if they were heading in the right direction.

Nor could he tell what might be laying in wait around them.

* * * *

Portenda came to a sudden stop, which also brought Collin and Shoryu to a halt. The Simpa Bounty Hunter rose to his bestial form, and sniffed the air for a long minute.

"We've just gained a shitload of time on them. I'm not sure why or how," he said, looking around the flatlands surrounding them. The trio had almost gotten to the Greenskin Nation's borders, and over the course of the last six hours, he knew that they had somehow gained roughly twice that on the Browler brothers. Shoryu wasn't aware of this change, but he did not possess the same supernatural powers of perception the Simpa enjoyed.

"Are you sure?" Collin asked excitedly.

"Yes, quite sure," Portenda said. "They may have all stopped to sleep, and instead of keeping a watch just all tucked in. Come on, we don't want to lose this somehow."

With that, he once again shifted shape, and led the way forward now that he had a better lead on the scent than the Cuyotai.

* * * *

"Sean," Reggie said from almost right next to Sean's ear.

The oldest Browler jumped nearly out of his skin, expecting to turn and see a monster of his nightmares lurking there, but it was just his brother.

"Sean, we're in trouble. This is some sort of demon magic according to my sensors, and no other relevant data has come up for a good ten minutes, best as I can judge."

"Best as you can judge." Sean raised an eyebrow and his voice over the wind. "What's that supposed to mean?"

"My clock is all out of whack," Reggie said, genuinely distressed. His instruments had never failed him before, but when he showed the clock display to his brother, Sean could understand his discomfort. The numbers on the digital display were running backward, then forward, then skipping entire hours and minutes and seconds, and then reset themselves to all zeroes before starting the cycle over again.

"That's never happened, has it?" Sean asked, feeling rather stupid for doing so.

"Well, the first time I activated it yeah, but I just had to manually reset it," Reggie replied, his eyes wide with panic. "Sean, this is bad, whatever it is! We have to figure out a way out of this, because I think this is some sort of magical trap set by a demon!"

Sean had suspected as much for a few minutes now. He'd tripped over the same rock at least half a dozen times now, and each time the rock felt less and less real, less solid.

"Don't worry, Reggie, we'll figure this out," Sean said with false confidence. "Go back and confer with Dean, see if he has any ideas. He's a clever one."

Reggie nodded and left Sean's side, and for the first time in quite a while, Sean Browler honestly thought he might die where he walked.

* * * *

Portenda and Shoryu shape-shifted into their bestial states the moment they spotted the Orc troopers on the road ahead. Collin slowed his stallion and dismounted, leading it by the reins for the time being. "This could get ugly," Collin said under his breath.

"Not necessarily," Shoryu offered. "I am a diplomat, don't forget. I'm sure I can reason with them."

No sooner were the words out of his mouth than a warning arrow shot landed scant inches from his foot.

"Hold your place," one of the Orc troopers called. Only eleven hours before, he'd been informed by the guards he and his allies replaced on the watch of this road that they'd allowed a group of Human men through with a covered wagon. They'd had a sealed letter from the king himself, stating that the men were to be allowed uninterrupted travel through the Greenskin Nation. Only the demons near Mount Toane could be allowed to touch the Humans if they were fool enough to get near that dreaded place, and nobody should be allowed to follow them, no matter whom.

"We are holding," Shoryu said in as polite a tone as he could muster. The troopers were clad as those they had replaced, but with a difference in combative equipment. The previous shift, the day watch, tended to lean toward axes and spears. This unit preferred siege crossbows and maces, each man wielding both weapons. The Orc who fired upon them started a slow approach, but stopped a good ten yards away from Collin, who stood slightly closer than his companions to the Orcs.

"What business you have in our nation," the Orc asked in broken Common. "Speak now, or be dead!"

"We are merely passing on northward, good sir," Shoryu said before Collin could speak.

That's fine, Collin thought as the Orc turned his attention to the Cuyotai.

"Doggy-man speak for all," the Orc asked, to which Shoryu nodded in harmony with the Bounty Hunters. "Doggy-man," the Orc said then, addressing the Councilor in the same way most Greenskins of his level of intellect did. "Where you go in north lands?"

"We are heading for Arcade, also known as The Port of Arcade," Shoryu said as smoothly as he could. He didn't twitch or flinch, or give any of the other subtle signs that he wasn't being entirely truthful. If he'd learned anything in the political arena, it was how to lie, and lie well. He didn't do it much himself, but he had watched others in the High Council and Her Majesty's Court do it so much that it had become a spectator sport for him. Who lies the best, and how grand is the lie? he thought to himself.

The Orc appeared to be thinking heavily on the response from Shoryu. He scratched his broad forehead with a thick green finger. "Arcade filled with thieves and brigands," the Orc said. "You no look like thief. What you do in Arcade?"

"Ah, you see, my friends are Bounty Hunters, actually, and we're tracking a group of fellows who are heading in that direction," Shoryu said. In the next instant he was using his thin short sword to stave off a blow from the Orc's mace, which came crashing down for his snout.

"Nice job being diplomatic, Councilor," Collin quipped as he blocked an incoming mace attack and performed a swift and brutal self-defense technique on the second Orc. The third Orc launched himself through air at Portenda, who simply knelt down and drew out his spear, thrusting it forward and up, right through the Orc's jaw and then the top of his head as his own weight bore him down the shaft of the weapon.

The Orc pressing down on Shoryu used his sheer strength to drive the Cuyotai back and then to the ground, and for a horrible moment, Shoryu was sure that he was going to be crushed. Then a burst of heat and crimson light shot out through the Orc's chest, and his body stiffened as Collin's breath weapon finished working its wonders on his nervous system. Before the Greenskin could fall atop him, Shoryu rolled out of the way, grateful when he heard the wet slap of the body on the hard ground.

"Well," Shoryu said, dusting himself off as he looked from one Bounty Hunter to the other apologetically. "Um, negotiations are finished. Shall we take our leave?"

"Yes," said Portenda, who grabbed Collin by the shoulder before the Draconus could remount his stallion. "But we'll be going on foot from here. Best to always be at the ready, you know?"

While he didn't like it, Collin agreed, and together they set off once more to the north.

* * * *

"It feels like we've been walking for hours," Dean complained as he came over to Sean's side of the wagon. The wind had died down, but the smog of green appeared to have become even denser than before, limiting their vision to about twenty meters on all sides. "And quite frankly, Reggie's starting to give me the creeps. He's falling apart on us, Sean, and I don't mean he needs a wrench and new bolts. This isn't rational, and anything that isn't rational doesn't fit in his little world."

"I'm well aware of that, Dean," Sean said. "Do you have any sutras or ninpo that can get us out of this?"

"I don't think so," Dean replied. "Also, Sean, I think the temperature is dropping. You see?" Dean blew air through his nuisance mask, and Sean saw that his brother's breath was steaming. "If the temperature drops again, it could be bad for the horses."

"Ben, stop the horses and untie them. Let them rest," Sean said to his younger brother. "Dean, go bring Reggie over to this side. We're going to figure this out before we take another step."

Dean nodded, Ben stopped the horses, and Sean sat down on the hard brown grass. *What's going on?* he wondered. We keep walking and walking, but we aren't getting anywhere. And that rock over there isn't real, he thought, seeing the same rock again to his left. Something about it just didn't feel right. It felt, well, fake.

Dean and Reggie came back around the wagon and sat before Sean, while Ben unhooked the horses, who looked about ready to drop.

The four Browler brothers sat in a tight circle, each man trying to figure out a way out of this trap. It was Ben who finally had an idea that proved useful to them ten minutes later, if Sean's sense of time wasn't off.

"Reg, that thing can analyze stuff, right? See if there's anything wrong with the soil we're walking on."

Reggie, while still a bit panicked, had his head on just tight enough to do as he was asked, and Sean would thank the gods for that later. He scooped up a handful of dirt, and underneath the soil, where he'd dug his artificial hand in, there was simply white space.

"What the hells," Sean asked with Ben in unison.

Just then, one of the horses dropped to its side, falling asleep. When the first loud animal snore escaped its throat, the animal disappeared altogether. "That's not right," Ben said.

Sean snapped his fingers, realizing in a moment of epiphany why they hadn't gotten anywhere, and why the rock had started to feel fake! "We're asleep! We've been put to sleep! The demon cast some sort of sleeping spell on us!"

Reggie looked down at his analyzer, and jumped up.

"You're right! My display just changed! It's a demonic sleeping spell! We have to figure out how to wake up!"

Before Sean could stop him, Dean shot to his feet and struck Reggie in the back of the head. When Reggie dropped, he disappeared in a cloud of smoke. Sean gave Dean a curious look.

"Well, it makes sense, if you think about it," the Ninja said defensively. "Sleep here, wake up there." He delivered a similar blow to Ben's neck.

Ben disappeared.

"And don't worry, I know how to do it to myself," he said, striking Sean upside his head.

Sean felt himself falling forward, and then being pulled up as his vision blurred and then came back into focus.

Awake, he thought, *I'm awake.*

A few feet away, he saw Dean slowly rising from the ground, and beyond the Ninja, Reggie and Ben were wrestling with some strange-looking creature. To Sean, it appeared to be a man made of mud, and its struggles against his two brothers appeared to be mostly in vain. "Sneaky bastard," Sean said aloud. "It knocked us out so that it could slither up and kill us in our sleep!"

"Should have seen it," Ben called over his shoulder as he and Reggie bore the creature to the ground. "It was sloshing along at about an inch a minute! Probably came all the way from there," Ben said, pointing toward the open mouth of Mount Toane.

Sean stomped over toward his brothers and the weakly thrashing mud demon, pulling one of his long knives from its sheath.

Sean looked down into the inhuman face of the mud demon, its grotesque mouth warping and stretching to make odd warbling noises. So enraged was he with this deformed weakling that he said nothing. Sean Browler merely buried the long knife through the demon's forehead, and watched as the monster steamed, smoked, and then melted into a pile of salt.

He looked back over his shoulder, and saw that the horses were up, but looking rather dazed and uncomfortable. They'd fallen asleep in their harnesses, after all.

"Come on, boys. We've got places to be."

The brothers got to the wagon, and Ben took up the reins once more. In order to rest the horses a little, the three other Browlers got up in the wagon, and Ben didn't urge them beyond a walking pace. It seemed the best thing to do for the time being.

The Elf-Queen's Bounty

* * * *

Shoryu loosed one last arrow, catching the final Goblin shock trooper of the bunch. "That makes twelve," he said with a sadistic grin, his canine lips pulling back far enough to reveal his gums. Nearly forty assorted Greenskins lay about the trio in pools of their own blood, a military unit running routine exercises when they'd spotted the intruders. From his perch atop a bloated Troll corpse, Collin lit his pipe and enjoyed the tang of the first puff.

"Nine over here, but you will observe that all of my kills are Trolls, Mr. Tearfang," he said with fake hauteur. "How about you, big guy," he asked Portenda as the Simpa put his foot against the chest of a dead Goblin who lay prone and impaled on his spear. Blood exploded out of the little man's mouth as he flew off of the weapon.

"Sixteen, including five Goblins, six Orcs, four Hobgoblins and a Troll," Portenda reported in militant fashion. He took a good whiff of the air, and found that despite all of the blood, feces and other bodily secretions of their fallen foes, he could still detect the Browler brothers. "This little fracas set us back about fifteen minutes, nothing more. But they are moving again," he said. "We're probably about eight hours behind. We'll wait for you to finish your pipe, and then we're out of here. No more fooling around with the likes of these. We'll go animus, Shoryu and I, and you'll run, hard. I'm not spending another day in their wake."

"Fair enough," the Red Draconus said chuffing away on his pipe. Collin's eyes were drawn once more to the first victim of the battle, the Troll that Portenda had felled.

When the Troll led the charge, Portenda had merely stood his ground while Shoryu leaped away, readying his bow. Collin hadn't seen Portenda draw his mecha weapon, but when the Troll got to within swinging range of his iron club, Portenda had made a single movement, and a gaping hole had blown open in the Troll's face, making a canoe out of his head. It then dropped so fast and hard that its comrades all hesitated, a mistake that gave Shoryu and Collin a chance to open fire on them.

Shoryu had proven to Collin once and for all how deadly and accurate he could be with his bow, landing arrows in at least one arm of every Troll and Orc on the field, thus hindering their ability to fight. This he'd done before the Greenskins closed to melee range, and in that regard, the Cuyotai had been able to hold his own as well, for the most part. When prepared for the fight, the Councilor moved around with speed and grace, taking his slashes and stabs where he could, playing conservative while he struck at his enemies' arms and legs. When the foe was properly disabled and slowed, he leaped away, drew his bow and arrow, and fired a single deadly shot to their throats. Time-consuming, but effective.

"Well, I'm done," Collin said, tamping out his pipe on the ground, grinding the ashes into the grass. "Lead the way, Portenda."

The Simpa took his animus form, and then charged ahead at almost top speed. To his and Shoryu's credit, the Draconus had some trouble keeping up.

Chapter Ten
Encounters in the Night

General Bergen sat up suddenly, giving his bedmate quite the surprise.

"What's the matter, my dear," the Queen asked from the cover of her sheets. "Is it your knee again?"

Bergen had injured his right knee many years before in a skirmish with hostile Minotaur invaders from the north who wished to annex part of the kingdom's forest for their own territory. He hadn't hurt it himself, of course- a four hundred-pound Minotaur with a mace and an attitude had seen to that. Still, said Minotaur had died by his blade that day, and the reminder of that brush with death was a dull throbbing that sometimes kept the General awake.

"Yes, I'm sorry dear," he lied, looking to the high glass window on the right side of the bed, his side. As he'd expected, a yellow flower hung down by a wire from the outer wall. "I think I just need to walk it off. Go back to sleep for now, my love," he said sincerely, looking at the Queen's lovely form beneath the silk sheets.

He donned his long johns and his robe, as well as his thick slippers, and headed out of Her Majesty's private quarters.

When he stepped out into the hallway, the first person he saw was Marielle, one of the Queen's personal attendants. A lovely young Elven woman, Marielle curtsied politely to the General, who gave her a warm, open smile. "Good evening, Marielle. I trust you have the, ah, item in a safe place?"

"Oh yes, General Bergen," she replied quietly, smiling ear to ear. "When are you going to ask her?"

"I was thinking tomorrow, at breakfast," he replied casually, his hands tucked into the pockets of the robe.

Marielle gasped with her hand over her mouth, but could not contain her girlish glee. Her cheeks were flush with color, and Bergen knew that the rest of the mansion staff would be expecting the proposal of marriage the next morning as they seated the Queen and future King of the Elven Kingdom.

Marielle giggled then, and gave the General an impish look before he headed for the stairs that led to the roof. "Shall I call you Your Majesty then sir?"

"Hmm, just this once, until tomorrow," he said playfully. "Now run along, Marielle, and inform Timothy that we'll be having a grand feast in the morning. I want to drain every last drop of suspense out of you and the rest of the ladies as I can, and a big meal should do nicely," he said, and she dropped another curtsy to the General before darting away.

Nice girl, he thought. *Too bad she's an idiot.* The General headed to the end of the east wing, and opened the door to the stairs that led to the roof.

As he expected, when he opened the door to the roof of the mansion, he saw nobody that shouldn't be there. As arranged, he went from one nearly invisible guard to another, telling them to head off of the roof for a short bit, because he wanted some time to think in peace.

All five guards did as they were told, and a single man only now joined him. "All clear, James," he whispered. James Svelk came out from his own hiding place, a spot on the side of the mansion that held a secret compartment for guards to hide out in. The hidden port had been put in by the first King of the Elves, but for one reason or another, the port had been forgotten.

A good thing we have it, General Bergen thought.

The former major looked the General up and down, and smiled lasciviously. "You smell like sex, good General. Already getting ready to sire the next in line for the throne, are you?"

"I thought I told you not to report here again, James. What news have you?" Bergen had thought he'd seen the last of James Svelk for a while after leaving him the precious gems in the Fiefdom of Lemago. That, apparently, hadn't been accurate.

"As you are aware, I have friends in a lot of places, General," Svelk said, walking a few paces away from the General. "Friends who keep me in information, sir. The Browler brothers are passing through the Greenskin Nation as we speak. They will finish the job, sir. Once they're in Arcade, things can proceed here as they have to."

"Is that all you came for, James? A quick progress report? Because I can tell you that it seems quite unnecessary to me."

"Oh, of course it isn't sir," Svelk said with a mischievous grin. He turned to face the General once more, his hands behind his back. "I was just wondering if perhaps, when the deed is done and the plan followed through to the end, I might be given a promotion when I'm pardoned for my abandonment by His Majesty the King?" He gave the General a sweeping bow that smelled of mockery.

"You should be grateful that you're getting the pardon and reinstatement, period," Bergen grumbled. "What makes you think I'll give you a promotion?"

"Oh, I think you'll be doing a lot of things for me under your leadership as King," Svelk said, still smiling as he tiptoed closer to the

General. "That document that I had Dean forge for you? Did I forget to mention that when I had the parchment magically aged to be believable, I also had a little fault put in it, in the paper itself?" Svelk's whisper came out in a rush of excitement.

"What?" was the General's baffled response.

"Yes, yes of course! You see, I still happen to have the first Bergen family history tucked away in a safe place, ready to be shown to Her Majesty by whatever guard I send for it. And if that guard should happen to want to know about the authenticity of palace's version of said family history? Why, I will gladly inform him that he need only hold it in a cloud of heated steam to reveal it for the falsehood it is." Svelk laughed quietly at the general's stunned countenance. He clapped his hands together twice, a tad too loudly, and thrust himself nose-to-nose with the General. "Now if you'll excuse me, General, I must head to my temporary home. Oh, and by the way?" He stepped away and flourished a grand, sweeping bow once more. "All hail the king, sir."

Laughing like a hyena, James Svelk disappeared from the roof of the Queen's mansion.

General Bergen realized that, like the Queen, he had been played for a fool.

* * * *

As Svelk arrived at the front door of his own temporary home, he realized how wonderful teleportation spell scrolls would be if they could be concentrated and placed permanently on an object. He was fairly certain he'd seen something like that at a magic shop once, a bracelet that allowed the wearer to teleport to anyplace they'd been themselves. He'd have to go purchase one with the rare gems General Bergen had given him as payment to the Browler brothers. After all, Svelk surmised, he'd never actually have to give the stones over to that pack of thieves. Once their mission was fulfilled, they'd wait for him to contact them in the Port of Arcade, in case he wanted more work done.

But he would never be contacting Sean Browler again, he thought as he entered the simple cottage that was his home for the last three years. He was careful to travel to and from his home only at night, so that the local patrolmen didn't see his face or get a good look at his general outline. He was, after all, a wanted man even in the territories he lived in. Svelk lived here under the name Trevor Augustus, and thus far all of his falsified papers had worked out all right. Of course, he'd only had to submit them to government offices via postal carrier, and not in person. This region's government worked wonderfully in his favor like that.

The city of Ja-Wen bustled and moved ever forward outside of his cottage in the tenth district, and James Svelk flipped a switch on the wall next to the door as he closed it. Electric light spread through the room from the overhead fixture, another gift of the technological knowledge that had survived the Fall of Mecha. His home was comfortable, furnished with just the right amount of furniture one might expect to see if he had a wife. That was one thing he missed, he supposed, even just a little bit- companionship. He'd lived alone since fleeing from the authorities in the Elven Kingdom, and most Elven women he'd met outside of the kingdom bored him to tears. They had no real appreciation for their culture or heritage when compared to a woman born within the kingdom.

James heaved a sigh, walking over to the liquor cabinet in his little living room and pouring himself a shot of scotch. He really could have gone for a nice drink of buren, but that was a drink exclusively made and served back in the forest of the Elves. It wasn't that he didn't like the drinks made by the Humans, the Dwarves and the Jafts; he just missed the finer things of his Racial history and culture. Living in Ja-Wen just wasn't the same, even in the district he lived in, which comprised mostly of Elves and Illeck.

James eased himself into a recliner and plucked from the floor next to it the book he'd been in the process of reading. *When the Bird Takes Flight* was the title of the novel, and it had been written in the early years of the Fifth Age, also known as After the Fall of Mecha. James himself had been born the year before the book had been mass produced and sold around the continent.

Svelk read a little while, and then headed off to bed with a stomach warmed with scotch.

"Empty," he said to himself as he looked at the narrow, single-man bed in his bedroom. Sure, he'd enjoyed the company of prostitutes in his years on the run, but the last couple of years had drained the joy from the meaningless sexual encounters. He'd had nobody to really call his own, and after his first year in Ja-Wen, he'd hit up most of the Illeck and Human professional ladies of the night in the area. They were all vapid, clueless creatures without any sense of culture or refinement, and their company now made him feel ill.

That would change, however, and soon enough he thought with a smile. He would be pardoned for his crimes by the new King of the Elves, and given his post once more. It helped too that he had said king under his thumb. Few manipulators throughout the history of the Elven Kingdom could have said the same.

The Elf-Queen's Bounty

As he removed his day clothes and changed into long johns and a gray nightshirt, Svelk wondered how much like the dark-natured Illeck that were his racial cousins he was. Very much so, he decided, and that didn't really bother him too much. After all, he had Illeck blood in his family lineage.

General Bergen's family history documentation had revealed to him and Sean Browler that the good General had the same problem, however. Nearly two millennia before, official law had declared that no Elf with Illeck blood in their lineage could rise into the position of King or Queen of the Elves. The discovery of such heritage in Bergen's bloodline would render him nothing more than one of the Queen's playthings, if she chose to keep taking him to her bedchambers. The future King of the Elves really should have thought of that before letting Svelk handle the handle the precious document.

His thoughts placed on his own bright future in the Elven Kingdom, James Svelk drifted pleasantly off to the land of slumber, comforted by his superior ability to scheme.

* * * *

Dean Browler, as a Ninja, had access to the arts of sutras and ninpo, special scrolls made by Monks and Ninja that contained magic-like powers. One of the ninpo, which were specific to the Ninja Class, he drew from his pack of prepared scrolls and placed flat on the floor of the wagon as it eased along. He brought his free left hand up under his chin in a sign of prayer, and the Ninja of the Browler Gang concentrated all of his chi on the task of activating the ninpo.

A small flash of green light came from the tiny scroll as it burst into smoke, and he gazed into the smoke.

An image of their pursuers appeared before him, little more than a crude animation, but it gave him an idea of how close he and his brothers were to being caught up to. He didn't like what he saw one bit. "Sean," he said, gaining his elder brother's attention. "They are only a few hours behind us. We've been taking this easy pace too long. If we stop to rest again, they'll catch us up in no time." As he spoke, the image of a charging lion, coyote, and a Red Draconus on horseback faded into nothingness.

"Ben, you heard the man," Sean said from his seat against the far wagon wall. "Get these horses moving on the double. I don't want to deal with the Bounty Hunters just yet."

Ben cracked the reins and gave Dean a raised eyebrow. "You look like you want to say something else, brother."

"Indeed there is, big brother," the Ninja said plainly. "This pass we're going through right now would be the perfect place for me to lay some traps for them. I could use another of those teleportation scrolls of yours and return here to the interior of the wagon after I finish setting them for the accursed Bounty Hunters and their Cuyotai friend."

Sean weighed the risks against the potential benefit they'd gain from shaking their tail, and decided that his brother had indeed come up with a good idea.

"All right, do it. But the second you smell trouble, you get back here to us, you understand?" he said with the full authority granted him by their mother.

Dean grinned and nodded, and after Sean handed him one of the scrolls, the Ninja leaped out of the wagon with his gear on his back.

Sean watched as Dean turned into a hazy dot on the horizon, and before long, they were completely out of sight of Dean Browler.

"I'm worried for him," Reggie confided after a long silence.

"So am I, but he knows what he's doing." Sean pulled out the deck of cards they'd been using for years. "Come on, a few hands of blackjack and then I'll relieve Ben. You and him can either play some more, or get some rest. I'd suggest you do the latter rather than the former, Reggie," Sean said. "You're starting to look a little on the tired side."

"I am," Reggie said through a yawn. "I'll tell you, though, I'm feeling a lot better since we got rid of that mud demon. That was a confusing mess, wasn't it?"

"Just a weak fool who thought he could pull one over on us," Ben said from his seat up front. "And as always, who came out on top?"

"We did, and amen to that," Sean said, dealing the cards.

* * * *

I've only got a couple of hours to work with here, Dean thought as he assessed the narrow path between the sloping hills around him. If the trio on their tail was following as closely and as tightly behind them as he'd seen, he had no more than that to set a few traps and get the hells out of there before they showed up. He didn't want to tell Sean how fast they were being gained on, but from what he'd seen thanks to his ninpo, the Bounty Hunters and Cuyotai were outstripping them for speed by at least six times.

The pocked, rocky sides of the hills on either side of him provided Dean with plenty of inspiration for a few nasty surprises for the pursuers, but would it be nasty enough to delay them by more than a few minutes? He had to think in terms of causing threatening injury to a Simpa, a Cuyotai, and a Red Draconus. While the dragon-man couldn't regenerate like his two companions, harming him would be enough of a task to be frustrating. What he wouldn't give for the consultation of his instructors, Thaddeus Fly and Markus Trent!

Trent had proven to be a master of traps and setting them, Dean thought. While Trent's Guild Headmaster had been quite the combat monkey (a term often affected in Tamalarian slang), Trent himself seemed to be the more crafty and cunning of the two. Dean hadn't been trained one whit by the mysterious Akimaru, but somehow he got the impression while he was in Desanadron that he shouldn't ask much about the white clad Ninja. Fly and Trent both seemed to shy from the subject of Akimaru, so Dean never pressed the matter.

Now, however, Dean found himself wondering if Akimaru might have had some piece of wisdom to offer about circumstances such as his. The environmental traps would be easy enough to lay in terms of causing a rockslide in the hillsides. However, he was lacking severely in supplies for setting more than a few other traps for the Bounty Hunters and Cuyotai, so he'd have to make them particularly efficient.

Casting aside his doubts, the Ninja set to work.

He spent a little over an hour of his time preparing the rockslides, which proved mostly a task in terms of ensuring that it didn't happen while he worked in the area. The area covered by the trap wouldn't be large, but that would work in his favor. When the three men came around a bend in the path, they would inevitably trip one of the wires that held the manually displaced rocks and small stopper objects that Dean had set in the hillsides. They would be pelted with stones and earth, and if the lycanthropes remained in their animus form, they might well be buried under the displaced soil, at least partially.

Heading up the path a ways from the rockslide trap, Dean opened his pack again and started retrieving the steel springs and attachments to set the next trap. At a particularly narrow point, which the wagon and horses his brothers traveled in had barely cleared, he dug up a shallow trench in the dirt with his boot heels. In this small depression he set several lengths of metal pressure plates, which he joined together with the springs. These he also strung bits of thin cord around, drawing the long cords out a short distance to a large outcropping of stones. In the stones he set two ranks of silver shuriken, all attached to a launching board, which would hurl them at their targets as soon as any pressure more than a couple of pounds came down on the pressure plates. He buried the pressure plates, careful not to put too much weight on the ground himself, and checked his timepiece.

Checking the timepiece proved unnecessary, however. As soon as he pulled the pocket watch out of one of his pouches, he heard the approach of the Bounty Hunters. Wasting no time, Dean withdrew the teleportation scroll, and vanished from the pass.

* * * *

Portenda led his two companions and the horse on a brutal, relentless charge now, so close did he feel he was to catching up with the present targets. The same litany kept circuiting through his mind as he ran along in his animus form—*catch them, they'll give you Svelk. Catch them, they'll give you Svelk.* For him, the Browler brothers were a means to an end.

For Collin, whose horse was starting to complain a little about the demanding pace, the thrill was ever greater. With the arrest and delivery of Ben and Sean Browler, he was looking at a combined total of eighty-thousand gold pieces, all of which would go to sustaining his apartments and other expenses for the next few years. It might even buy him a new pipe and some booze, he thought wistfully. Reggie Browler would probably show up as a bounty head in the Fiefdom of Lemago soon enough, but he was going to hand deliver that little weirdo to Captain Jugura. The half-Jaft Samurai deserved that much after giving them the information that had led to the battlefield, where Portenda and Shoryu had first picked up the scent of the Browler brothers.

Shoryu felt none the worse for wear despite all the running on four legs. Though he was a little cramped, true, and perhaps more winded than he wanted to admit, he was having the time of his life. Here, out in the wilds and flatlands of Tamalaria, he was engaged in work that didn't require him to really think too much. Even the battle with the Greenskin military unit hadn't exactly been taxing on his ability to think, as it was mostly fueled by instinct and training. He held the title of a diplomat, but his true calling always seemed to be the lure of adventuring. If he had any real big complaints, they only came in the form of his thoughts on the little meals the trio had taken while walking, saving time by not really stopping.

"Looks like we've got a bit of a narrow pass to head through up there," Collin called ahead to the animals running in the lead. "We'll have to go single file." Because he had the better senses of perception, Portenda's lion body took the lead, with Shoryu following close behind, and Collin on his horse in the rear. The ground level slightly dipped as they started to head between two hills that gradually sloped up while the pass sloped down.

The first stretch of the pass flashed by Portenda's eyes in something of a blur. He had the Browlers' scent, and one of them in particular stood out from the other three. Normally, he would have stopped to think about that, but the mighty Simpa had spent far too much time in his animus form, and his instincts called out over his long years of training. *We're hot on their heels now*, the voice of instinct called. *Don't stop now!*

Reminding himself that he had to keep a pace that the others behind him could follow, the lion plowed forward at the same charging pace.

A bend in the path up ahead. He kept his body moving but prepared his legs for the change in direction. *Right up there*, he thought, *one of them was right up there until only a minute ago.* Why was that? Why did one scent among all four stick out so much? Had he been in his bestial form, he might have paused to think through that bit of information, but as he was not, he did not.

He charged blindly around the corner with Shoryu and Collin in tow, and only when his front right leg felt a slight tug against it did he slow down.

Oh shit, came the clear, rational voice of his bestial form in his own mind.

The first stone that flew from the displaced stoppers struck Portenda squarely along his left flank, bruising a few of his ribs. Collin's horse whinnied and reared up, throwing him off as the stallion turned and bolted back in the direction they'd come from.

"I paid good money for you, you son of a bitch," the Red Draconus raged from his flaring back. "Get back h-," he managed before a large amount of rocks and dirt started to pour atop him from the right hillside.

More rocks flew, and as Portenda and Shoryu shifted up into their bestial forms, they discovered that loose earth had already covered them up to their waists, restricting their movements.

Shoryu heard a thick, thunderous booming noise as one of the larger stones on the left hillside, closest to him, came free of its earthen moorings and dropped right at him.

The Cuyotai managed to lunge just a little forward before the stone landed, striking him in the lower back and pinning him into the loose soil. Through the pain in his head from getting pelted by much smaller rocks, he managed to hear Portenda shouting something about digging down into the soil.

Collin, already half-buried in the soil, tried to stand up and was clobbered for his efforts by another large stone. The trap hadn't quite run its course yet, apparently, and his forehead split open from the blow, blood trickling down into his reptilian eyes. Collin did then what seemed the sensible thing, since his senses were a little dazed; he listened to what

Portenda had to say. He started to lie back down, forcing himself through the loose dirt and chunks of earth, until he was entirely buried.

By this point both Collin and Shoryu felt their lungs cramping, the lack of available air crunching in on them. The Red Draconus knew how he'd get out of this predicament after a minute of hard thought. He wondered what solution the Cuyotai had, if any.

"Can you still hear me," a voice called. Portenda, he thought.

"Yes," he called back, trying not to swallow too much of the dirt around and over him.

"Hmph," came another nearby reply.

Okay, Collin thought, *so the Councilor is still with us as well.*

"Good. Shoryu, I'm coming to get you," the voice called. "Just keep making some sort of noise and I'll locate you! Don't try too hard to breathe or open your mouth to speak! The landslide is over, but stay put! There may be other problems," Portenda's voice informed the Cuyotai and Red Draconus. "Collin, I think I know how you're going to get up and out."

Well, I don't want to disappoint him, Collin thought, opening his mouth just a little and blowing a wide cone of flames from deep in his stomach through the dirt and rocks over his body. He could hardly believe it when he saw how deep he'd been buried; at least three feet of dirt and rocks covered his body!

Extending his arms as well as he could, Collin Caulkins hauled himself up out of his makeshift grave, onto the loosely packed earth from the landslide trap. He spotted Portenda, who was down on all fours, listening to the ground every now and again.

Collin saw on Portenda's face something he never thought he'd seen before, or would see again—flat panic.

I've never lost anyone before, Portenda thought the moment he'd seen Shoryu get struck by one last stone before trying to dig into the soil to safety from rock projectiles. The stone had appeared to knock the Councilor out, but his body had sunk into the loose soil under and around him like he was being pulled down into it. If the Simpa Bounty Hunter didn't act fast, the Cuyotai might suffocate in the dirt of this deadly trap.

Not in all the years I've worked in this field, he thought again, desperately trying to listen for any sounds from Shoryu.

The Councilor had grunted something a minute ago, if only out of pain and discomfort, but Portenda hadn't heard anything else. The lack of sound from the Cuyotai Hunter burned on his nerves with each passing second, and he knew he was losing control of his calm, icy demeanor. Though he didn't show feeling to others in his line of work, he was aware that his panic was as readable on his face as the words in a book. He looked up one second, and for what felt to him like a lifetime, a silent message passed from Simpa to Draconus: *this is my fault, I got him into this.* No longer able to control his actions entirely, the Simpa started heaving up enormous showers of grit and rock with his bare hands.

Hmm, Shoryu thought a minute after being buried in the sucking soil. *This is odd. The ground seems to actually be swallowing me up. I should probably go with it.* The stone struck him in the head only a moment earlier, just after Portenda had instructed him to bury himself a little under the collected soil. He understood Portenda's instructions; burrowing shallowly into the collected dirt would spare him from further damage from flying screed and stones. But the stone hit him, and as the insistent soil tugged at him, the Cuyotai simply let go.

"Come to me," the soil said into his furry ears as he was dragged down.

Funny, he thought in reply, *I've never heard the ground talk to me. Especially not in my wife's voice.*

"Come into my arms," the soil said, speaking to him once more.

Okay, I'm game, he thought back, certain now that he could communicate with the soil and screed around him.

Shoryu was pulled down, and thought he heard Portenda's voice far away.

"I'm down here," he tried to shout, but heard himself only make a loud, "Hmmph," sound. His mind was addled from the blow to his head, he knew.

From that point, he heard nothing from anywhere but the soil, and the ground's words were conveyed to his mind directly.

"He's looking for you," the ground said to Shoryu, once more in the tone and voice of his beloved wife, back in Whitewood. "He's lucky that Mother Gaia sent me a vision the moment that wicked man set to making her part of the plan to destroy you all. He looks to be going into quite a fit," the ground added. "I think we'll let him squirm a little before I help you to the surface."

Shoryu slowly became aware that there was a small pocket of air around him in the surrounding soil, and when he turned his head slightly to the left, he could see the rutted marks of a wagon's passage directly beneath him. He couldn't immediately put one and one together, but something about this situation seemed familiar.

Where are you watching him from, he thought to the surrounding earth.

"From an exposed root in the hillside," came the reply of the earth.

Finally, Shoryu was able to make sense of his circumstances. The Browlers, or one of them at least, had set a landslide trap for the Bounty Hunters and him. When Mother Gaia, Ellen Daires-Tearfang's chosen goddess, had become aware of what the Browlers intended, she'd sent Ellen a vision. The Elven Gaiamancer had been in the middle of scolding Toshiya for one of his immature little pranks. The vision hit her with such force that she'd actually told him to just get out of her sight and see her in the morning.

Focusing her mana, Ellen allowed her mind's eye to follow the trail of tangible energy that her goddess had left, all the way to her husband. Through an exposed root in the side of a hill she viewed the entire incident, and used her considerable powers of magic to work the ground and protect him. Had she the strength from afar, she would have aided the Simpa and Draconus as well, but she knew her own limits. So she saved the obvious choice.

"Shoryu, by the will of all the gods above willing to hear me, say something," Portenda bellowed almost at the top of his lungs. He'd dug right down to the road in several spots, but could not locate the Councilor.

Ellen had a hand in that; she'd used her small sanctuary of protection around Shoryu to good effect, and moved him away from the Bounty Hunter. She realized she shouldn't be toying around this way, as her mana supply was draining fast, but she couldn't help it.

All right, she thought, *enough is enough*. She parted the soil around her husband with her powers, and then severed her connection from the root in the side of the hill that overlooked the scene of the Bounty Hunters and her husband.

Portenda, stilled by the sudden shifting in the dirt, looked on in awe as Shoryu Tearfang came up out of a hole that had appeared in the mound of soil he stood half sunk in.

"Hey there," Shoryu said with a sheepish grin. "Um, perhaps I should explain."

Collin and Portenda both made a dash for the Cuyotai, and were asking him a hundred questions about injuries he might have and if he could breathe on his own okay.

Shoryu would have laughed if not for the strangeness of Portenda's reaction. *Wow*, he thought, *Mr. All Business really seems shook up. Was he actually worried about me?* He couldn't make out the exact questions they were asking, but Shoryu noticed that Collin was hissing something in his native tongue, and Portenda's eyes were closing slightly, his demeanor returning toward the sort of cold, calculated aloofness that he always displayed.

Inside the Simpa's mind, order was swiftly being restored. His heart ceased thudding like a child on a new drum, and his blood pressure was coming down. The cold sweat that had broken out on his thinly furred forehead evaporated and his sense of urgency started to climb back to normal levels. In addition, his senses of perception, although decreased due to his outbursts, had not become so dulled that he couldn't smell the silver nearby. Another trap lay close to the trio, and they would all have to be careful to avoid it, especially the Councilor, whose health he was personally responsible for. He'd promised Ellen Daires-Tearfang the safe return of her husband, and he intended to deliver on his word.

"What?" Shoryu asked to one last question from the Simpa Bounty Hunter.

"I said, are you well enough to travel again?" Portenda put a reassuring, steadying hand on Shoryu's shoulder. The archer had been under the soil for a good while, and he didn't want Shoryu to push himself too hard if his lungs had indeed been cramped from his submersion.

"I will be in a short bit," Shoryu said, being honest with Portenda and himself. His head started to throb, and when he felt the back of it, he found a very tender spot.

"Good. Collin?" The Red Draconus was about to light his pipe, and Portenda slapped it out of his hand irritably.

Shit, the Simpa thought, still not entirely in control of myself. "Sorry, but that can wait," he said to the stunned dragon-man. "Help Shoryu back around the corner of the path for a few minutes. There's still another trap set up around here, and I smell silver."

"You do know that'll hurt you, too, right," Collin asked in a hushed tone. "Look, this wasn't your fault. You didn't get us buried and pounded by rocks." Collin put one of Shoryu's arms over his own shoulders, supporting the Cuyotai's weight easily.

Portenda turned his back on the two of them, sighed, and hung his head slightly.

"This *is* my fault," Portenda said evenly. His tone had the edge of frost that indicated to him that he finally had control of his emotions again, which in turn meant he had control of the situation once more, which was more important. "I blindly led us around the corner without regard for our safety. I focused too much on the scent of the Browlers, and not enough on my own surroundings. I should have seen the tripwire. Now go back around the corner."

"You don't have to do this alone," Shoryu began.

"GO BACK AROUND THE CORNER," Portenda said, his voice eerily unpleasant and commanding.

Shoryu, dazed and confused, blinked and found himself standing back up the path they'd come down, around the corner as he'd been told to do. When he looked at Collin, the Red Draconus had the same perplexed expression he felt forming on his own face.

"What did he just do?" Shoryu asked.

Collin merely shook his head, reached for his pipe in his pouch, and remembered that Portenda had swatted it from his hand. He considered going back for it, thought about the feeling that had coursed through him when Portenda had spoken his command that second time, and decided that the best course of action would be to wait.

Portenda, around the bend in the path and descending the far side of the landslide, sniffed the air heavily, taking his steps slowly and gingerly. He knew a fair deal about traps and the setting of them, though he usually worked with indoor traps of a faster and definitely less lethal nature. He could detect the hated scent of silver, but could not see any telltale glints of metal in the narrow pass between the hills. He cursed himself silently for opening his mouth and speaking so much; had he reserved his perceptive power, he might have a better look around the area. He didn't have the time to waste waiting for that power to build up again though, and he would have to press on with this task without the help of his supernatural abilities.

The hillsides were naturally steep at this point in the pass, so he kept a close eye on them in case a second landslide trap had been set. However, he assumed that the Browler brother who'd done the earlier trap wouldn't be so unoriginal, or have the time to do that. No, that had taken a lot of time and planning, and so the second trap would have to be something simpler. The first trap had been designed to injure and stall the trio; the second trap would be something more businesslike, something designed to cause severe harm or death in a moment's time.

So, he thought, what sort of trigger will it be this time? Another tripwire? Still he lurched forward slowly, cautiously. A timed trap, set to go off a specific amount of time after the first one? No, that seemed unlikely, as the equipment required took time to set up. Thinking about the Ninja of the brothers, he considered then another possibility. There could be sutras or ninpo barely concealed under the dirt path.

Luckily for him, Dean Browler hadn't thought of that.

However, as invulnerable and omnipotent as he sometimes seemed to others, when he stepped down on the pressure plate and felt it click into position, he knew all too quickly that he wasn't.

Ten silver shuriken flew from a large rock up the path, each one scoring a hit up and down his body except the one he ducked, which would have put his eye out permanently.

Each silver projectile landed painfully in his arms, legs, or chest with a hiss of burning flesh and fur, and he let out a howl of agony, dropping to his knees. This too turned out to be a bad move for him, as it pressed another shuriken deeper into the injured leg.

Blinded by searing pain, he dropped onto his side, unaware that even then Collin Caulkins was tearing the projectiles free of his flesh.

Blood spewed from each wound in small rivulets, staining the scrubby ground beneath him.

"How bad is it," he heard Shoryu asking the Red Draconus.

"Not too bad," Collin responded.

Portenda's vision started to clear, and he could just make out Shoryu's worried face and singed claw. He'd been the first to try to remove one of the shuriken, and had been burned by the weapon for his efforts. He'd known it was silver, but couldn't see as such at first. Dean, knowing that the scent would be permanent, had at least painted the weapons black before bringing them on this trip. He knew most Bounty Hunters were lycanthropes these days, and always kept a set on him.

"He's tough, and the armor kept these ones from doing too much damage," Collin said, referring to the shuriken he drew from Portenda's chest, the last of the bunch. "Plus, he does regenerate his wounds."

"True, but wounds made by silver take longer to heal than other wounds." Shoryu knelt near Portenda's head, and waved his damaged hand in front of the Simpa's face. "Can you hear me, Portenda? Can you see my hand?"

"Yeah," the Simpa replied, ashamed at the strained sound of his voice. "Looking a little short in the flesh and hair departments," he added.

Though the weapons had been silver, Collin's assessment about the chest wounds had been spot-on. Already his body worked its regenerative gifts, closing the shallow piercing wounds. "My leg feels like total shit, though," he said, easing up into a sitting position. He looked down at his leg, and could see the bone of his knee exposed to the open air. It could have been worse, but Shoryu had opted to burn his hand on that shuriken when he pulled it out first. It was, overall, the most grievous wound, made worse by landing on it when he'd fallen to his knees.

"Well, it didn't hit the bone," Collin said, pointing to the wound with his pipe in hand. "It could have been worse. We're going to have to stay put for an hour or so before that sucker closes up enough to get moving again. We may as well have a hot meal while we're here." He shuffled away to breathe fire on the scrub grass.

Shoryu used the flames to set up his cooking gear and prepared a simple stew while Collin returned to the prone Simpa. "By the way, what the hells was that little trick of yours back there?"

"What trick?" Portenda asked, playing dumb. He knew he didn't do it well, but when the words were delivered with as much ice as he'd put into them just now, few would brave asking further questions. Then again, Collin happened to be one of the few.

"Whatever it was you did with your voice," the Red Draconus pressed, chuffing blue smoke into the air.

The full force of night had come upon them, the darkling of evening now past. Portenda looked around him at the walls of the pass, and wondered how many traps he might have laid for the Browlers if they managed to get ahead of the thieves. He was trying to remain quiet and avoid the question posed to him, but he'd known Collin for too long, and owed him at least a half-assed explanation.

"It's something I sort of inherited," Portenda said quietly, keeping his eyes away from Collin's. "Every now and again, when I really concentrate, I can use it to make people do things."

"You used it on that Troll when we got into it with the military unit," Collin said, making it a statement, not a question.

Portenda nodded and lowered his head.

"What did you tell it to do?"

"I told the Troll he must have lost his mind to come at me swinging," Portenda said with a wry smile. "You know, I didn't expect those sort of results. I intended to have him just go crazy and confuse his comrades. I didn't think his brain would make a forced exit out the back of his head."

Collin laughed a little at this dark bit of comedy, and thanked Shoryu as the Cuyotai handed him down an earthenware bowl of stew.

"Here you are," Shoryu said, handing another bowl and spoon to Portenda. "You know, we're going to lose a little time on them again."

"We'll catch up," Portenda said. He'd realized something about the Browler brothers when he'd encountered the second trap. They were trying to stay ahead of the trio and stall them, instead of turning around and facing them head-on. Sure, they might just be scared, but that didn't fit with Sean Browler's profile. He'd lead his brothers into battle against other Bounty Hunters and policemen who'd gotten close to them. The troopers in the Fiefdom of Lemago had been unfortunate enough to bring the fight to the Browlers, who had a secret weapon in Reggie. They were buying time, and that only one thing to Portenda.

"What makes you so sure?" Shoryu took a bite of his food.

"Because," Portenda said, voicing his suspicion. "They haven't quite finished their work for James Svelk, and they need to do that before they deal with us."

Chapter Eleven
Three On Three

Dean Browler could hardly believe what he saw in his revealing ninpo when he gazed into the images being shown to him. The Simpa, Portenda the Quiet, had survived being struck by nine silver shuriken, and after only an hour or so of rest, the Bounty Hunters and Cuyotai were on their way after the Browlers again! The only benefit seemed to have been the fact that the Red Draconus's stallion had injured its legs badly in the landslide trap, so he had to ride the Simpa in his animus form. Still, that didn't seem to be slowing them.

Ben gazed ahead at the road, and saw in the middle distance that the horses would take the wagon into a small woodland, still following the path they were set upon. He knew, as did Sean, that these woods marked the northern border of the Greenskin Nation. They had made good time through the country ruled by Goblins, Orcs, Ogres and the like, only spending a couple of days within its borders. *However,* Sean thought, *we still have a few days at least until we reach our destination.*

The eldest of the Browler brothers withdrew his map, and unrolled it on the wagon floor, checking their position, and beginning a brief calculation. At their present pace, it would still be four or five days until they reached territory in which it would be safe to travel openly. After that, it would be another three days until they reached the village where they would pull off their diversion for Svelk.

"We shouldn't bother," Reggie said from his seat across from Sean, as if reading his oldest brother's thoughts. "The Bounty Hunters are after us right now, big brother. Svelk isn't their concern."

"Now Reggie," Sean said, not looking away from his notepad and his calculations. "We never flake out on a client." He rolled up the map. "What would mother say?"

Reggie looked away from his brother, whom he knew to be right. Mother had never turned away a job when it came her way, and neither had their father. Mother had taught her boys to have a certain degree of honor, and to follow the code of rules she'd laid down for them. One of the most important rules she gave them was, 'Finish what you've started'. Sean didn't want to stray from those teachings.

"Big brother, we have a problem," Dean suddenly said from right next to Sean's ear.

"Jeez, back up you pajama-wearing creep," Sean blurted as he flinched sideways. "What's the problem, Dean?"

"Big brother, my traps did not have quite the holding or deadly effect I'd hoped for," the Ninja confessed in a harsh whisper. "From what I just saw in my ninpo of farseeing, they are almost back on pace with us! We are approaching the woods on the northern border, yes?"

"Yes, we are," Ben said in reply as he slowed the horses and led them through the first flanks of trees along the narrowing path. They would have to travel through the woods for the better part of a whole day, and since their pursuers hadn't stopped coming altogether, the four brothers and the horses hadn't had a decent rest in almost a full twenty-four hours.

"Sean, they will catch up to us here, in these woods, in only four or five hours." Dean's eyes starting to widen with the first telltale signs of panic. "I would strongly advise that if we want to complete our given task, or rather, if you want to accomplish the task we have been given by James Svelk, that you should take one of the horses and go ahead of the three of us. Besides, no offense, but in a fight like this, you might not be able to help us out all that much, doing what you do."

For a long moment, Sean's mind screamed at him to take the opportunity that his brother was trying to give him and run. However, if he did that and then completed the portrayal of being James Svelk in the village north of here, he would be contradicting his promise to take care of his younger siblings. His promise to his mother and her rules, laid down and immutable, raged against one another. *What to do?* he wondered, *what to do?*

"He's right, big brother." Reggie's voice was as even and monotone as whenever he worked on a new piece of equipment. Reggie popped open his long black trunk, and rifled through it, pulling out a pair of shimmering metal legs. These artificial limbs, unlike the ones he was presently using, were built for speed and range of movement than stability and strength. "You may have made a promise, but mother was already on her way out of this world when you made it," he said, sounding perfectly rational and reasonable. "Her rules make it pretty clear that we have to finish the job. You're the only one who can play the part of Svelk, brother." He lay flat on the wagon floor and handed Dean the fake legs. "You have to go ahead and let us stop these Bounty Hunters."

Dean took hold of Reggie's left upper thigh, pulled down toward the back of the wagon and twisted counterclockwise. There came from Reggie's leg a hiss and a pop, and then Dean grabbed the booted foot and pulled the fake leg out of Reggie's trouser leg. He took one of the thinner, more acrobatically designed legs, and ran it home. He repeated the process for the right leg, and then Reggie stood up, regaining his balance with the speed-type legs that he hadn't donned in a few months.

"What about you, Ben," Sean asked the Pickpocket of the group, who continued to guide the horses with the reins. "Will you join them?"

"Whatever you want me to do, I'll do it Sean," came Benjamin Browler's reply.

Sean remained seated, and hung his head until his chin touched his chest. If Reggie's memory hadn't been so clear, Sean could have told them that their mother had instructed him to watch after them. But that wasn't how it had actually happened. In their mother's last minutes, Sean had promised her that he'd keep them safe, and that he would continue to follow her rules until the day he died. Between his promise and her well-established rules, he had to choose her rules, because they had always been there, while the promise could well have been muddled words that she didn't really hear. It was simply a matter of being logical, like Reggie.

Sean desperately wished he'd purchased more of the teleportation scrolls that would return his brothers to his side, but he hadn't foreseen a greater need for them. He'd already given Dean the two he had, and now his brothers would be on their own to escape if and when they could from the Bounty Hunters. Finally, he looked up into each of their faces, one by one. "All right," he said finally. "Ben, stop the horses."

Ben did that with a tightening of the reins.

The three brothers in the back grabbed their gear and emptied out of the wagon, and Ben came around with one of the horses, handing its personal reins to Sean.

"Listen boys, and listen well," Sean said, huddled close with his kin. "If the heat gets to be too much from these pricks, you cut and run in different directions, hear me? We'll all meet back at the usual place, right?"

"Right," his brothers chorused.

Sean gave each of his younger brothers a fierce hug, ending with Reggie.

"Big brother, we'll wait for you there for a while, but if you're not back in a week or so, we'll come looking for you," the mecha-enhanced Human added when he let his eldest brother go.

"I know you will," Sean said, mounting the stronger of the horses. *Ben had made a good judgment on this one*, he thought. "Well boys, see you back home," he said, turning the horse about on the woodland path and charging off north, away from his brothers and the wagon.

The Elf-Queen's Bounty

The second horse would have tried to follow suit, but Ben hadn't undone it from its harness.

"We have to get ready for them," Dean said when they could no longer see a trace of Sean on the northern path. He pulled his packet of ninpo from his hip, and started rummaging through it for the most useful ones at his disposal. He snatched two from the pile, and handed them to Ben, who looked at the cards quizzically.

"When they come upon this location, you will press those ninpo to your forehead, and concentrate on the word 'strength'. They will then activate, and give you a burst of additional strength."

"Are these magic?" Ben asked, tucking the cards into his pocket.

"In a way." Dean looked through for a couple more that might assist himself or Reggie, though he didn't really think Reggie could use the ninpo. "You see, in the martial arts, it is taught that each and every living thing has a certain amount of chi in their body. This chi is spiritual energy, and everybody has a limited amount dependant upon their Race, their Class, and the amount of training they have done with their body, as well as the body's condition." He finally found a pair of ninpo that could help enhance his own performance.

"I think I follow so far." Ben crossed his arms over his chest. "It's like mana, like magic-users have, right?"

"Yes," Dean said, just to make things easier. "The difference being, everything that lives has chi, whereas only magic-users have mana. Mana is something that you can develop as well, but it takes more mental study and effort than physical training and practice. Now, Reggie," Dean decided to forgo trying the ninpo on his little brother and simply say what he suspected. "Your own chi is too hectic and disrupted by all of the mecha that you employ in your body to use ninpo. However, I saw what you can do with those arms of yours, and I know why you chose those skinny legs of yours. Those are your speeders, right?"

"Affirmative," Reggie said plainly.

"Good. You'll need more speed than power with these Bounty Hunters, brother. They're very powerful indeed, and they know how to fight. At least, the Red Draconus does, and we all know that."

The Browlers, when they learned that Collin Caulkins had been assigned to Sean and Ben's bounty, did background checks on him, and discovered that he had once been a Monk. Martial arts skill and training was on the dragon-man's side, but Dean hoped to counter that with his own skill in the arts of ninjitsu.

He also had another trump card that he could play, one that none of his brothers knew about. He had altered the forged document that he'd given Ben to sneak into the Elven Kingdom's royal mansion. If he or his brothers were in danger of being rounded up by the Bounty Hunters, he could use this information as a bargaining tool to secure their release and get them a good head start in running. That, and he knew exactly where James Svelk lived, thanks to Ben's extensive network of informants.

After all, though they had an obligation to have Sean pretend to be Svelk, they had no obligation not to sell the Elf out.

* * * *

The sun had almost come up over the horizon by the time Portenda brought the three of them to a halt. Collin dismounted the Simpa, and both lycanthropes shifted up into their bestial form. "There, in those woods, and not very far in," Portenda said, snuffling at the air once again. "It would appear they're waiting to ambush us and finish what they tried to start back at the pass."

"I thought you said they'd try to finish their business for Svelk first," Collin said, lighting his pipe once again.

"They may already have done that," Shoryu said. "I don't know if they had any business with the Greenskins in the area, but we did pass by a few villages on the way. That one in particular stank of Orcs," he added, the olfactory memory still haunting him. Dirt, grime, and bodily fluids had been pungent only a few hours back, and he'd been able to make out the odor of Orc flesh just beneath those scents. But the Orcs used an irrigation-style system for their waste management, and the stream not far south and east of them now had been clogged with Orc waste. He'd almost stopped to throw up.

"That's true," said Portenda, looking off to the woods about half a mile away. "But I don't think they stopped into any of the Greenskin camps. I only smell three of them up ahead, so I think one of them, probably Sean, went on while his little brothers stayed behind. He'll finish their job on his own, if he can."

"So, what do we do then?" Collin asked. "I still want to get my hands on Ben, and I'm sure Reggie will be worth something in the Fiefdom one of these days soon. Shall we go waltzing on into their ambush and destroy them?"

"Not just yet," Portenda said. "Collin, do you have that artifact of yours, the compass?"

The Draconus grabbed the compass artifact from its pouch and held it up to his mouth, breathing lightly on it. Portenda did the same, and then held it before Shoryu.

"Good. Shoryu? How good of a shot are you?"

The Elf-Queen's Bounty

The Cuyotai Hunter, a skilled archer in all circles, viewed this question almost as a challenge until he thought about what Portenda might have in mind. He grinned like an imp, and drew his bow from his back and a pair of arrows.

"I think I know where you're going with this," the Councilor said, looking at the compass display and then closing his eyes. He raised the bow, and notched one of the arrows, keeping the other tucked behind his ear. He opened one eye to look at the compass, and then looked with that eye into the woods. Taking careful aim, and checking on the speed of the wind by watching the fur on his extended arm flap lightly to the east, Shoryu breathed slowly, rhythmically. Finally, he launched his shot, waiting to hear the telltale report.

* * * *

Though most trained archers don't like to admit it, a certain degree of luck goes into making long-range shots with a longbow. Admit it or not, the element of luck is there. Though none of the men up the road could see it, Reggie Browler's extended left arm glinted and glowed maliciously as he took aim at them with his energy cannon.

Only halfway through its charge, however, a single arrow rammed into his palm, the arrowhead splitting the barrel end wide open and thrusting far enough in to ruin the energy storage cartridge. The sound that issued from the mecha-enhanced Human, however, was not the scream of pain that Shoryu was waiting for and wouldn't hear. It was, instead, a pair of words that Dean, perhaps twenty yards away and up in a tree, didn't want to hear; "Oh, shit."

* * * *

"I don't think I hit anything," Shoryu said, his face drawn tight, his irritation clear in his tone. "Just a wasted shot, and now they definitely know we're here."

"Oh, you hit something," Portenda said with a smile. "You hit Reggie, and probably someplace important." His heightened sense of hearing had served him well. "But remember, he's got fake arms of mecha. He wouldn't feel any pain if you hit him in the arms."

Remembering this, Shoryu's scowl quickly transformed into a bloodthirsty grin.

"Give it a minute, Shoryu," Portenda said, knowing full well that the Councilor was itching to close the gap and begin the fight in earnest. "I want to see if they'll bring the fight to us."

Off in the woods, Dean Browler was hoping that the trio up the road would bring the fight to him.

* * * *

"This is utter nonsense," Ben said to himself as he urged his horse on at a slow trot, trying to keep the noise of its hooves down. He looked down at the object in his left hand, which Reggie had given him, and shook his head. "Just looks like a dog toy or something," he said, unaware of the destructive power of the device. Still, if Reggie said it would do some damage, his older brothers tended to trust his judgment and leave it at that.

A couple of hours previously, Dean had put together a loose battle strategy with his brothers. Ben had been assigned the task of being a surprise flank attack, much to the Pickpocket's dislike. Reggie, however, had pulled something off of his hip, and handed it to Ben. "It's called a fragmentation grenade," the mecha obsessed brother told him. "You pull that little ring off, and then throw it at your target. Make sure you stay well away from it once you've tossed it."

"And then get right back to us," Dean said. "Hopefully, the device will injure them a bit, or at least stun them and make them slow, groggy. Reggie and I can take care of things when they first get here, and with those ninpo I gave you earlier, you can provide some use in hand-to-hand combat. Trust me on that one," Dean said. He'd explained that the ninpo would make Ben as strong, if not stronger, than a Werewolf in full lycanthrope rage. While fascinated by the idea, all Ben could think was, sure, great, but what good is strength if I don't know how to use it? I don't know how to fight!

But he didn't argue. Arguing wasn't his strong suit either, and since Dean was oldest brother present, his orders were final.

Ben stopped the horse then, hearing the muffled sound of conversation just over the lip of the hill he was using to flank their foes. He dismounted slowly, cautiously, and crawled on his belly to the lip. He poked his head up slightly, and spotted the three of them, a Cuyotai with a bow, a Simpa with an impressive arsenal, and a Red Draconus. Something about the Simpa bothered him, and immediately he saw what it was; the Simpa had several grenades on his hip, just like the one that Ben now held!

If the Simpa saw the mecha weapon, Ben knew that he would be able to avoid the effects of it as a weapon. Ben himself wasn't aware of what sort of damage could be done with a grenade, as he knew little about mecha in general. However, he knew instinctively that if he wanted the weapon to do what it was designed to, he'd have to make certain that he didn't let the Simpa see it.

Trusting to his own sense of accuracy, Ben pulled the pin.

* * * *

"They aren't coming out," Collin said, irritated at waiting. "Let's go in and nab the little pricks," he said, stepping forward.

"Fine." Portenda was himself surprised that none of the brothers had come out of the woods. Yet, he thought he could smell one of them to the west of their position, and being curious, he turned just in time to see something coming through the air at the trio. "Run, now," he screamed to his companions, both of whom had already thankfully been in motion.

Sprinting ahead, Portenda and Shoryu had a definite speed advantage over Collin, who lagged a few paces. When the grenade exploded behind them, the concussion force of the blast struck all three men, sending them all to the ground with bruises already forming on their bodies. Collin, closest to the blast, received the worst of the injuries, landing wrong when he tried to break his fall and thus breaking his left wrist. The flames that singed his clothes didn't bother him one wit; he was, after all, a Red Draconus and immune to all but the most powerful magical flames.

The bones in his wrist crinkled like a plastic bag, the volume of the break horribly loud to his own ears. "Lords above that hurt," he grumbled as he got once more to his feet, looking around in surprise to see that the wave of force from the grenade had thrown the three men nearly a hundred yards. He turned to find Portenda and Shoryu both rising slowly to their feet, the hair on the back of Portenda's head slightly crisped by the flames that had managed to reach him, and Shoryu likewise scorched. "You guys okay?" he asked.

"Just dandy," Shoryu replied, rubbing the back of his head. "That was a bit of a surprise. What was that?"

"A frag grenade." Portenda squinted to bring his eyes back into focus. He was still hurting from the silver shuriken the evening before, and now a concussion wave had done a little more damage, mostly jarring his recovered knee. "Let's get into those woods and take them down. Remember, we won't kill them if we don't have to." He charged ahead of the other two men. "If we do, though, make sure it's nice and bloody," he added, thinking about the Ninja and his traps.

* * * *

"It didn't make a direct hit, but it's going to hamper them," Dean said to himself. He looked down at Reggie from his perch up in the tree, and saw that his youngest brother had managed to pull the arrow out of his cannon arm, and wasn't replacing the limb. Probably not enough time, Dean mused, which turned out to be correct. Ben returned a moment later, applying the ninpo scrolls to his forehead and activating them. He flexed his arms as the ninpo vanished, their chi energy merged with Ben's own, and he marveled at the feeling of brute power in his body.

Unfortunately for Ben, admiring his newfound power left him wide open for the brutal punch that Portenda landed to his chest when the Simpa charged into the woods.

Portenda's fist slammed directly into Ben's breastbone, sending him screaming nearly twenty yards deeper into the woods, slamming at last into a sturdy oak tree and landing in a heap at the bottom of the trunk. Portenda stood where he'd delivered the blow, and couldn't quite move out of the way of Reggie's initial cannon blast.

Searing heat and light slammed into Portenda's ribs from the hand cannon Reggie Browler had employed against the troopers of Lemago. However, the energy leak from his power cartridge had appreciably depleted the power of the cannon, thus only yielding results similar to Portenda's punch to his brother Benjamin.

Reggie silently cursed the well-placed shot the Cuyotai had made, and began powering up another charge in his cannon.

Shoryu arrived on the scene a moment later, volleying another arrow at Reggie, clipping him in the left leg. The armor plating of the artificial limb did its job in deflecting the arrow, but the shot did distract the mecha-enhanced Human.

Reggie waited another two seconds, as Shoryu jumped about to make himself a harder target to hit, and blasted at Shoryu, who avoided the beam.

Now, Dean thought, launching into action.

As Portenda got up and made ready to charge at Ben, who was back to his feet, Dean landed a foot away from Portenda, and delivered a series of quick, shallow stabs with his kunei into the Simpa's stomach and legs.

Damn he's fast, Portenda thought as the blows hit home, but thank the gods he's not using more silver.

The wounds were minor, each stab only half an inch deep, and they did little damage overall to the Simpa's powerful frame. He made a claw swipe at the Ninja, who proved nimble enough to duck the blow. In turn, as Portenda's body came forward after the swipe, Dean thrust both of his hands, wrist to wrist, into Portenda's chest. The counterattack thrust him back a few yards, his arms flailing to maintain his balance.

"Let me handle this Ninja." Collin stepped in front of Portenda, who was now blocking incoming punches from a ninpo-strengthened Benjamin. The Red Draconus cracked his knuckles, and then his neck. "Think you've got what it takes to face a real martial artist?"

"I've got what it takes and then some, Bounty Hunter," Dean rasped, moving forward and delivering several snake-style attacks, each parried or hard blocked by the Red Draconus. Shoryu, meanwhile, rolled out of the way of another force blast by Reggie Browler, who was becoming agitated with the Cuyotai's agility.

The two of them, Human and Cuyotai, continued to dance back and forth, Reggie blasting and missing, then Shoryu firing his bow and barely missing due to Reggie's artificial speed. The legs the Browler brother had chosen were being put to good use, and when one arrow more hit the right leg, it was again deflected by the armor plating. They were, for the time being, evenly matched. The trees around them, however, were feeling the brunt of the battle, with arrows sticking out of them in places, and scorch marks scarring them in other spots.

Portenda ducked and dodged Ben's incoming attacks, both with and without knife in hand. The Simpa hard blocked one of the hook punches, and he felt the power behind it in his bones. *He's got power, sure*, Portenda thought, *but unlike his brother Dean, he has no finesse, no speed, and no true skill.* This he thought as he parried and wove in and out of close range with Ben, until the Pickpocket used one of his few notable talents. Portenda ducked a left roundhouse punch that he saw coming a mile away, and felt something tug at his hip.

When he stood back to his full height, Ben used Portenda's revolver, which he'd just snatched, to fire a round directly into Portenda's stomach.

The Simpa Bounty Hunter felt the slug enter his abdomen, a metallic intruder in his body that seemed to be on a mission of pain and punishment. Muscles ripped and tensed as the bullet passed through his body, the powerful shot throwing his body back in what felt to him like slow motion.

Point-blank shot, he managed to think through the pain in his lower abdomen. *Of course it's going to throw me back, but there's got to be a way to turn this to my advantage.*

His blood sprayed across Ben's cheek, and the Pickpocket, horrified at the sick splash on his face, didn't hold on to the weapon, letting it clatter to the ground.

When Portenda finally landed on his back about eight yards away, he kick-flipped to his feet, a course of action that caused more blood to come out of his ragged bullet wound. He saw the expression on Ben's face, and he knew that he had an advantage, if only for a moment.

"What's the matter?" Portenda asked, his voice cold and flat despite his momentary pain. "Never shed much blood, have you? Well here, you can have some more." He cupped his hand under the wound and threw a handful of his own crimson lifeblood into Ben's eyes.

The Browler brother howled in horror and flailed backward.

Portenda seized his opportunity, and charged forward, bull-tackling Ben into an oak tree. Portenda felt several ribs giving way under his enormous weight, and heard the wheeze of Ben's air being forced from his lungs. When Portenda pulled away, Ben was unconscious, the wind knocked out of him.

Collin, meanwhile, had quite the contest on his hands. While he was at least three times stronger than Dean, and a tad faster, he wasn't quite as crafty as the Ninja. When he managed to land a hooking kick, Dean wrapped his arm around the offending leg, bringing his elbow down hard on Collin's leg. The Red Draconus let out a grunt of pain, and lanced a stream of fire from his mouth toward Dean, who ducked and swung Collin's own leg into the jet of fire. While it didn't hurt him, it certainly put Collin's back to Dean, who used this to his own good. Dean plunged a kunei into the back of Collin's right shoulder, and the Red Draconus felt the knife going in handle-deep, parting the muscle tissue and letting out blood with relative ease.

Collin leveled a back kick into Dean's chest and the Ninja flew back from the impact, screaming in pain as his breastbone cracked from the pressure. Dean landed in a three-point crouch several yards away, and he looked to his left, watching as the Simpa tossed blood into Ben's face.

Well, Dean thought, *we had a pretty good run, now didn't we? We're probably all as good as dead, so I may as well use one last good ninpo.*

Collin spun and lunged at Dean, who brought up one last ninpo and placed it on Collin's forehead as the Draconus crashed his right fist into Dean's stomach, forcing the Ninja to throw up all over his arm and the ground.

Light flared from the ninpo, and Collin felt lightning crackle against his scaly brow. The power surged then through his whole body, and both Ninja and Bounty Hunter fell to the ground, unconscious.

"Brother, no," Reggie cried, and in the moment of distraction, Shoryu drew out one arrow and shoved it into the end of Reggie's hand cannon.

The mecha obsessed Browler turned to face him, a scowl of such savagery on his face that Shoryu almost forgot that he was about to harm himself instead of the Councilor.

Reggie let loose a blast from his cannon, and the power rebounded back into his own arm, blowing the entire assembly apart. Screws, bolts and scraps of metal flew through the woods, twisted and contorted into different odd shapes as the power cartridge melted and smoldered only scant inches from his feet.

Unable to recover quickly enough from the shock, Reggie Browler went down to a single punch that Shoryu threw into his face.

The Cuyotai felt the sick crunch of nostril cartilage under his knuckles, and felt as well the tears spatter his soft facial fur as Reggie stretched back from the blow. He could smell the coppery odor of nasal blood as well, and he could hear the groan of passing from consciousness to the realm of slumber deep in Reggie's throat.

Reggie landed on the turf, and his body went strangely stiff before going limp. His left arm from the shoulder down had been blown apart by the backward flow of his own energy cartridge, and Shoryu shook his head in dismay and concern.

How could the man have done all of this to himself? Shoryu wondered as he took a brief look into the bottom cuff of Reggie's pant legs. How?

"Good work," Portenda said as he approached Shoryu, holstering his gun and checking on his own bullet wound. It was already in the process of healing, though slowly. "Collin's okay, so don't let the appearance fool you," Portenda added.

Shoryu looked to where the Draconus lie atop Dean Browler, crackling lightning energy still flowing off of his dragon-like tail.

"Shoryu, are you all right?" Portenda asked after a moment.

"Yeah, I'm fine," Shoryu said, feeling his outer body with his hands, checking for injuries he might not have felt. "You?"

"I'm a little banged up, but I'll heal. In the meantime, help me tie these three up," Portenda said. "We're going to get some information out of them, so help me gods we are."

"What about Sean? Are we going to go after him?" Shoryu was, in truth, more than ready to go home, because this whole business of apprehending James Svelk had gotten out of hand. He'd fought a bladeron, traveled almost clear across the continent (though much of the distance was covered by the Alchemy of Jonah Staples), been fired upon by a deadly mecha weapon, and had the evening before been struck by stones in the body and head and then buried. He'd fought and killed several Greenskins, who had attacked them without provocation, and though that fight hadn't yielded him any injuries, it had pushed him to the limits of his physical endurance. He was tired, and wanted to sleep in his own bed, with his wife.

He was ready to hear the Simpa Bounty Hunter tell him yes, they were going after Sean.

Instead, Portenda said, "What we need to know, one of these others can tell us. Besides, Ninja don't often go out without information to exchange for safe travel." He looked over at Dean as he pulled rope from his own rucksack to bind Reggie Browler to a tree. Before tying him up, however, Portenda got Shoryu to help him figure out how to dismantle the artificial limbs, thus rendering Reggie much less capable of escape.

When they finished tying the three men together to a tree, Portenda got some smelling salts from his pack and waved them under Collin's nose.

The Red Draconus came around with a groan, sitting up and blinking at the two of them. "Where are they?" he managed to ask before pushing the salts aside and searching his pockets for his pipe and tobacco.

"Over there." Shoryu pointed to the trio of brothers lashed to a mighty pine tree. "We'll be questioning them when they come to. Don't worry. We already disarmed them all, and took away all of Dean's little gadgets. Portenda apparently knows a lot about hidden weapons," Shoryu said with a shudder.

"Like the throwing needles embedded in the backs of his hands?" Collin asked.

Shoryu nodded, and Collin lit his pipe. Portenda knew his job all right, Collin thought. *I wonder if he'll let me ask the boys any questions.*

* * * *

Dean Browler and Benjamin Browler were both brought awake by their little brother Reggie's screams of terror.

"They dismantled me, they took me apart," their little brother was bawling. "They took me apart!"

Dean turned his head as best he could to the left, and saw that it was true; they'd literally taken Reggie's arm and legs off. They had evidently also found his trunk of replacement parts and gear, and had piled it all a few yards away, out of any of their reach.

Dean tried to reach for his throwing needles, which he kept tucked just under the skin on the backs of his hands, but found he couldn't move his hands even in the slightest. He felt a piece of paper on the backs of his hands, and knew what was there the moment he looked up into the smug smile of the Red Draconus. "Binding sutra," the former Monk said. "I still know how to use the mystic scrolls of the Monks, you see, and we didn't want you trying anything funny."

"Were you by any chance looking for these?" The Cuyotai stepped into view, dropping the throwing needles to the dirt. "Already got those taken care of. Anything we're forgetting?"

"Just these." Portenda stepped between the Draconus and Cuyotai, flipping the deck of ninpo at Dean's face. Each ninpo had been cut in half, rendering them useless. Portenda the Quiet crouched down, getting as close as he cared to and lowered his voice. "Ben, I've got your lock picks tucked nicely away in my rucksack." He faced the Ninja but addressed the Pickpocket. "It's a nice set, I must say. I'd give them back, but Collin here intends to take you in for the guaranteed bounty on your head."

"What do you want," Dean growled, spitting in the Simpa's face.

Portenda reached back without looking and plucked the handkerchief that Shoryu held to him.

"Are you after the bounty on Sean's head?"

"No," Portenda said flatly, gracing Dean with a grin of the psychotic type, the one that stretched his lips almost back to his ears. "I couldn't care less about your brother. What I'm interested in," he lost his smile, "is your employer. James Svelk."

Dean shivered slightly. Ben had pissed himself upon seeing that grin. Dean could smell it on his brother now, and the stench almost gagged him.

"He has something that belongs to my Cuyotai friend here, Councilor Tcarfang," Portenda said, letting the Cuyotai's title hang in the air like a veiled threat. "Beyond that, I think he has something else going on behind the scenes. Now, what you're going to do is simple. I'm going to ask you a couple of questions, and you are going to answer them. Each time you give me trouble, one of your brother's trinkets goes the way of the tewonoo bird."

On cue, Shoryu took one of Reggie's replacement arms and set it in a loop that he'd set up in a tree branch. Collin stepped over, and blew a stream of fire just next to the loop, leaving it and the attachment undamaged.

Reggie let out a low, animal-like mewling sound of misery. "Brother, don't let them do it. Please don't let them destroy it all!"

"Oh, we aren't that cruel." Shoryu held up a pair of simple-looking legs. "These look to be pretty basic models, so we'll let you keep these. Of course, it'll be rough trying to eat with no arms, won't it?"

Dean cursed Reggie's obsession with all things technological for perhaps the hundredth time and looked into Portenda's eyes. What he saw there made his insides squirm, and he quickly looked at the ground.

"Do we have an understanding?" Portenda asked.

Dean nodded, miserable but unwilling to cause his little brother further trepidation.

"Very good. Now, what is the real intent of James Svelk? Why did he steal from the Historical Society building in Whitewood?"

"It was a distraction," Dean answered, uncertain now if he really could withhold anything from the Simpa. What he'd seen in Portenda's eyes had been so strange, and so frightening, that perhaps he would be better off just confessing everything and saving his skin for another day. "While Sean and Svelk were robbing the Historical Society, Ben broke into the royal manor and smuggled out a family history document. I made a forged duplication of the document with the alterations I was instructed to place in it."

Hold onto something, Dean told himself. *Just something.*

"Whose family history did you steal and then alter, and why?" Portenda ask.

"It was the Bergen family history," Dean said.

That caught Shoryu's attention right away. General Bergen had always struck Shoryu as a clean and honest man. Was Svelk out to damage the General's reputation? What if he was trying to do something to damage the General's relationship with Her Majesty the Queen?

"What did you do?" the Cuyotai asked, coming toward the Ninja fast, scowling and growling low in his belly. "What did you do to the document?" He was snout-to-nose with Dean, and the Ninja wasn't certain which lycanthrope he should be more afraid of. He no longer blamed Ben for pissing himself.

"I was instructed to alter the family history and ensure that the Illeck bloodline of Bergen's family was replaced with pure Elven breeding."

Dean's words rocked Shoryu to the core. He stood up and started to walk away, when Portenda came up behind him, putting a gentle hand on the Councilor's shoulder.

"Is this something important?" the Simpa asked.

"I'll say it is. If an Elf has Illeck blood in his family line, he can never be married into the royal family. It is forbidden, and has been since the discovery that the Illeck and Elves are related, but are two separate Races. General Bergen could still hold his post as a General, but could never marry the Queen if we discovered his Illeck heritage."

"Wouldn't marriage make him king?" Portenda asked flatly. Suddenly, it all made sense to Shoryu, and Portenda. Bergen had hired Svelk, who had in turn hired the Browler brothers, to get the document and alter it. In order to distract the city guard and the High Council, Sean and Svelk had broken into the Historical Society and stolen priceless treasures of the kingdom. "What would Svelk get out of the deal, anyway?"

"The new King of the Elves could grant him a pardon and let him back into the kingdom," Shoryu said with disdain. "He could even give him his old post back, with full rank. This is bad, Portenda, really bad. We have to get back to the kingdom and warn Her Majesty!"

"Just a minute." Portenda crouched in front of Dean once again. "Is there a way to prove all of this?"

"Steam," Dean said. "If you hold the family history in the archives in steam, it will reveal the message I tucked into the history. It says, 'Ha ha, you've been had!' Not very original, I know, but it was an insurance policy that Svelk wanted in place, so he could force the new King to look on him with favor."

"One last question," Portenda said, and whispered the question into Dean's ear. The Ninja smiled his best, most knowing smile. "I'll let you and Reggie go if you answer it. Ben has a bounty on his head, and as you can see," Portenda said, pointing to Collin, who at that moment was hauling the bound Pickpocket to the horse that Ben had taken from the wagon harness. "Collin's eager to collect. Now, where does Svelk live?"

"Come closer," Dean said, and whispered the exact location of James Svelk's home in Ja-Wen into the Bounty Hunter's ear. "Are you satisfied now," he asked.

"Almost," Portenda said. He turned to Collin, who had returned from the horse to the pile of Reggie's artificial limbs. "Shoryu, you have the legs set aside, right?"

"Yeah." Shoryu stepped away from the larger pile with the two approved legs.

"Do it," Portenda said, and Collin Caulkins breathed devastating fire onto the pile of assembled artificial limbs.

Reggie started gibbering and crying the instant the flames started to burn through the mecha, but Portenda did not give Collin any signal to stop breathing his flames. On poured the fire, eating through the armored plating, through component boards, melting wires and fusing entire sections together. At almost the same power of a Red Dragon's breath weapon, Collin's tunnel of fire could destroy most anything, given enough time.

"You said you would spare him this if I told you what you wanted to know," Dean screamed over the fire's roar.

"No, I did not," Portenda said, not deigning to look at the Ninja, but instead watching the metal melt and pool together. "I said that each time you caused me trouble, one of these trinkets would go away. There appeared to be a total of about three replacements per limb there, if you don't include the basic legs that the Councilor set aside. That's nine troubles," Portenda said. "The first trouble you caused me was working for James Svelk. That's one out of nine," he said, still holding his eyes on the flames jetting from Collin's mouth. "The second trouble you caused me was running, so that's two out of nine. The third trouble you caused me was trying to strike me with a shuriken while the Councilor and I dealt with a bladeron, which was not a fun experience in and of itself, thank you," Portenda said, finally looking away from the wrecked mecha.

"In my defense, you shot that shuriken down, and then tried to blow me up with an arrow weapon of some sort," Dean said with a shrug.

"True enough, but we're not going to get into that right now. Next, you buried the three of us in a landslide trap, which was very cleverly done might I say," Portenda said, giving Dean an appreciative look.

"Thank you." The Ninja tried to nod his head in a futile attempt to bow graciously.

"You're welcome. Now, that's three troubles, Dean Browler, putting you at a count of six. You then managed to snare me with nine silver shuriken, which would put you up to fifteen troubles, out of nine limbs. You see where I'm going with this?" Portenda asked, making the circular motion with his right hand that normally meant 'get on with it'.

"Yes, okay, you're being very generous to leave me with a damaged brother who can at least walk," Dean said. "What about our food? Our camping gear?"

"Oh, we left that stuff intact back over by the wagon." Portenda pointed between the trees to the abandoned wagon. "As I said, we're not entirely cruel and unusual men. Now," he said, cutting the robe that bound Dean and Reggie to the tree together. "Stand up, get some feeling back in your legs and ass. You've been on the ground for a while."

Dean did just that, though he didn't need too much reworking of his lower half to get feeling back. "So that's it? You're going to let us go," Dean said, somewhat perplexed.

"Well, there's no official bounty out on Reggie's head yet," Collin said, pointing down at the untied but crippled brother. "So even though I'd love to turn him over to the authorities, there's no profit in it at this time." The Bounty Hunter calmly puffed on his pipe. "No profit, no bag. So for now, count your blessings."

"Yes," Portenda said. "We are Bounty Hunters. The only time we hurt or kill someone or something, is when it gets in the way of our job. You were getting in the way. Now, you've helped us out a bit, so we'll turn the other cheek. By the way, were you aware that you had a ninpo in the middle of your pack that teleports directly to Ja-Wen," Portenda asked.

"I was," Dean said. "I figured I'd use it as a last ditch bargaining chip, giving you Svelk in exchange for our release."

"Well then, things worked out pretty fair in the end then, right?" Shoryu asked with a shrug of his shoulders. "After all, we didn't destroy all of your ninpo outright. We wanted to keep the ones that could come in handy."

Dean then helped Reggie by putting on his two basic leg units, and they hobbled toward the wagon together. As they did so, Collin approached Shoryu and Portenda.

"Well, gentlemen, I'll be taking off now to drop this guy off at the nearest bounty office." The Red Draconus tucked his pipe away now that it had cooled. "Hope you guys don't mind."

"Business comes first." Portenda gave Collin a pat on the shoulder. "You go do what you have to do. We're heading to Ja-Wen, and then we'll be taking a nice quick trip back to Desanadron. Are you aware that Jonah has a partner in Ja-Wen," Portenda said to Shoryu as they turned around and walked a short distance away, in order to ensure that the ninpo didn't drag Collin along with them.

"I didn't know that," Shoryu said, pulling the ninpo out of his pocket. "Then again, I don't know much of the goings-on outside of Whitewood and the Elven Kingdom. Who is he?"

"Well, the guy runs things a tad different. You see, he's a mage, not an Alchemist. Runs a little magic supplies shop in the city, does pretty well for himself. His name's a hell of a thing to try to say, but he's a nice Kobold fellow."

Shoryu held the ninpo toward Portenda, and they concentrated on their destination as both men took a firm grip on the card. A flash of light and cloud of smoke later, they were gone.

Chapter Twelve
Wrapping Up Business

James Svelk arose early in the morning, and once again began his daily ritual. He marveled at the collection of items stolen from the Historical Society, most of which he kept in the closet of his humble little bedroom, and then showered. After cleaning up, he sauntered into the kitchen, where he made himself a light breakfast. At least, most mornings he made himself a light breakfast. This morning, he could plainly see, wasn't going to be like most other mornings.

A pair of bruised and rather fatigued gentlemen was sipping coffee from rather large earthenware travel mugs at his table. When he entered the room, the fellow seated at the head of the table (Svelk's usual morning perch) looked up at him and gave him the most hideous smile he'd ever seen. The fellow seated facing the doorway squarely didn't smile at all, but stroked the bow that belonged to his family line for generations as it rested in his lap. Said gentleman had retrieved it from the rack in James Svelk's living room, where he'd hung it as a special reminder of his hatred for said gentleman.

"Well, good morning sunshine." Portenda maintained the grin of doom he saved for situations such as this. "Pull up a chair, have yourself a cup of Joe. Where you're heading, only the guards get the good stuff." Portenda let his tone go from insanely perky to cold and flat along with his expression.

James Svelk had always assumed that, given such circumstances, he'd be able to do something to defend himself, get away from the authorities. Now, curiously, he simply shuffled forward and took a seat across from Shoryu Tearfang, member of Whitewood's High Council.

"You are aware that we're going to arrest you, right?" Shoryu asked politely as he took a sip of coffee.

"Yes, I believe I am aware of that," Svelk pulled his chair in closer to the table. "I have been something of a bastard now, haven't I?"

"Oh, more than something of one." Portenda got up and stalked over to where the Elf kept his mugs. He set a cup of steaming coffee, with creamer and sugar, down in front of his target. "You tried to rig the future royal dealings of the Elven Kingdom, my friend," the Simpa went on, all in his dry, businesslike tone. "That's bad business."

"On top of that," Shoryu added, "I'm well aware of how General Bergen feels about non-Elven Races. He despises the heavy Cuyotai and Human presence in the Kingdom's borders. He's tried three times to pass legislation that would expel my people from the major cities, along with Humans and the few Jafts who make their homes inside of city walls. The High Council always shoots him down, though, even though I'm the only non-Elf at the table."

"That's why the two of you decided to work together, isn't it?" Portenda asked as Svelk took a half-hearted sip of his coffee. "Because you're racists? But the only way to get your half-baked ideas into law would be for one of you to be King, and only Bergen stood a chance in hell. But having Illeck blood would make things difficult for him to get into that position."

"So you offered your assistance," Shoryu said.

"No, actually," Svelk said plainly, his face slack with disbelief. Why was he going to tell them this? *Because they've got me dead to rights*, he thought in reply to himself. *May as well tell them the way things were.* "Bergen and I served together a long time ago, when the hostile Minotaur tribes attacked the Kingdom's northwestern quadrant. We both had the same ideals, and he and I often discussed these things during the officers' meetings, though it clearly didn't float too well with the rest of the units."

"I'm guessing you were the second-in-command during the campaign," Shoryu said.

"Yes, so we often cut the officers' meetings short after the first week of the campaign. He and I thought a lot alike about non-Elven Races, and we had some brilliant ideas for using the present conflict to run them out of the cities. It worked a little when we got back home after the months spent on the front, as the King at the time was a very reasonable fellow, but also a very reactive one."

"King Shelton the Third," Shoryu said, more for Portenda's benefit. He reminded himself as he said it that Portenda wouldn't have even been alive back then, much less Shoryu himself. "Two monarchs ago," Shoryu said.

"Yes, Shelton." Svelk drained his coffee and pushing the mug aside. "When we argued against non-Elves in the cities, he responded to half of our suggestions, which was more than we really could have hoped for."

"So how did Bergen get a hold of you for all of this?" Portenda silently offered Svelk another cup, which the Elven man took in kind.

"Actually, he found me through a network of spies that the Kingdom has planted throughout the other lands," Svelk said, a statement that Shoryu filed away in a mental cabinet for later discussion with Her Majesty. He and the High Council weren't aware of any such spy network, and if the military was using one without their knowledge, it constituted a breach of protocol. The High Council had to be informed of all military activity, at all times.

"Instead of having me arrested by the spies, Bergen explained to his men that they weren't official, and couldn't affect an arrest, but he wanted to know exactly how to get a hold of me. Some years later, he finally did, and he sent a letter with his grand idea.

"'What if we could do what Shelton started and the Queen knocked out when she came to the throne,' his letter said to me. 'I've devised a way to do it, and doing it requires that I become King of the Elves. You'll have to help me,' the letter said. He then went on to explain how this could be done, and I accepted the job on the spot. By the way, for not being an Elf, you make terrific coffee," he added to Portenda.

"It's his lifeblood," Shoryu said.

Portenda let the jab go unnoticed, or at least deigned to not respond to it.

"Now, what were you going to get out of all of this? Your old post back, I assume that much," Shoryu said matter-of-factly.

Svelk nodded.

"But that wouldn't have been enough, would it? You would always and forever have an edge on the King of the Elves. You would use your influence to get command of units and brigades to go start some sort of stupid Race war, wouldn't you?"

"I must admit, the idea had more than crossed my mind," Svelk said, some of his old hatred bubbling up to the surface of his emotions and face. "The first thing I'd do would be to drive you dogs out of our cities."

"And those married to Elves," Shoryu growled.

"Court-ordered annulments, all around," Svelk said with a grin.

Shoryu lashed out then, kicking him under the table, hard.

"Ow! What the piss?"

"Sorry." Shoryu sat up straight. "Foot must've slipped. I think we've got everything we need." He opened one of his pouches and handed a strange mecha device to Portenda. "Wouldn't you say?"

"What is that?" Svelk asked, completely unfamiliar with the lost technology of the Age of Mecha.

"It's called a tape recorder," Portenda said cheerfully. "It makes a copy of conversations, including this one. I snagged it from Reggie Browler's collection of trinkets, because I have one of my own, but it's busted beyond my ken. Now, finish your coffee, and get up." Portenda tucked the device away and got to his feet, drawing his broadsword as he did so. "We're going to be escorting you to the local bounty office, where you'll be prepared for shipment back to the Elven Kingdom."

His words sent a shiver of fear down Svelk's spine.

Afraid though he was, James Svelk conducted himself with dignity all the way down the streets, and through the booking process at the bounty office of Ja-Wen. He only panicked when he saw that his guides back to the Elven Kingdom were two royal guards. "How the hells did they get here already?"

"Oh, a Kobold friend of mine," Portenda said simply as he collected his payment, forwarded to him by the same Kobold. "You see, he uses magic to teleport people and objects, including letters of warning. I had him send a letter of warning to the Queen, and she sent these fine gentlemen to come collect you. They'll be taking the same service to get back to the Elven Kingdom, as shall we. But we're going to be coming along a day or so behind, because we both need some sleep."

"Amen, brother," Shoryu said with a sigh.

Portenda handed one of the guards the tape recorder, with instructions to the Queen on how to play it. It held Dean Browler's confession, as well as James Svelk's, and would be all Her Majesty needed, for the time being. Portenda folded the scroll that was his payment and led Shoryu out of the office, and when the guards took a gibbering and crying James Svelk north up the street, Portenda and Shoryu headed south.

After a short walk, they arrived at his apartment building, and headed up to his place. Portenda pulled out the spare cot, and Shoryu flopped down onto it. Before he passed out, he had to ask one last question of the Bounty Hunter. "By the way, what was your payment?"

"Oh, this," Portenda asked, holding up the scroll. "It's the deed to an apartment building in Whitewood. The place has been on the market for a while, and the government was about to auction it off, so I took it instead. You see," he said before Shoryu passed out. "It's always nice to have work on the side of your normal business. It'll be a good retirement career."

Portenda the Quiet laid down, and for the first time in many moons, went to sleep immediately.

* * * *

Sean Browler had arrived at the other side of the woodland and continued on through most of the night before he realized that the horse needed to rest, badly. He dismounted, and made himself a small camp on the northern border of the thick woods while his mount got some rest. His mind toiled over what may have become of his brothers, and as his thoughts tumbled into the realm of unconsciousness, he allowed himself to drift off to sleep.

Late the next morning, a light nudging at his shoulder brought him awake with his knife in hand. He'd used his pack as a makeshift pillow, with one hand tucked beneath so that he wouldn't be ambushed without a fighting chance. However, when his hand came up with the weapon, it was stopped by the grip of his brother, Dean Browler. "Good sweet heavens," Sean exclaimed. "You boys are all right! Oh, gods, what happened to Reggie?" Sean saw that his youngest brother, miserable and defeated looking, had no arms on.

"It was the Draconus," Dean said flatly. "At about dawn this morning he destroyed the rest of Reggie's limbs. We were left with our rucksacks, and I still have a couple of my concealed ninpo in my pack. Nothing much, but they'll get us back home in a blink."

"What about the job," Sean asked.

"Don't bother," Reggie interjected, his mood slightly lifted at the prospect of heading home. He had a large number of reserve parts back at momma's house. "We gave up Svelk's location and the whole plan. The Draconus took Ben, too," Reggie said, his tone severe. "No idea where they'll be holding him."

"Probably in Palen," Sean said, rubbing his chin. "Let's get back to the house, and then we'll find out where Ben is. We'll let him stay in for about a month, and then we'll go retrieve him. After all," Sean surmised, stretching. "The break from his hobby might do him some good."

All three present Browler brothers gave a good laugh at this.

Dean pulled out three ninpo that would return them each to their mother's old home, and handed one to Sean, slapping the other onto Reggie's chest.

The cards flared with chi energy, and Sean had time for one last comment. "Home again, home again, jiggety-jig." With a flash of light and puff of smoke, they were gone.

Epilogue

Shoryu Tearfang returned to his home and to his work the very next day, and the capital was in quite a state of chaos. The Queen had placed General Bergen under arrest herself, and was mostly broken hearted over the discovery of his betrayal. She had thought rather highly of him, and would have accepted his proposal for marriage, had it all been genuinely felt. However, the incident also made her take a step back into her role as wise ruler of the Kingdom, and she decided to rescind ALL of Shelton the Third's ridiculous laws regarding Racial policy.

Portenda stopped in to the Tearfang family home to pay them all a visit, and he talked and dined with the family as a welcomed guest. He managed to smile throughout the visit, and even kept his temper in check when he fell for one of Toshiya's simple pranks. He didn't appreciate a bucket of water on his head, but he wasn't about to go ape-shit on the boy for something so harmless (he was fortunate that Toshiya was out of itching powder, or he'd have been in trouble).

And so life moved forward in the Elven Kingdom. Shoryu kept his appointments with the High Council (always the last one to show up, running late all the time), Portenda started renovations on the apartment complex that was newly acquired (more building code violations than he could count on two hands) and Ellen reared her children without the fear of her husband not coming home (both son and daughter worried her a lot more these days, though).

A month later, in a township north and several days to the east of the Elven Kingdom, Benjamin Browler made the return to his mother's old house, where the Browler Brothers Gang prepared for its next heist.

And James Svelk? James Svelk was becoming accustomed to the life of a prisoner in the dungeons beneath the main military barracks in the city of Blackwood in the Elven Kingdom. Part of acclimating to that lifestyle was the fact that most of his fellow inmates were also former military members, as he'd been charged and processed as a major in the Elven army. He supposed there were some small mercies left to him. Take his sentence, for example. He was a little over five-hundred years old, not a bad age for an Elven gent, when he was sentenced.

He'd be just over a thousand years old when he got out. As he made his way down the chow line at breakfast one morning, he reminded himself that he should add 'if' to that particular equation.

The End